VANDELLA

VANDELLA

M.CH.LANDA

LANDA PUBLISHINGS

Edited by William Boggess and Julie Tibbott
Proofread by Lara Kennedy
Cover art based on an artwork by Ernesto Barba

PRAISE FOR "VANDELLA"

"Any book that truly makes you ask questions and holds your interest until you find the answers is a great book, and this one goes way beyond that. It should be added to everyone's list of must-reads, not just those who enjoy the Fantasy genre." — **Feathered Quill**

"Dark, intriguing, and guaranteed to tug the heartstrings, M. Ch. Landa's Vandella is a young adult paranormal romance novel packed with mystery, danger, and highly relatable characters." — **San Francisco Book Review**

"The writing in Vandella is exquisite. The narrative is fascinating, dramatic, dark, and engaging. I wish M. Ch. Landa would write more books of this caliber because Vandella is such a fantastic story." — **Readers' Favorite Review**

"Paranormal YA readers will absolutely devour Vandella. It's emotional, dark, surprising, and fun. Landa has this wonderful skill of shocking readers with every chapter." — **Independent Book Review**

"Strong worldbuilding and an engaging teen protagonist ground this fantasy in real emotion." — **Booklife Reviews**

"Vandella is a refreshing, gentle read that explores human connection and the will to survive." — **Literary Titan**

"Vandella by M. Ch. Landa is a masterpiece when it comes to creativity. The author created a world we can easily lose track of time in." — **Online Book Club**

"In the lush, baroque tradition of such classics of the macabre as Interview with the Vampire." — **Booklife Prize**

Dear reader, thank you for purchasing a copy of *Vandella*. As an artist, your economic support, honest reviews, and sincere recommendation to your close ones are what allow me to continue this writing venture.

That's why, as a token of gratitude, I want to share with you the short story **"The Man with a Thousand Names,"** intended to be read before this novel. Please visit my webpage, **www.mchlanda.com**, and subscribe to my newsletter to download it for **FREE**.

Thank you again, and I hope you enjoy it.

Sincerely,
M. Ch. Landa

For my late father,
my example of fortitude and selflessness

CHAPTER 1

"YOU LOOK HORRIBLE," I said to the person inside the mirror.

She remained unmoved—she already knew that.

The bags below her eyes had bulged and darkened after weeks of restless dreams. Her forehead and nose were oily, with pores clogged by a swarm of blackheads. Her teeth were discolored and uneven, even after two years of torturous braces. Her lips, pale and dry. The crooked grooves of her frown separated poorly populated brows.

"I don't hate you," I said with brutal honesty. "But you and I… we had a pact." I gulped. "A-and you—do you *want* to look cadaveric and bald again?" I struggled to contain my tears.

I swung my auburn hair to the side and saw the bump on my neck, just below my ear. The bump was the size of a walnut, firm and rubbery. I pressed it, squeezed it, and kneaded it. Painless.

"Just one more day…"

I will not spend another seven hundred seventeen days and one morning wishing this thing gone. Not anymore. I've had enough suffering for a lifetime.

"I'm not sick. That's the only truth," I declared.

The swelling was just a sequel of the flu I'd suffered a few days ago, or maybe an ear infection, as suggested by a webpage when I

Googled the symptoms.

"I'm not sick and never will be… again."

My hands clung to the washbasin, and I inhaled deeply, glancing through my collection of fashion magazine clippings pasted around the mirror, dreaming about having the pictures' perfect smile, in a perfect face, attached to a perfect body, living a perfect life.

"Why does life have to be so unfair?"

I carefully arranged my hair to conceal the bump. And finally, I rehearsed my smile until I found a more pleasing expression.

"Maia, dear, are you ok?" my grandmother shouted, knocking at my door. "It's getting late."

"I know, I know! Sorry, I'm coming."

I unlocked and opened the door.

"Maia, do you feel ok?" My gran peeped into the bedroom with wide eyes, magnified by her bifocals.

"Yes." I continued combing my hair to ensure the bump remained hidden. "Just tired," I said, displaying my rehearsed grin.

"How can you be so tired if you got home *so* early last night?" My gran's sense of irony always rose before the sun.

I rolled my eyes. "Sorry, I was at Shelly's. I lost track of time."

"You have to stop walking alone at night—it scares me."

"It's just two blocks away!" Never mind that the blocks were almost a quarter mile each.

"I don't care if you're next door, to me it feels like China." Even tempered by her ear-to-ear grin, her words made me feel guilty. "Well, hurry up! You may be late to school, but you will never miss breakfast." She squinted at me over her glasses, wobbling her cane before leaving.

"I'll be down in a minute," I answered with feigned enthusiasm.

I dressed in a flash. I picked up my school things on my way downstairs and followed the smell of omelets and toast.

"I warmed your milk, Ruddy Bear, it's freezing out there," my gran said.

"You don't have to do that." Her coddling only made me feel worse.

"It's the only thing I have *to* do." She sat at the table, funneling her weight on her cane.

"You have a million things to do besides worrying about me." I disliked the idea of her doing dull chores and attending to her granddaughter instead of resting in some kind of old lady paradise.

She had turned reclusive since the passing of her best friend, Mrs. Thompson, less than a year ago. Since then, she seldom left the house beyond doing her errands. "When are you going to get that cottage at the beach?"

"Someday." She stirred her coffee and took a slight sip.

"Oh, right, I forgot. Someday." She always said that.

"*Someday…*" she repeated and gave me a know-it-all smile, "you will manage to meet your curfew."

I frowned at her. "You know I'm responsible." I hated to be treated like a child, like I wasn't seventeen.

"Responsibility is about fulfilling promises."

"We were having fun," I grumbled. "I bet you did the same at my age, didn't you?" After a long silence, a mischievous grin popped up on her face, and I cut into my mushroom omelet.

I heard Shelly honk twice out on the street.

"I have to go." I drank the warm milk in a gulp and grabbed my things on my way out, leaving the omelet steaming on the table.

"Where do you think you're going, Ruddy Bear?"

I rushed back and kissed her creased forehead—our old custom. "I'll see you later."

Shelly was immersed in her phone when I hopped in her car.

"Ready?" Shelly grinned.

My gran swung out of the house to say goodbye to us. With each passing day, I sensed it took a greater effort for her to make it to the porch, but she never missed a morning farewell and always managed to draw a smile out of me.

The streets were shades of gray, absent of greenery and sunshine. The frosted windshield of the white Corolla predicted the first snow was right around the corner.

"How did last night end?" I asked.

"You know, the usual. Jase came by."

I had goosebumps just hearing his name. *Jase.*

"But Rick said Jase wasn't coming."

"Well, whatever, he made it."

"What did he say?" I was afraid of the answer.

"Guess."

He loves me? I shook that reflexive, hopeful, stupid thought out of my head. "He asked you to convince me to team up for the research project?"

"Yeah, he mentioned that…" I crashed back to reality. Jase was passing biology thanks to me—I'd happily pulled an all-nighter writing his part of our last team project. "But first he asked where you were," Shelly added.

"Ugh, like he cares. He just wants to get out of studying cellular respiration." I rolled my eyes, trying to seem like I was brushing it off.

"Maia, I promise. He *really, really* likes you. Maybe he doesn't know it yet, but he does."

"And I would *really, really* believe that if he'd done a single thing to show it."

"Maia." She frowned. "C'mon."

How many times had I heard that? Shelly always lectured me about self-confidence, arguing that I was prettier than her, but I knew she was being patronizing. After all, it was *her* jaguar-print leggings that the guys' gazes followed. I was just a miniskirt-over-tights kind of girl. I guess I wasn't mad at her for trying to pump her best friend up a little.

"Don't worry, Rick told me Jase is done with Samantha."

Shelly's boyfriend, Rick, was Jase's best friend and football teammate. But even with Shelly pulling strings behind the scenes, we hadn't crossed over from being acquaintances to potential love interests. It felt as if we were Quasimodo and Esmeralda—but I was the hunchback.

Jase was the quarterback of the school football team. And he wasn't just any ordinary QB; he was being hailed by scouts as *the next Tom Brady*, which was reason enough to be besieged by women, even while he was dating Samantha—a slim girl a year older who surprised everybody when she chose to go to Penn State over moving to New York to become a model. Like all long-distance relationships, things must have been difficult, putting Jase back on the market—and into every schoolgirl's delusions, including mine.

"You just need to be brave and open yourself—"

"And break through a thousand rows of fan girls," I interrupted.

"I have a hunch he's going to ask you to the prom."

My jaw hit the floor. "Did Rick tell you that?" I shook Shelly's shoulder, risking a car crash, but it didn't matter.

"No, I'm just guessing." I knew I should not have high hopes, but I was starting to tingle a little. "But Jase did say he wanted to hang out with you," Shelly said with a sassy smile.

"No way." The tingles exploded through to my fingertips. "When? Where?"

"He said maybe tonight, but that's all I know." Shelly winked and exploded with laughter, driving through the school parking lot like a crazy cabbie. If we slammed into a school bus, I would die satisfied, knowing he wanted to see me.

Shelly parked, and I walked after her, besotted, absentminded, gorging on the possibilities created by my crafty imagination.

A car honked so we'd get out of the way before getting run over. Lisa—our third musketeer and Skrillex impersonator—leaned out the window, showing her new tongue piercing that matched her gauged ears. She parked and joined us just a minute later.

"What's new?"

"Maia and Jase might have a date tonight," Shelly said, proud of her accomplishment.

"I'll believe it when I see you two making out like fools," Lisa said.

"Me too." I sighed.

"You need to make a clear statement of interest if you want to make it out of the Friend Zone," Lisa said matter-of-factly.

"How many times have we discussed this?" Shelly rebuked. "She only needs to be herself. Men love confidence, and Maia can keep Jase interested." Great advice, considering how well being myself had paid off in the past.

We joined the river of students flowing through the school hallway.

"Hey! How you doing?" Rachel—our fourth musketeer, lover of argyle sweaters, cuffed jeans, and cats—adhered to us with her signature braced grin, always on the edge between happiness and torture.

"Great, Rachel," we answered in unison.

The crowd parted as Rick and Jase made their triumphant entrance, accompanied by their entourage, making every girl sigh as they headed our way. *Oh, my God.*

Shelly hooked my arm and whispered, "Just work your magic."

My field of vision fastened on Jase in his football jacket, tightened around his stout torso, with his fine-featured face that I would kill to kiss. His luminous eyes aimed at me, and I realized how much trouble I was in. I was slobbering, spellbound by his charm. *Don't ruin it this time*, I urged my inner self, but my heartbeat drowned everything out.

We charged, tribal armies clashing in *Braveheart*. Shelly went straight to Rick, slashing a kiss. Lisa handled John, and Rachel grinned.

"Hi," Jase said, and my confidence collapsed. I was only able to stare at him intermittently.

"Hi-i, how are you?" I said gingerly.

"Great, and you?"

"Fine, and you?" I blundered. *Retreat, retreat! Before the casualties become catastrophic!* I looked around for an open locker to vanish into Narnia for life but instead caught a glimpse of three smug witches gossiping about me: Barbara, Sophie, and Marie-Anne. There was no need to hear their words—gossip was so natural to them that their venom flowed through their movements and gestures. Their beauty and glamor were matched only by their devotion and resourcefulness to destroy, and I was in the crosshairs.

"I didn't see you yesterday," Jase said with what appeared to be concern.

Wait! Don't retreat, don't retreat! "I had to leave earlier."

"I heard that. Are you sick?"

"What?" I babbled. "No, I'm just tired, that's all." I ran my fingers down through my hair, feeling the bump below my ear, making sure to keep it covered.

"Too tired to partner with me for the biology project?"

"Yes!" I answered, overexcited. "I mean, no, I'm not that tired—"

"Hi, Jase," the witch Marie-Anne interrupted us with her honeyed voice. "How are you?" She stood between us, turning her back to me.

"Hey, Marie-Anne," Jase chuckled, and I became invisible.

"Jase." Marie-Anne fondled her hair like a cat grooming herself. "My car was making a weird noise on my way here…" *Yeah, sure, your brand-new Mustang was making any sound.* I could not avoid rolling my eyes at the spoiled-brat-in-distress act. "…and I was wondering if you could be so kind and help me check it out after practice?" She fluttered her mascara-saturated eyelashes. Marie-Anne had joined the cheerleading squad after Jase's breakup with Samantha with the sole ambition of getting close to him.

"Yeah, sure, no problem." And Jase, like all men, fell for a pretty girl's trap.

"Cool, I'll see you later." Marie-Anne peered at me over her shoulder scornfully with a pretend smile before departing. My blood was boiling and my jaw twitching, but before I could stammer anything out, the bell rang.

"Let's go." Rick tapped Jase's shoulder.

"See you tonight, then?" Jase asked.

"Yes."

"Ok, I'll text you."

Jase winked at me before Rick hustled him away. That gesture converted my tribulations into fluttering butterflies like a magic trick—the power of *l'amour*. I was astonished at my spoils of victory: he'd invited me out, even if it was just for the project, and hopefully our meetup would even be outside of school instead of at the crowded library, like last time. It was an epic win, even if I was the underdog to Marie-Anne. The smug witches spied me from a distance, plotting retaliation. I could not afford to show frailty, so I chinned up and walked tall.

"How was it?" Shelly pulled me to her.

"It was one small step for humanity, but a giant leap for me."

"Really?" She grinned. "Are you going to see him?"

I nodded, grinning stupidly.

"Great, Maia." Shelly's grin turned into a frown. "But please do me a favor and cut all the nerd crap tonight, will you?"

"Ok." Great, so I should just be myself, but also not be myself.

"What the hell was Marie-Anne doing?" Shelly asked.

"Being Marie-Anne."

We arrived at Mr. Mankell's history class, but while listening to a recount of the lives of Roman Emperors Tiberius, Claudius, and Caligula, I absconded from reality, thinking of nothing else besides Jase. I imagined the scene that night countless times, mentally changing the outcome each time. Finally, I constructed the perfect scene, in which I was glamorous, confident, and appealing and he invited me to prom in front of everybody. I accepted, confessing my feelings, and he drew me in close. But when we were about to kiss, Marie-Anne always invaded my fantasies, sliding her boastful smile between us. In my daydreams, I was brave enough to slap her.

But by the end of the school day, I had dragged myself back to reality. I knew that Marie-Anne was going to date Jase, and there was nothing I could do to prevent it. I had to go to work, so I boarded the bus downtown, hoping a torrential rain would flood the field, ruining their practice.

It never hurt to hope.

Bahiti's Cabinet of Musical Curiosities was set up in a classy Victorian row house with a terracotta brick facade and tall, arched windows displaying a broad array of instruments. The annoying electronic doorbell welcomed me, playing Johann Strauss II's "Egyptian March"—it was the first piece I learned when I came to work here last summer, because it was a favorite of the owner, an Egyptian composer named Fred Bahiti.

"Fred is working again," Griselda, my coworker and partner in misery, said as she snuck out for a coffee break. Mr. Bahiti had been composing his first sonata for the past fifteen years. Some "connoisseurs"—as he referred to his friends—considered him a perfectionist, but I had a feeling he was just short on talent. He blamed everybody and everything, from a passing plane to a fly, for disturbing his zen environment. Griselda and I were the victims of his constant gripes.

"Maia!" Mr. Bahiti shouted.

"Yes, I'm here." I crossed the maze of instruments: cellos, violins, lutes, zithers, harpsichords, and some weird antique stuff worthy of being displayed in a museum. Most people visited the store to admire rather than buy. Charging an entrance fee of one dollar might help to recoup the two hundred bucks Mr. Bahiti had paid the technician to put Strauss in as the doorbell tone, but my suggestion was not well-received by management. "That would be prostitution!" Fred had declared.

He was at the end of the room, seated at a Steinway piano with his wild hair and wearing chained glasses that hardly fit on his cob nose.

"Bring me a coffee," he said, browsing through the mess of scores plaguing the piano. He lifted his bushy eyebrows. "Did I speak in Arabic?"

"No, sorry." I rushed to the kitchen. He always dressed in white *gallebayas*, a long tunic that looked like old pajamas. According to Griselda, his family belonged to a tiny Egyptian minority who had been exiled because of cult persecutions.

I brought the boiling coffee to him, as ordered.

"Leave it on the table," he said, fondling his beard, immersed in his chords.

I stumbled, spilling the coffee over the scores. He slammed the piano keys, and a string broke with a strident sound.

"What?" Mr. Bahiti tossed the scores into the air and pulled his hair. "Another distraction!"

"Mr. Bahiti, I'm so sorry," I said clumsily, trying to correct the damage by blotting the pages against my clothes.

"This is a conspiracy to prevent me to finish my masterpiece!" He waved his fist high in the air, blaming—fortunately for me—whatever God he believed in.

"Bring me a .007 spring steel!" he demanded. "You can find them in the basement."

I hesitated before I nodded and turned to head for the basement. I had been down there just a couple of times with Griselda, and every time, I felt as if somebody was following me, breathing on the back of my neck. It was terrifying even in her company, but I feared Mr. Bahiti's temper more.

The creaking door revealed a dark pit, and the light didn't turn on when I pulled the chain. The windows were planked, leaving the scant sunbeams that strained through the cracks as the only source of light. I took a deep breath and used my cell phone as a lantern. The basement was crowded by dust-glazed boxes and furniture that seemed older than the building itself. The structure shuddered with the cars passing on the street, and the echoes reverberated like moans, drowning in the pools of water that dripped from the rusted pipes.

At the far end of the room, I found the blue metal cabinets containing the spare parts and a box labeled *Piano Wire* above a moth-eaten wardrobe. Even standing on my tiptoes, my fingers barely touched the box. I dragged over a drum and stood on it, but even once I could reach, the weight of the box forced me to tip it off the shelf. Once I got it moving, its momentum was too strong as it tipped down, and I hopped back to keep it from crushing me as it fell. I held my breath and waved my hand to disperse the cloud of dust, which revealed a deck of powdery cards scattered over the floor; they must have been stacked on the box. I picked up a card and brought it close to my phone to see it clearly.

"Reversed Devil," someone behind me said hoarsely. My heart

tried to escape through my mouth but collided with the scream in my throat. My cell phone lit the pitch-darkness, revealing an old woman in a floor-length black garment.

"Don't be afraid." The woman opened the lid of an antique brass oil lantern and brought it close to her face.

"You scared me to death." I coughed, trying to expel the dust I inhaled in my panic. "You are Mr. Bahiti's mom, right?" It was the first time I had seen her in person, but I immediately recognized her from the picture hanging in her son's office. It was difficult to forget those profound eyes framed by dark bags sunken in her skull, and her prominent nose had clearly been passed on to the next generation. "What are you doing down here?" I asked, perplexed.

"I'm visiting my son and came down looking for some old belongings." She glanced to the cards dispersed over the floor.

"Hmmm… sorry, I made a mess."

"Do you believe in divination, Maia?"

"I never told you my name."

"My son speaks a lot of you." *He does?* "He says you have a gift." *He said what?* I struggled to think what my gift could be. Brewing coffee?

"Yes, Maia, everybody has gifts." She pointed at the cards strewn over the floor. "Mine is reading the tarot. Do you want me to tell your fortune?"

"I'm not really into that stuff. Nothing personal," I added, but rejecting her made me feel uncomfortable, considering the fact that she was my boss's mother, so I tried to be polite. "And I don't have money. I'm kind of broke."

"I bet you have a ten-dollar bill in your right pocket."

Skeptically, I slid my hand in my pocket and took out a creased ten-dollar bill. I could have sworn I didn't have any money on me. "How did you know?"

She smiled briefly and turned dead serious again.

"Reversed Devil." Mrs. Bahiti turned to the cards, all facing down but one, displaying a number fifteen. The card depicted two demonic figures facing opposite directions, their long, serpentlike tails entangled around an inverted crucifix. "The snake is knocking at your door and brings news of chaos. From the bowels of heaven descends the beautified angel that remains an eerie creature, ravenous to feed on dreams and souls, with snares of romance and lust."

I didn't understand a word of what she said, but it gave me a bad feeling.

"Maia, you are being watched."

"Watched?" I asked, trying to grasp how someone could be interested in my boring life.

"Not in the way you think. *He* observes you from beyond." The image of a pervert watching me through a telescope was the only thing that came into my mind.

"Who? How can I recognize him?"

"You can't."

"So what am I supposed to do?" I asked with frustration, but old Mrs. Bahiti stared at me in silence.

"Great. Thanks for the fortune." I rummaged in the box for the piano wire, for once eager to get back to Mr. Bahiti.

"*He* is a messenger," she clarified.

"What is the message?"

"The only way to know is to pick another card."

The cards were lying harmlessly on the floor. *What is the worst that can happen?* I picked another card.

Oh God! I thought when I flipped it over.

"Reversed Death." Her gnarled finger pointed to the grim reaper with his black hooded cloak circling around a full moon. In his hands were a needle and thread, knitting his own robe. The card was crowned by the Roman numeral thirteen. "You are afraid to confront the end."

"The end?"

"You live in dread of the implacable truth that will bring you to your final destination. Your inner demons now are dwelling in plain daylight behind false masks, feeding from your negative feelings, the fears that fish from the murky well of your soul." She brought the lamp close to my face so her distressed eyes could run over me from head to toe and finally sniffed me. "Maia, you are plagued by the scent of death."

I wanted to laugh her off, but my shivering hand reached the bump below my ear. My heart froze and my entire body numbed with a spine tingling that felt like a centipede crawling up my back.

"H-how do you know?" I stammered.

"It doesn't matter how hard you try to hide it; Death is a hungry hound, which no chain can bind. And once you have been marked…" She trailed off, seeming lost in her thoughts.

"What?"

"It's just a matter of how fast you can run."

"*Run?*"

"Maia!" Mr. Bahiti's shout permeated the basement.

"I-I have to go back upstairs."

"Maia." She held my arm. "Don't tell him you saw me down here."

I nodded.

The old lady closed the lid of the oil lamp, restoring the darkness in the basement.

I left without turning back, telling myself not to believe in what she said. I didn't have time to start being superstitious. Upstairs, a ravishing piano melody welcomed me. A cheerful waltz dyed with nostalgia engulfed the entire place with oddly familiar chords. Chopin, maybe?

"Maia, that's it!" Fred yelled feverishly from the second floor.

"Chopin?"

"No, I've finally got it!" He must have been referring to the missing chords that would complete his sonata, something he endlessly moaned about. In his hurry, he slipped, stepping on his *galle-baya*, and rolled downstairs, landing at my feet. My hand flew to my mouth, horrified, and the piano went silent.

"Mr. Bahiti!" I propped him up.

"The piano, who was playing it?" he mumbled. I had assumed it was him, but it clearly was not, since he was lying in a heap in front of me. I gently led him to the Steinway. The bench was empty, and there was not a single soul in the store.

"You frightened the customers, Mr. Bahiti." I giggled, but he gave me a look that made me swallow my laughter.

Griselda shouldered the door open, cradling a fast-food bag and slurping a soda. "What?" she said, bewildered, watching us like statues while the "Egyptian March" played at the door. I wondered why Strauss had not played for whoever had been playing the piano.

Fred didn't say a word about it and returned to his staff paper. I buckled down to dust the instruments, keeping my mind busy to avoid thinking on what had occurred.

That evening, Fred allowed us to leave earlier than usual. He wanted to compose undisturbed. "See you tomorrow," Griselda said and kissed me on the cheek as we closed up shop. "You need to rest; you seem tired." She ran to her boyfriend, who was waiting for her across the street, leaning on his shiny bike. She flung her arms around his neck and kissed him effusively. For a moment, I almost died of envy, wishing Jase could be the one waiting for me, but my cell phone said otherwise, displaying neither missed calls nor messages. He was probably busy with Marie-Anne.

I keyed his number but couldn't press send. I was terrified of confronting my expectations about Jase. To realize he would never be real to me. To discover that my place in his life was at a distance, in the background, and never by his side.

Maybe I was just created to contemplate life, not to live it, I concluded glumly.

I shielded my hands inside my pockets from the biting wind, finding the creased ten-dollar bill.

Trembling, I reached for my neck below my hair but retreated before touching the bump.

I felt a cold blow on the back of my neck, as if it were somebody's breath. I turned around. The street was empty. Maybe Mrs. Bahiti was right, and I had to run, but where could I go?

The only place that came to my mind was the one I loathed the most.

The very place I wished never to return.

It doesn't matter how fancy and welcoming a hospital is; nothing can ever get rid of the smell of the sanitizer, and the white worn by the staff will never conceal the funeral black.

I browsed through the directory on the board at the entrance of the medical office building and picked a name listed with the medical specialty that would suit my purpose.

"Hi, I'm here to see Dr. Wolk," I said to the receptionist.

"Do you have an appointment?"

"Yes."

"Name?"

I never was a good liar. "Foster, Maia Foster."

"I'm sorry, I'm afraid there is no appointment under your name."

"Can you give me one?"

"Let me see…" Her striking long nails surfed the agenda. "Is next Tuesday, five p.m., ok for you?"

"Is it possible to fit me in today?" I shrugged and grinned.

"I'm sorry, I can't—"

"Please?" I reached for her hand. "It's important."

"Ok…" She retrieved her hand cautiously. "Please have a seat and let me see what I can do."

"Thank you."

She dialed the doctor while I took a seat among the patients in the waiting room. One was an old man fat enough to rest his head on his double chin, breathing like an out-of-tune trombone, and the other an emaciated woman in a wheelchair with a bag full of medications toppled over in her lap. Quite a different picture from those all-smiles people portrayed in the meds ads on the walls.

My phone buzzed with an incoming message from Jase:

See you at Wingy's at 8?

I squeezed my cell phone against my chest, and my eyes elevated to the ceiling. I sighed, and my heart bloomed with the sublime taste of elation.

YES, I answered immediately, followed by a smiley.

Everybody in the room was staring at me. I regained composure and put on a poker face to hide my excitement. I wanted to scream; I wanted to kick and run and dance. I was so blissful that I could kiss Mr. Trombone and take Mrs. Wheelchair for a ride around the entire hospital.

"Miss Foster?" the receptionist called.

"Yes." I jumped off my seat.

"Dr. Wolk will see you after finishing his remaining patients."

"Ok." I wondered if I should wait and waste the precious time I could be spending getting ready to meet Jase. However, staring at Mrs. Wheelchair's unmovable expression reminded me of the purpose of my visit.

The handles of the clock circled with the speed of a snail, and hearing the screech of the wheelchair and the heavy breathing of my companions only fed my eagerness to be out of there. The seats emptied one by one until the door finally opened.

"Foster," a voice called, and I ventured forth, holding my breath and clenching the straps of my backpack.

"Welcome, Miss Foster. I'm Dr. Wolk." He greeted me at the door with shining loafers, unwrinkled attire, and a dental-care-commercial grin. "Please, have a seat."

"Thank you."

"I owe you an apology for the long wait, but your visit was unexpected." His young appearance contrasted with the wall tapestried in credentials. "What can I do for you?" he asked, folding his arms over the desk.

"Well, I…" I stammered and ducked my head. "Sorry, I shouldn't be here."

"Don't worry, everybody feels the same way. What brings you here today?"

I cleared my throat, thinking that the sooner I started, the sooner I could leave.

"I-I came here, Doctor… because I need to know that I'm not gonna die."

CHAPTER 2

IT WAS THE MORNING OF NOVEMBER 25, my seventh birthday. My gran rushed me to the hospital in howling wind and rain. Dr. Emmerich rigorously inspected my neck and lifted my thin arms to tickle my armpits. I had to undo my dress to let him get a full inspection.

"As soon as we finish, we can go back home to celebrate your birthday party, Ruddy Bear," my granny said to cheer me up before the nurse inserted the enormous needle in my arm to take blood. I shut my eyes and imagined myself biting the piano-shaped chocolate cake and unwrapping my presents among my school friends to distract myself from the pain.

It didn't work.

We returned to an empty house. "I'm afraid we will have to postpone your party for a few days," my gran said, packing up the Happy Birthday signs, the musical hats, and the sheet music-themed tablecloth. "Doctor said that resting is best."

My eyes turned watery.

"Don't cry, my dear." My granny knelt and cupped my face in her hands. "You should be happy."

"Why?"

"The entire cake is yours!" she said, pushing up the corners of my mouth with her thumbs to draw a smile. "And I will buy another for when your friends can come."

My gran brought a massive slice of cake to my bed, along with the presents she and Mrs. Thompson had bought for me. But I was afraid to extend my curled arm to take them, fearing I could bleed to death through the hole the needle had left. I ate half the cake but left the presents unopened, considering myself the unluckiest girl in the world.

Three days after I went to the hospital, one more present arrived. "Hodgkin's lymphoma," I overheard Dr. Emmerich explaining to my granny. "It's a type of cancer that begins in the cells of the immune system."

"And that was how it all started," I explained to Dr. Wolk.

"I'm sorry," Dr. Wolk said, handing me a tissue to dry the stream of tears.

"I need to know, Doctor," I babbled.

"We need to perform some tests in order to corroborate—"

"Please, I need to know," I begged.

"Well, Miss Foster…" He paused and exhaled. "Your lymph node has been swollen longer than what is attributable to normal causes. The tiredness, weight loss, and night sweats you are experiencing are also clear symptoms, but most importantly, given your medical history, you have a high probability of relapsing."

"How high?"

Dr. Wolk remained silent.

"But he said it was over," I spluttered, remembering the words of Dr. Emmerich when he'd declared me victorious.

A champion.

Cancer-free.

"Please, let's not jump to conclusions…"

I zoned out Dr. Wolk's words and remembered the lamentations of my gran, coming out through the half-closed door of Dr. Emmerich's office. I was admiring the goldfish floating around the fish tank on the reception counter when I saw my granny shielding her face with both hands, as if she were ashamed of crying. I didn't really understand what was happening. But I knew it was bad. And

I knew I had caused it.

"…I'll need you to come to the laboratory tomorrow…" Dr. Wolk handed me a piece of paper, but my quivering hands rejected it, and I jumped out of the chair, fleeing back through the waiting room.

"Miss Foster? Miss Foster!" the baffled receptionist shouted, but I didn't stop. I escaped from the claustrophobic maze of rooms and halls of the hospital, evading the looks of nurses and patients until I made it to the exit. I jaywalked through the passing cars to the park across the street.

Finally, I found myself alone. I moseyed across the carpet of rustling leaves down to the riverbank, where an arched bridge extended over the rushing water. After climbing the steep bridge, I succumbed to exhaustion. I clutched the railing while I regained my breath. The gargantuan river flowed below my feet, not yet frozen by the winter.

Tears dropped from my chin into the river, leaving behind the salty taste of the dreadful memories of my battle against cancer. I shook the railing, imploring myself to wake from my nightmare.

"Please, Miss Foster!" Dr. Wolk yelled with labored breath, approaching the bridge and waving his hands. "Don't jump." He had left his comfortable office and crossed the park, dirtying his impeccable loafers in pursuit of an unknown girl—a gesture that I appreciated, even in my current state.

I released the banister and stepped back. He rushed over and secured me in his arms.

"I'm sorry," I said, shielding my face. "I shouldn't have run away. It would be rude of me to die before paying your bill."

He laughed meekly.

I delved into my pocket and felt the creased ten-dollar bill.

The wings of the night settled over the town as Dr. Wolk and I sat at a diner, his idea for calming ourselves down. It was barely ten past eight of the longest day of my life, and I was submerged in terror, deliberating whether it was still worth going to see Jase. *Could he still be waiting for me at Wingy's?* But even if he was, what would I say? *Sorry I'm late, but I was diagnosed with cancer—again.*

Pathetic.

It was time for me to let go of my foolish dreams.

Of course, he wasn't waiting for me, or even worse, maybe he'd never showed up. Why would he? I was just the nerd friend of his best friend's girlfriend.

I turned my phone off. It was better that way.

"Buck up. Long faces are not allowed," the overenthusiastic waitress said, chewing her gum while placing my strawberry tea and a decaffeinated coffee for Dr. Wolk on the table.

I smiled back, but Dr. Wolk looked troubled.

"I hope the tea helps you feel better," he said between sips of coffee.

"I'll be fine, as long as I can stay away from the hospital." He frowned. "Sorry," I said, still embarrassed by my behavior.

"Don't worry." He chuckled. "Miss Foster—"

"Maia, just Maia."

"Maia," Dr. Wolk rephrased, "would you believe me if I tell you I used to hate hospitals too?"

"Actually, I pictured you as the six-year-old asking for a dissection kit for Christmas."

"Hardly. I wanted to be a news anchor." After a long pause, he continued, "But finally, I chose to go to med school."

"What made you change?"

"Life," Dr. Wolk said, with his eyes lost on his coffee.

"But you love it now, don't you?"

"Most of it. There are things that I still hate. But overall, yes, I can say that I love it."

"I know the feeling."

"You want to be a doctor too?" he joked.

"No," I chuckled. "It happens to me with horror films. I hate them, but I cannot stop watching them. It became some kind of masochistic hobby. Since I was a little kid, I remember covering my eyes for the scariest scenes but refusing to turn it off. Eventually I realized that sounds could be even more frightening than images."

"That's called Gestalt," Dr. Wolk said. "It's a psychology theory that explains how your mind recreates the scenes for you, using a few parts from the original—in this case, the sound. And I have a feeling your mental version was even scarier than the actual movie."

"Probably," I admitted. "Eventually, I had to start fast-forwarding through the terrifying parts."

The hands of the big clock on the wall of the diner read eight thirty.

"I guess you have things to do," Dr. Wolk deduced from my obvious expression of concern. "You better go before your carriage turns into a pumpkin." He gulped his remaining coffee.

"I wish I could," I said, touching the swollen lymph node with my fingers.

"What do you mean?"

"Do you know Wingy's?" I said, playing with the tea bag, plunging and pulling.

"The sports bar?"

I nodded. "A boy I like asked me out for the first time." To discuss the research project, of course, but it still counted as a date—at least to me. "And right now, I should be sitting there instead of here."

"You better hurry, then," Dr. Wolk said.

"It's too late now."

"I'm sure he will understand your delay was due to extraordinary…" Dr. Wolk went silent, using his Gestalt psychology to decipher my expression and guess that Jase didn't know about my condition. "I-I'm sorry."

"I'm tired," I acknowledged. "I wish I could fast-forward the cruel parts of my life—"

"And slow down the happy ones," he finished the phrase with a shallow sigh. "It would be splendid if we could, but both come all mixed up, and you will miss the good parts trying to avoid the bad ones." His voice, charged with nostalgia, made me remember how many times that, when I had fast-forwarded movies, by the time I uncovered my eyes, the credits were already rolling.

"It was my mother," Dr. Wolk said with great effort after a long silence. "I became a doctor hoping to save her. But I couldn't." His eyes reddened, but he managed to suppress his tears. "She passed a week before my graduation. Lung cancer." He forced a grin.

I didn't know what to say to him. Or maybe I knew enough to realize there were no comforting words in such a situation.

I sipped my tea. It was cold.

I hauled my marathon-tired feet home. My gran was in the greenhouse in the backyard. She was a respected floriculturist, and her flowers were her priority, morning and night. They were her second love, just after me—but not by much.

"What are you doing?" I helped her drag a flowerpot with a beautiful purple flower in it out of the greenhouse. "It's freezing," I said, concerned. The canopy was too flimsy to shield the flower from the incoming snow.

"I'm tired of hiding from winter, my dear," she said, petting the flower as if it were a dog.

"But it will die."

"It's a *Masdevallia coccinea*," she said. "A mountain orchid. It grows at thirteen thousand feet in the South American Andes in temperatures below minus four degrees Fahrenheit."

I gave a second glimpse to such an extraordinary flower, doubtful of how something as beautiful and ephemeral as an orchid could brave those extremes.

"Supper is on the stove, Ruddy Bear," she said, dutiful as always.

"Thank you, but I'm not hungry."

"Are you ok, my dear?" She adjusted her spectacles.

"Yes." I looked away before she could spot my eyes. "I'm just tired. Good night."

I kissed her forehead and withdrew to my room. I hung the *Do not disturb* sign on the doorknob and twisted the lock. I leaned against the door. My room felt immense and cold. I plummeted to my bed in a sort of catatonic state.

Tears sprouted, but I didn't sob.

I lay awake for hours. Through my window, I watched the wind slowly spinning the night away, bringing dawn, as if the sky were a rotating diorama.

It was fatigue that finally shut my eyes, only to replay, rewind, and replay again and again the memories that I strived to forget.

The next morning, I woke up perspiring with fever, so I skipped school and work. It was a good way to evade Jase—and not just him, but myself. I was not in the mood to see anyone, but my excuses didn't dissuade an obstinate Shelly, who dropped by after school to see how I was doing.

"How did it go?" she asked anxiously, waiting to hear everything about my romantic night with Jase.

"I-I didn't go." I lowered my eyes. "I felt terrible and didn't show up."

"Oh, my goodness! Have you gone to see a doctor?" Shelly said, touching my forehead. She knew me enough to know that the only way I would skip a date with Jase was if I were literally dying—though she didn't know how right she would be.

"No, no, no, really, I'm fine. Just a sore throat, don't worry." It felt miserable to lie to my best friend, but it was better that way. Kept in the dark. I wanted her to enjoy being with me as much as possible.

"You have to get well as soon as possible—remember that Brendan's party is tomorrow, and we need to plan your comeback. You'll look so fabulous that Jase won't even remember you flaked on biology." Shelly tried to cheer me up with the courage of a football coach whose team is losing the game at halftime. I faked enthusiasm to disguise my dread, and my answer was convincing enough that Shelly left satisfied, making plans for the weekend.

Thinking too much was exhausting. I entangled myself in my bedsheets, wishing I could fall asleep and dream about being someone else. A better person in a better world. Living a simpler life.

I tried to divert my mind into my place of power, *the calm meadow*, as I'd been uselessly taught in my cancer support group, but I found myself crying. I punched the pillow, mad at myself.

A comforting hand rested on my back. Gran was sitting beside me—I had forgotten to lock the door.

"Hush, hush, my ruddy bear," she said as she stroked my hair.

"I'm sorry," I mumbled.

"Why are you sorry?" She set her cane against the bed and cleaned her spectacles with her age-worn handkerchief. "The first time I laid eyes on you, you were just like this, kicking and crying." She gasped. "It seems like yesterday when I held you in my arms. You haven't changed a bit."

"I think I've grown a few inches, at least."

"No, your clothes just make you seem bigger." Her words once again broke the spell of my tears, and a laugh sprouted. "You are and will always be my ruddy bear."

My grandmother told me often that I came into this world with my umbilical cord wrapped around my neck, just seconds away from dying asphyxiated. I was completely red, with white blots on my cheeks that resembled those of a red panda—that cute creature that looks like a breed between a bear and a raccoon. That was the origin of my nickname. Only my gran called me that.

"I remember lulling you to sleep while the doctors and nurses tried to save your mother's life." Gran's eyes turned glassy, looking at the portrait of my mother on the nightstand. After delivering me, my mother passed out on the operating table. Her heart stopped for no evident reason, as if her sole job was to deliver me into this world, only to abandon me a minute later.

"That day, my heart broke in two," Gran said. "I held my tears and squeezed you against my chest to prevent myself from falling apart."

"Why didn't you cry?"

"You were sobbing, my dear, and one person shedding tears in the room was enough."

I hugged her and rested my head on her lap.

"What was she like?" I glanced at my mother's portrait with a familiar uncertain mixture of feelings.

"I have told you a thousand times." But for me, I could never hear about her enough. "Luvena was a lovely girl, full of energy and eagerness to experience life and discover the world." She caressed the picture. "Oh, my poor baby, you made me so happy…"

I knew that in her youth, my grandmother had been diagnosed as incapable of having children. It was hard, but over time she put aside the idea of motherhood and channeled her passion into her job as a floriculturist and enjoyed her marriage the best she could. Then, when she turned fifty, her doctor communicated the unbelievable news that she was pregnant. It was a shock, as unexpected as my grandpa's passing a year later. But happiness, my grandmother always said, "is a bumpy road." She raised my mother all by herself, just like she did with me.

"Was my mother popular with the boys?"

"Oh yes, she was very beautiful, just like you."

"I'm not." Not in a million years. "I'm so dumb. I ruined the chance I had with the boy I like."

"Don't worry, my dear, nothing is lost. If you need to apologize, that's ok. If you are honest with him, everything will be all right." She patted me.

I wished I could, but I knew that telling the truth would doom everything I'd fought so hard to recover. I didn't want to be sick again. Furthermore, I didn't have the right to make my grandmother endure all that suffering. She didn't deserve it. I couldn't cause her the pain of losing another.

All of this was my fault. And I would have to go through all this alone.

My gran stood with effort and extended her cane to reach the *Do not disturb* sign hung on the doorknob. "Hearts are like doors: the hardest to open are those locked from inside."

Her words echoed in my head.

Maybe she was right.

"I'll fetch your lunch, my dear."

No, she *was* right. I owed Jase an apology.

That Saturday, I scrutinized my reflection in the mirror for the twentieth time: a striped shirt and a slate-gray wool peacoat matching my tight black denim and contrasting with my ice-blue leather boots. My accessories included a grass-green satchel, a tube scarf, and a knit beanie. I meticulously hid the traces of past nights' insomnia with a concealer and powder. After finishing, I looked once more and realized I already hated my outfit.

Shelly hit the horn twice, announcing that the moment of truth had arrived.

Relax, Maia, you have to do it, I repeated my mantra, focusing on my breathing. I reached the door, and my hand froze holding the knob.

"Maia!" my gran yelled. "Shelly is waiting for you."

On the way to Rick's house, I avoided speaking about Jase, which was really difficult with Shelly.

"You are not chatty today, are you?" Shelly said.

"It's nothing. I'm just edgy."

"Chill out. Tonight is your night, Maia." She squeezed my hand.

Rick's street was a congested parking lot, forcing us to park blocks away, but even from that distance, the music was as loud as if there were a concert at his house.

"This party will end early," I thought aloud.

"Why do you say that?"

"Police bait."

"The music? Maybe the neighbors like it."

"And Rick's parents?"

"On vacation. It's my night too." Shelly winked, handing me the car keys. "You know the way back home. I'll pick it up from you tomorrow."

The entire school was at the party that night—not a surprise, considering both Rick and his brother Brendan were so popular. Shelly held my hand, and we waded into the house. I hated crowds; they made me feel observed, uneasy. Thankfully, we found Brendan in the living room. He was a chubby, shorter copy of Rick. The party had just started, and he was already drunk. Did I mention why he was so popular? Drinking was his sport.

"Happy birthday, Brendan!" Shelly shouted, grabbing everybody's attention. She was definitely not the subtle type.

"Hey, Shelly! Thank you." Brendan staggered to hug her.

"Happy birthday, Brendan!" I imitated Shelly's enthusiasm but shrank back when I sniffed the stench of alcohol.

"I'm glad you came by."

"Where is Rick?"

"In the kitchen. Please serve yourselves, ladies." He raised his red plastic cup in a toast.

The whole football team was gathered in the kitchen, along with their fans—all except Jase. Shelly gave Rick an affectionate kiss and greeted everyone. I spotted the witches, Barbara and Sophie among them, so I detoured to the backyard.

My heart stopped.

There was Jase, in the middle of a group of people, smiling and running his hand through his scruffy hair in a way that made him look so sexy. Perfect. Unattainable.

The plans I had mentally rehearsed thousands of times vanished.

I wanted to run as much as I wanted to stay.

Shelly pushed a cup into my belly, which I held with clammy hands. She winked and returned to Rick. The cranberry vodka offered a solution to my lack of courage—my best option, even considering that all my past drinking had ended catastrophically. I drank, repeating to myself the power of the *law of attraction* as I'd seen on some pseudoreligious videos on YouTube. I snagged another cup of vodka and marched over with my gaze aimed at him. He looked at me with a mystifying air, and I stopped short. There was no doubt we were connected. Fated.

I made the last steps and started talking before anything could ruin it.

"Hi, Jase, I want to apologize about the other night. I stayed late at work and didn't feel well, so I went home. Sorry for not calling you." The couple of seconds I waited for his answer lasted an eternity.

"Hi, Maia. I tried to call you," he finally answered. "Your phone was off—"

"Of course it was off," Marie-Anne interrupted. I hadn't noticed her appear in the group. "She was having a romantic date with some old guy and didn't want to be interrupted." She flaunted her conceited smile. "Right, Maia?"

Marie-Anne's words left me speechless, with my insides twisting at the thought of being seen by her while I was with Dr. Wolk that night. *What did she know? What had she heard?*

"Why don't you tell us how you jilted Jase to be with some lame dad?" Marie-Anne swaggered, capturing the attention of everybody around us. My jaw clenched, and my nails dug into my palms as I wished to erase her pompous smile. "I didn't know you preferred such mature men," she teased. "Is he *married?*"

My ears pounded with each word, and my eyelids shivered. The last thing I wanted was to cry in front of Jase. I had to go. I turned around, but Marie-Anne grabbed my arm. "You're not even going to try to lie your way out of it?" she said boorishly.

I spilled the reddish vodka on her, staining her white sweater, and she retaliated with a slap that stung my cheek. I tried to strike her in return, but she rammed over me before I could hit her. We fell on the lawn and struggled, while laughter roared all around us.

"Calm down!" Jase pulled a kicking Marie-Anne off me.

I stood up, ashamed, surrounded by inquisitive looks.

I ran away, blaming myself for not listening to my inner voice that had told me to stay at home. I didn't stop until I reached the Corolla. But there was no time to sob in the car; I needed to be away from everybody and their stupid laughs. I turned the ignition and hit the gas, and within seconds the car was moving fast. The road was a constellation of lights through my sodden eyes.

The green lights turned yellow and then settled into red, but I didn't stop.

A flash shone at my right side. I slammed the brake and turned the wheel away, but a loud clang deafened me, and I was shaken violently. The lights revolved around me while I floated among a shower of glinting glass shards, until the car landed on the pavement.

I opened my eyes. Tears were running down my forehead. I was hanging from my seatbelt inside the upside-down car. The windshield and side windows were shattered, limiting my visibility to a portion of the concrete and the broken mirror, which reflected the wasted car.

My efforts to free myself were futile. I was stuck.

"—are you?" I heard bits of an almost inaudible voice.

"Ple-please help," I babbled.

"I was hanged too." The voice sounded like a woman's, and it drew closer, but I saw nobody. My sight was shading, and I fought to not lose consciousness. "You are in pain. You need to be freed," she said.

"Yes, yes, I want to get out."

I turned to the mirror and saw bare feet walking over the shards of glass. "I can help you if you promise me to do what I say," the voice said.

"Yes, yes, I'll do it, but please take me out of here! It hurts!"

"I will stop your suffering. All you have to do is call my name."

"I-I don't know your name, please, take me out!"

"Fear not, soon all this will be over."

That was the last thing I heard, and then there was nothing but darkness.

CHAPTER 3

AM I DEAD? I was in an endless corridor of cool granite walls embossed with intricate golden vines. Each column was crowned with infant seraphim, their hands supporting a vault garnished by paintings. On one side of the aisle, windows revealed a beautiful garden maze soaked in moonlight. On the other side, mirrors and doors adorned the wall.

Was this… heaven?

I saw myself in one of the multiple floor-to-ceiling mirrors. I was wearing a scarlet silk gown that hung from my shoulders and ran tight in a pronounced V to my waist, with flower-patterned decorations. I revolved on my exquisitely embroidered satin shoes, and my crinoline skirt billowed. My hair was tamed inside a voluptuous headdress, with silver hairpins that matched my pearl necklace. I could not conceal my happiness; I looked gorgeous.

The wooden doors opened, revealing my golden velvet heaven: a nineteenth-century ball, like something out of *Pride and Prejudice*.

The entire hall quieted at my entrance.

A courteous gentleman welcomed me with a bow. In exchange, I performed a dull curtsy. I held his hand, and he conducted me through the crowd.

Among the attendees, I saw Shelly looking flawless in a white-

and-yellow satin gown, accompanied by Rick, both posing as if they were on the cover of *Vogue*. Next in line was Lisa, pretending like she was having a good time, but her frown told a different story. It was hard to blame her, forced to wear a kitschy costume that didn't match her hipster taste. Then I saw Rachel, all smiles and spirit, encouraging everyone to clap. Following her were the three smug witches: Barbara, Sophie, and Marie-Anne, gossiping behind their ivory folding fans. But this time, envy corroded them. This was *my* heaven.

More acquaintances and strangers greeted me on my way to the heart of the ballroom below a magnificent dome with hanging chandeliers that shone like stars accompanying the halved moon aloft in the sky. A piano melody flooded the place with celestial chords; an assembly of violins, cellos, and flutes joined later to form a magnificent waltz. I recognized some notes.

Mr. Bahiti's completed sonata!

I slid back and forth and heel-turned on the sleek marble floor, carried by the music like a swan on a lake, swapping from hand to hand of various handsome gentlemen.

An intriguing man with a white bowtie and dapper tuxedo drew my attention. He made his way through the courtiers, half hiding, averting his eyes before our gaze could meet, revealing only his wry smile. He lurked behind the women's coiffures and hats, the flower arrangements, chandeliers, or whatever other decoration suited his purpose.

The waltz steered me around the ballroom, and with each turn I made, he subtly swapped places to anywhere I looked, like he was teleporting. His presence became overwhelming, maintaining a precise distance to keep me both frightened and fascinated.

I grew impatient to uncover his identity. It wasn't Jase. Yet, somehow, he made me feel the same way. I thought I'd never feel that way about someone other than Jase.

My Mr. Darcy, I thought, feeling like Elizabeth Bennet.

An uncanny being, more dream than man.

Just the idea of dancing with him made my heart race. I bit my bottom lip and licked it to quench my dry mouth and alleviate my impatience for him to come and take my hand. But the song ended, and he remained in the shadows.

Why? Did he prefer other women? Why not me? I hit the brake on my thoughts and glanced upward to avoid seeing him. Outside, dark clouds covered the night sky, churning just like my stomach.

Suddenly, my perspiring hands clung hard to my dancing partner, while my dizzy head tried to focus on the multitude, all murmuring, their strings being pulled by the witches, who waved their fans with boastful grins and conceited poses, plotting to destroy my facade and expose me as an impostor. I searched for Shelly, Lisa, or any other friendly face without success. Even my Mr. Darcy faded away.

A void grew at the center of the clouds, creating a hungry but silent hurricane that pulverized the dome. I asked for help from the people surrounding me but found oblivious faces seemingly unaware of the destruction.

Mr. Darcy was heading out of the hall. I nudged my partner away and gathered my skirt to run after him. Various gentlemen stepped in my way with extended hands asking for a dance, but I despised them, eluding everyone interfering. Someone seized my hand and pulled me back, and I landed in his arms.

It was Jase.

My heart stopped.

Finally, I was in the arms of the man I wished to call my love, but now all I could focus on was running after the unknown man. Jase read my treacherous glance and held me tighter.

"You have to let me go," I said, shoving him away with all my strength. He let go suddenly, and I fell to the floor. The music stopped. My reflection on the floor showed me gaunt, mapped with deep wrinkles, the bump on my neck the size of an apple. I ran my hand over my head, terrified, pruning patches of hair. I became surrounded by everybody's scorn, incapable of lifting my chin, horrified by the reflection of their monstrous guffaws revolving around me, each time faster, until a painful tingling in my stomach announced that I couldn't hold it anymore.

I puked, but my pain was not eased. The diabolical laughs made me realize I was not in heaven. I had fallen into the most elegant of hells. *Why? Why?* I asked myself. Tears sprang from my eyes but didn't drop. I squeezed my fists, wishing with my whole being that the hurricane could suck everybody out and leave me alone. But they lingered.

With my last trace of strength and fueled by agony, I stood and made it to the door. It was latched. I hammered at it, crying, while the maelstrom of despair devoured all the good and beautiful things, and with them, all my hopes.

I closed my eyes, waiting for the swirl to rapture me, putting an end to my suffering.

I opened my eyes to the 100%-polyester-germproof-light-blue curtains that I loathed so much. I was confused by how long I had been unconscious, unsure whether the sun was rising or sinking. But at that moment, having a window was the sole thing that mattered. Nothing is more depressing about the hospital than the lack of scenery.

My grandmother rose from the armchair in front of my bed and reached for my forehead with her cold hand. "How do you feel, Ruddy Bear?"

I gulped. "I'm sorry—"

"Shhhhhhhh." She stroked my hair. "I know. I know. Everything will be fine, my dear."

I inspected myself—aside from a splitting headache, I was in one piece. Then I pulled the blue curtain and realized that I wasn't in the hospital solely because of the car crash. My neighboring patients were two bald boys. *Welcome back to the cancer ward, Maia*, I said to myself.

I felt a hollowness in my chest when I realized that all my attempts to shield my gran from knowing had failed. "How—how?"

"You are so brave, Ruddy Bear," she said. *Brave?* I would have run away right then if not for the catheter that had me chained to the bed. "Cheer up, you have visitors." She cupped my face in her hands and pushed up the edges of my lips with her thumbs. "Your friends are here to see you."

I guessed I couldn't avoid them.

"Gran, please, don't say anything."

My gran obeyed, under protest. I knew she wouldn't like the idea of keeping my disease a secret. "Being sick is not a crime," she always said.

A minute later, she returned with Shelly, Lisa, and Rachel carrying a bouquet of tulips, two get-well-soon balloons, and a huge cardboard sign with the names and good wishes of everybody in class that made me smile.

"They're beautiful. Thank you."

"I'll leave you in good hands, my dear," my gran said before walking away.

"How do you feel?" Shelly held my hand, worried, unwittingly throwing a look toward my neighbors.

"Ashamed. I don't have words. Shelly, your car—"

"You don't have to worry about that. Insurance already took care of it. Besides, my father had promised me a new car after graduation, so you kind of did me a favor and sped things up."

"You only need to care about getting well." Lisa handed me the cardboard covered with messages. "Everyone is worried about you, as you can see." My happiness deflated when I found Jase's signature was missing. Lisa noticed my reaction and snatched it from me, placing it on the table with the flowers. "You'll be back kicking ass at school very soon."

"Hopefully. I can't stay in this place a single day more."

"It was just a scratch, right?"

"I guess so." My mind traveled back to the incident. "How is the other driver?"

The three exchanged disconcerted looks.

"What happened? Tell me, please," I demanded.

"*She* is ok, Maia." Shelly held my shoulder reassuringly. "Don't trouble yourself with that."

"Girls, thank you for coming to visit," my gran interrupted. "I would like you to stay, but Maia needs to rest."

"You don't have to say it, Mrs. Wainwright," Shelly said, caressing my hand. "I'll drop by to see her tomorrow."

"Anything you need from us, please just ask," Lisa said.

"Bye, Maia, hope you feel better." Rachel waved before departing.

"You are truly blessed to have such caring friends, Ruddy Bear."

Even desperately yearning for solitude, part of me felt empty after their departure.

"Afternoon." A forty-something nurse with permanently knit brows came in carrying a cup. She shoved the over-bed tray table in front of me, almost hitting me. "Move up," she said, adjusting my bed. "Drink it," the grumpy nurse commanded while supervising the IV's levels.

Following her uncomfortable visit, I forced myself to try it. I was pleasantly surprised; it was a strawberry tea.

"I hope it's not cold this time." Dr. Wolk walked in wearing immaculate medical scrubs.

"It's perfect, thank you."

"Mrs. Wainwright." He bowed his head to my gran, seated in the armchair.

"Doctor," she answered.

"When will I be able to leave, Dr. Wolk?"

"I know you don't want to be here, but I'm afraid it's complicated—"

Looking at his expression, I guessed where the conversation was heading. I braced myself to slide back into the hated old habit of talking about cancer. "Dr. Wolk, please, no sugarcoating. I want the truth, doesn't matter if it's harsh... I deserve it."

"Ok," he said. "We performed a tomography and identified a swollen lymph node in your abdomen, besides the one in your neck. A biopsy is scheduled. If positive, that makes you at least Stage III, and..."

"And?"

"Hodgkin's is an unpredictable disease, and it seems your accident may have weakened your immune system. We must act quickly. We can start your treatment with purveying monoclonal antibodies through IV infusion, but I'm afraid we will need a more aggressive solution," Dr. Wolk said with a grim look.

"Do you mean radiation?" I said, troubled.

"Maia, I understand you may be against radiotherapy because of the side effects. However, if you refuse, our sole option at hand would be high-dose chemotherapy."

Bad news: My gran was on the brink of tears. The word *chemotherapy* seems to have that effect on everybody. The good news was that chemo now came in supersize! Because half-bald was not enough. This was the kind of medicine that should be cataloged as a WMD by the UN.

"But before that, we need to perform a stem cell transplant to keep from hurting your bone marrow cells, Maia."

"Transplant? Am I going to need a donor?"

"No, it's what we call an autologous stem cell transplant, in which the stem cells are removed from your body and frozen a couple weeks prior to treatment. After the therapy, the cells are pumped back into your bloodstream, returning to your bone to help in the regeneration process of the new blood cells. It requires a long stay in the hospital, which makes it expensive."

The worst thing that a doctor can do after telling you you have cancer is to mention the word *expensive*. I wanted my grandmother to have some purpose in life other than to pay for my medical bills.

"What are my chances?" I felt like I should start writing my demise in my planner.

"Stage III, in a five-year window…" He paused a few seconds to consult his crystal ball. "Around eighty percent."

I didn't dare ask about stage IV probabilities. "And if I don't take the treatment?"

"You will be treated, and you will make it through, Maia," Dr. Wolk answered firmly. "Everything is going to be all right."

It was *déjà vu*. I traveled back in time to when the same words were pronounced by Dr. Emmerich, and now, ten years later, here I was, begging for another extension.

"You have to raise your spirits more than ever, Maia. As a doctor, I can assure you that long faces don't improve your condition. So cheer up. You know I'll do everything I can to help you." He squeezed my arm. "Now, if you'll excuse me, I have to see other patients. Mrs. Wainwright." My grandmother didn't answer. She remained silent, battling her tears.

My gran cradled my head in her arms without saying a word. My ear against her chest heard her tired heart pumping like a Japanese *taiko* drum. "I'll fetch a coffee, my dear," she said before leaving.

Maybe she was giving me a moment to cry alone, but I didn't.

I was not sad; I was angry.

I remembered how much I hated cancer. I hated to be different, to be bald. I hated the looks of pity. I hated being segregated, being alone. I'd fought for almost two years to get rid of the disease and start life over, moving to a place where I wouldn't be called *Maia the cancer girl*.

But enduring all that a second time?

"Excuse me, can you do me a favor?" said the kid from the adjacent bed. He was standing at the end of my bed wearing a Yankees cap.

"I'm sorry?"

"Can you do me a favor?" he repeated.

"Um—well, yes, if I can," I said, not feeling helpful in my state.

"Can you give me a smile?"

"What—" I smiled, surprised, and he smirked. He was probably a bit younger than me, but the loose hospital gown emphasized his slenderness, and his bald head made him look like a grown-up child. He was still cute, though.

"What's your name?"

"Maia."

"Thank you, Maia."

"For what?"

"Well, I bet my bro Gary"—he pointed to the boy in the other bed—"that you have the most beautiful smile in the hospital."

I moved the curtain to see Gary.

"Hi, Maia," said Gary, adjusting his eyeglasses on his pug nose.

"Sorry you lost," I said to the first kid, hoping I didn't blush.

"Oh, I definitely won. Forget the hospital—it's the most beautiful smile in the world."

I went mute. I didn't know whether my flushed cheeks were from his compliment or the cancer. But I started to like these guys.

"I'm Darrell, by the way."

"So what did you win, Darrell?"

"I can't tell you."

"Why?"

"First rule of the club."

"Club?" I said disgustedly, thinking of all the support groups I'd hated, which I'd probably have to join again. Nothing personal, but being around sick people didn't make me feel less sick.

"It's like *Fight Club*," Darrell said.

"But with diseases," Gary clarified.

"So, a Fighting Disease Club?" I asked.

"Yes, sort of." Darrell nodded, arms folded.

"But cooler than that—that sounds kind of lame," Gary said sheepishly.

"And what do you do in your club?"

"Can't tell you," Darrell said and returned to his bed, pushing his IV pole and closing the blue curtain. After two steps, he poked his head out. "Just kidding!" He drew the curtain again and lay down languidly on his bed. "Truth is, we are ghostbusters, and since he lost, Gary has to confront the biggest challenge we have ever faced."

"Which is?"

Darrell sat on the edge of the bed and half whispered, "Find out if there is life after death."

I wanted to laugh out loud, but I controlled myself. "Yeah, nobody has ever wondered that before," I said sarcastically.

"It's not a joke," Darrell said, deadpan.

"Of course not," I answered with a staid expression. "I'm *dead* serious about it." I exploded in peals of laughter.

Darrell looked irked.

"What? You like my smile but not my laugh?"

"You don't understand. This is not about us going, Maia. It's about *them* coming."

I wanted to laugh again, but my recent experiences had chipped at my iron incredulity. I thought about Mr. Bahiti's mother in the basement. "You mean like *real* ghosts?"

Darrell sat up straight. "When I came here, there was an old man three rooms away down the corridor. His name was Farrell. Yankees fan. Good guy. *Too* good for pancreatic cancer. His wife was by his side, day in, day out. One of those nights, a girl came instead, saying Mrs. Farrell was ill at home. Then, the day after, Mr. Farrell was found dead on the floor. Mrs. Farrell got here and was devastated at not being present for her husband's last moments, just like had happened with her daughter. Apparently, she'd drowned years before, when they were on vacation. I tried to comfort her. She showed me a picture of the family, and I couldn't believe it, but it was *her*."

"Her?"

"The girl who stayed with old Mr. Farrell that night when his wife wasn't there was their dead daughter."

His story had me at the edge of my bed with a chill in my bones. "So you saw a ghost?"

"She was no ghost," Darrell said gloomily. "Her name was Iris. She was nice. We chatted and joked and snuck a cigarette in the stairway."

"You smoke, having cancer?" I asked, irritated with him.

"What? I don't have lung cancer," Darrell grumbled, but Gary coughed. "Sorry, bro," he apologized. "But you are missing the point, Maia. She was real."

I was not missing the point. "So where do you think she went?"

"How am I supposed to know?"

"Maybe she went to the morgue to wait for the next shift," Gary said, laughing.

"Well, I hope you never figure it out," I said, wishing a long life for them. "I'm tired. I need to rest." I closed the curtain, but my wandering mind didn't allow me to relax.

Could it be true? Could this somehow not be the end? Not that I didn't believe in miracles, but I was also a natural skeptic.

I rubbed the swollen lymph node on my neck, now the size of an egg, and my hand descended in search of a bump on my navel. The second nail in my coffin.

I must have closed my eyes, and when I opened them, I was there again, in my golden velvet heaven. In my beautiful dress, I swayed with ease around the ballroom of brandy-colored chandeliers and gilt walls, the place where my elusive charming prince was a reality.

My dream unfolded exactly the same, but this time the hurricane grew fiercer, devouring my bliss in an even more violent fashion. It wrecked the bricks and ripped open the jammed door that had impeded me from running after *him*.

My charming prince strolled gallantly at the world's end. I hurried, calling after him with my voice drowning in tears. After each step, the tiles of the terrace detached from the ground, floating into the maelstrom. The tips of my fingers almost reached him. I was so close to falling into his arms. So close to being protected. To being told that everything was going to be all right. That I would not die. But I couldn't reach him.

It didn't matter how fast I could run or how loud I hollered, even my dreams announced with frightening certainty that my time had run out. Going to college, traveling the world, loving passionately, and having children were desires that would remain unfulfilled. Even if God were kind with me and spared my life, the aftermath for cancer survivors is painful. Traumatic.

It was better to surrender and drown in the peaceful darkness.

I woke up soaked in sweat in my hospital bed, wreathed in the drapes of my blue cocoon. The lights were dim, and the room was chill and silent, with only the beeps of the medical devices disrupting the quiet night.

"I have asked for nothing in my life. But I have lost everything," my grandmother murmured behind the curtain. "That's why I beg you to help me." I guessed that she was praying. "I would do as you command," she continued. "But please, promise me…" She started sobbing. "You have to promise me—please."

As she fell silent, there was a tightness in my chest. I was accustomed to the feeling. I had hoped before for God to hear my prayers, but I was always met with the same silence.

I bit the sheets to release my frustration.

But then, someone actually answered.

"I'll keep my promise," a male voice said.

I opened my tired eyes wide and looked toward the gauzy curtains, which projected a faint silhouette of a man standing beside my grandmother.

"Tomorrow night, then," she replied.

"Gran?" I called.

"What is it, Ruddy Bear?" She peeked through the curtain with a concerned expression. She walked to me and placed her hand on my forehead.

"Who are you talking to?" I asked.

"Oh my God!" She called the nurse station. "You are burning in fever!"

"Who is he?" I asked again, but she ignored me.

The grumpy nurse flung the curtains wide open and checked my vitals. I just contemplated the empty space where the man had been.

Who was he?

Maybe he was a moneylender, come to seal a deal to take the house. When my disease was diagnosed ten years ago and treatment was prescribed, my granny had to sell her old house in order to pay for it. We were forced to abandon the property with big oaks where I'd lived the happiest moments of my girlhood.

Worst case scenario, the man was Dario. I refused to call him my father, because the only thing I had in common with him was my surname. No newborn who was abandoned while she was still in the womb deserves to carry the name of a neglectful father. My grandmother argues that he felt guilty after the passing of my mother and insisted on giving me his name, but I believe it was just to indulge himself, posing as a righteous man. His quick departure afterward proved that he only cared about appearances and what people might say. The last time I saw him, he stood before me at the end of my treatment offering "financial aid," as he called it—fortunately, I was recovered enough to reject it. Maybe now his remorse obliged him to act in advance, hiding in the shadows to prevent me from seeing him. Dario knew that even on my deathbed, I would reject him a thousand times.

The following day, my condition worsened. I was drifting in and out of consciousness because of sedatives and medication. It was like a time-lapse video from dawn to dusk. The visitors sitting in the armchair switched one by one, until the image of my gran sleeping calmly granted a bit of peace to my preoccupied soul. The window was ajar, welcoming the chilly wind that blew the curtain softly.

A hand rested on my granny's forehead. A man's hand.

I leaned to the side to see the figure concealed by the half-drawn curtain. It was a young man in a raven-black frock coat. He was probably my age, but something in his manner made him seem older. I sat on my bed to get a closer look, which called his attention. He stared at me with mesmerizing olive-green eyes that reflected the scarce light coming through the window. He walked to the foot of my bed.

"Y-you were the one who was here last night?" I stammered.

He remained silent, staring at me with an odd expression of fascination.

"What is it you want with my grandmother?"

"I'm here to take her," he said with a serene voice that made me feel wrapped in velvet.

"Why? What do you mean? Take her where?" I demanded, but he seemed unconcerned. "It's because of me, right?"

His silence fed my anxiety.

"If I confess to you a secret," he finally said, "you won't tell anybody else?"

I shook my head. "Ok, I won't."

"Your grandmother has fulfilled her time here."

"Is she going to die?" I said without thinking, as if the words were whispered to me. It sounded crazy, but somehow, deep inside, I knew he was speaking the truth. "I overheard her yesterday, asking you for a promise." My voice trembled.

"She asked to be allowed to see you again."

"She—she can see me now," I said, trying to compose myself.

"Not now. Later."

"Later? But you just said she is gonna… do you mean she's going to die?"

Darrell's story about the daughter visiting her dying father bubbled to the front of my mind. *Could it be?* I was uncertain if I was delirious and what I was witnessing was a side effect of the drugs pumped into my system, but it felt terrifyingly real.

"Souls need to be shepherded in and out of the *waking* world."

"Waking? You mean the living?" I asked abruptly, but he didn't reply. "Are you an angel? A demon?" He remained unchanged. "Death?" I said, discouraged, knowing I had answered myself. I already hated Gestalt psychology. "I never imagined Death would look so *young*."

"I didn't say who I am." He looked toward the window, and his tousled hair waved in the chilly wind.

"But you came here to claim my gran's soul. So you are Death." He didn't deny it.

"Can you at least let me know why you took my mother?"

He turned, intrigued. "Do you miss her?"

"How could I miss someone I've never met?" I said. I remembered her image only through photographs. "But I've suffered her absence my entire life." Then it occurred to me. "If you can bring dead people into the living world, could you bring my mother for me? I want to meet her."

"You already know your mother."

"I was minutes old, too young to remember her," I explained. "I want to see her."

"Everything has a price. How much are you willing to pay to see your mother?" His eyes illumined with curiosity. "But more important, how much are you willing to pay me to spare the soul of your grandmother?"

My grandmother was all I had. The idea of her passing was something I could not bear.

"I-I don't have money."

He cocked his head. "Not even the riches of the entire world would be enough to trade a soul."

"Then what? I don't have any possessions."

"You have one." He stepped closer and reached for my hand.

His was ice-cold. "A soul for a soul," he whispered.

CHAPTER 4

"MY SOUL?" I GULPED.

Was that even possible? That meant souls were real. But, even as abstract as the concept of a soul might sound, the idea of trading mine was bloodcurdling.

"Yes," he said serenely. "Imagine your grandmother has been sentenced to death. But you have the power to take her place on death row and sacrifice yourself to the capital punishment. Then her life will be absolved."

I turned to my gran, sleeping soundly out of exhaustion, and realized she had sacrificed enough. It was my turn now. Besides, I was already dying. It would only mean speeding things up. Making it easier. Simpler. On second thought, it was a fair tradeoff—even in her eighties, my granny probably had a greater life expectancy than me.

"If I accept…" I took a deep breath to control myself. "Do you promise me I'll reunite with my mother?"

"What makes you think that you are in a position to bargain?"

"I beg you."

Thoughtful, he observed my hand in his for a long time. "Ok, I promise you'll see your mother."

"Then… I accept."

"Repeat after me: I offer my soul in exchange for my grandmother's."

I squeezed my fists. "I offer my soul in exchange for my grandmother's."

"*Fait accompli*," he pronounced and headed toward the door. "Now hurry up, we have to leave."

I didn't hesitate. I extracted the needles, detaching the cords and hoses that kept me captive. The ECG flattened with a continuous beep. *Was I dead now?* I felt no difference at all, but being out of bed, back on my feet, relieved me. It also reminded me that I couldn't go anywhere in this hospital gown—not even to the afterlife. I closed the blue curtains and dressed in the clothes my gran had brought me. She was still peacefully sleeping in the armchair. My chest tightened, and my limbs trembled. Should I say goodbye? I wanted to wake her up and reassure her I'd be back soon, but it would be a lie.

I leaned to kiss her forehead, but the man grabbed my arm and pulled me out of the room.

"Wait, I have to—"

"Your time is up," he said brusquely.

"Wait!" I glanced back at my granny, Gary, and Darrell with uncertainty.

The night was dead quiet. The hospital corridors of beige walls and polished blue floors were deserted. The nurses at the station seemed frozen in time; they didn't even blink. How was that possible? Was this what death was like? The clock on the wall was fixed at 1:30 a.m., the second hand not ticking. Among the collection of living statues was the grumpy nurse pouring coffee, which floated, suspended, from the stainless-steel thermos into the cup. My fingertip burned when I touched it. It was *real*.

"How—"

"Don't question."

He took me through the stairs, a couple of stories down, and then into a corridor. At the end, double doors, there was a sign that said "Morgue."

"You've got to be kidding me," I said.

"Death is no joke." With exaggerated chivalry and a sardonic smile, he motioned me into the cold hall. I shielded my nose from the formaldehyde stink that lodged in my nasal cavities. We were alone—except, of course, for the corpses lying on the metallic trays and the ones stored in the stainless-steel refrigerators. I thought I was about to faint.

He sauntered down the aisles, peeking beneath the sheets over the corpses. "There you are!" he exclaimed, unveiling a corpse like a magician revealing a trick.

I quickly closed my eyes, but it was too late—the grotesque image had been engraved on my mind. The body belonged to a girl my age with a huge, bloody wound on her forehead. I recovered my composure and opened my eyes to see him undressing her.

"What are you doing, you pervert?"

"If we want you to pass for dead, you should look dead," he said in a soothing voice.

My stomach churned.

"Do I not look enough dead for you?"

"But you are not dead, not yet," he said, handing me the girl's white dress and her denim jacket. "Camouflage."

"I'm not wearing this, it's disgusting," I complained, holding up the bloodstained dress with the tips of my fingers.

"Do you have a better idea to fool the Ferryman?"

"Ferryman?" I said, remembering Charon from my literature class, the character who helped Dante to cross the river into the world of the dead using his barge. The man's don't-mess-with-me look dissuaded me from further questioning. I withdrew to an office and changed my clothes, grumbling about the mortuary apparel. At least the clothes were my size—he had a keen eye. I came out of the office to see a black rubber cadaver pouch on the floor—*Oh shit!*

"Come here," he ordered, and I reluctantly obeyed, standing three feet away from him. "Closer." I stepped forward, and he eyed me from head to toe. I rolled my eyes, feeling uncomfortable with the low-cut dress, too revealing for my standards. "Close your eyes."

"What?" I moaned.

"Close your eyes," he repeated. I obeyed and felt his overwhelming presence invading my personal space.

"Don't peek," he whispered in my ear and drew his hand through my hair from my forehead to behind my ears, transmitting shivers to my entire body. His fingertips fondled down my face with delicacy and to the back of my neck, arousing goosebumps on every square inch of my body. *Oh God!* It felt so good that I wished it would never end—but then his fingers started to stick to my skin. I opened my eyes and saw his fingers were covered with the dead girl's blood. I stepped back, ready to throw up again, but I managed to stop myself. "I told you not to peek," he said. "You need camouflage."

"Jesus, this is gross."

"It's just blood." He unzipped the cadaver pouch. "Step inside. I need to take you out of here."

"No way, I'm going to… suffocate… in there."

"You just traded your soul, and now you're worried about suffocating?" He made a point. "Okay, fine, I'll keep the zipper down to let you breathe. I promise." I took a deep breath and lay down.

He dragged the zipper over me, leaving just a three-inch gap of light and air. After three seconds in the bag, I remembered my claustrophobia, but it was too late. "Be quiet," he said and swung me over his shoulder with ease, with my legs hanging in front and my head swinging against his back. All I could see were his feet and the moving floor.

The hospital was still dead silent. I wondered why we had to use this stupid bag for getting out, when everybody was petrified. The frustration combined with the blood pressure descending to my head made my travel unbearable. I pulled the zipper down to make the hole wider.

"No peeking," he scolded and took a corner quickly, bumping me against a doorframe.

"Hey, watch out!" I punched the bag, aiming for his back, and he retaliated with a swat against my legs. "Douchebag!" I kicked and struggled, enraged. A refreshing cold breeze strained through the gap. We were outside. He walked for a couple minutes more before dropping me.

"Hey!" I undid the zipper, furious. I found myself in the park across the street from the hospital, surrounded by thousands of snowflakes suspended in the air, locked in time just like the nurses. The first snow had arrived. "Wow," I marveled, admiring the constellation of snow.

"Wear this." He put a coat over my shoulders and walked, leaving a trail in the snowflake's field and sitting on a swing beneath a streetlamp. We were at the playground on the river side of the park. I followed the figure-shaped cave after him.

"Now what?" I asked.

"Now we wait." He looked to be admiring the buildings reflected on the river, which created the illusion of a floating city.

"Wait?" Maybe it was his indifferent answer, the bloody dress I was wearing, or everything all at once, but I exploded. "You kept me from saying goodbye to my grandmother because we were in such a hurry, and now you ask me to wait?"

"You wasted your farewell time dressing yourself. Where we are going, there is no need for that."

"Then why did you force me to wear these clothes and dip me in blood?"

He didn't reply, and it was not his silence but his calmness that infuriated me.

You unabashed, unapologetic, egocentric weirdo, with your charming eyes and Morgan Freeman's voice. You won't fool me anymore, I thought, picking up a snowball and throwing it at him. "Do you think it's funny for me to look like a corpse?"

"Actually, you look lovely in that dress." He grinned.

His grin connected something in my brain.

It was *him*.

The smile I dreamed of, the uncanny being, the dream of a man, my Mr. Darcy. *No, no, no, no. Maia, hold your horses. This* prick *could not be him.*

"Your outfit only needs one last touch." He extended his hand to offer a gold-circled medallion with an engraved pentagram and five small orbs embedded at each vertex—blue, red, green, yellow, and black at the top. Carved on the other side was my gran's name, Emma. It was too light to be gold. "This is what you need to wear to fulfill your part of the bargain."

"This is how I save Gran?"

"You need to wear it as you take your grandmother's place in the pilgrimage of death."

"Pilgrimage to where?"

"To Mt. Touriel." The name didn't ring a bell.

"What's there?"

"Death itself," he said with a cryptic tone. "Samael, the archangel of death."

"So, what, I bring him this necklace, and I save my gran?"

"Your sacrifice. The offering of your soul is what will save your grandmother."

"Sacrifice…" My thumb fondled the engraving, and I put it on without hesitation. As soon as I had it hanging from my neck, a vicious smile popped up on his face.

"Good. Now your life belongs to you no more, so please stop behaving like a spoiled little brat and sit down," he said.

"How dare you?" His gallantry was just a mirage. He really was a prick. "You have no idea who I am."

"Yes, I know you. You are Maia Foster. You are a spoiled brat who thinks you deserve special treatment. But tell me, what puts you above all the people on the ward? What makes you different from the girl at the morgue? Do you think she wanted to die? That she deserved it and you don't?"

"How dare you?" My insides quivered. "You have no idea—"

"Tell me, Maia," he interrupted with a bold voice. "Are you here to save your grandmother or to put an end to your suffering?"

I could not answer.

I ran back to the hospital, away from him but not from his words, which haunted me in my escape. "Spoiled brat? Me? An orphan? Ha! *Sure.* He has no idea what I've gone through. What I've suffered… What my gran has suffered!" There was a weight on my chest, and I struggled to breathe until it forced me to limp, and then it became so crushing that ten steps later, it forced me down to my knees. The medallion felt like it weighed a thousand pounds. I tried to tear it off, but it was welded to my chest. I crawled, but the burden increased with every step. *God, what have I done?*

Finally, I understood the severity of my situation. My life didn't belong to me anymore. It was *his*. And the medallion would keep me from escaping his grasp.

I turned around, and the burden vanished as I returned to my captor. I sat on the swing beside him in silence, trying to digest my unavoidable fate. He knelt in front of me and took a white handkerchief out of his pocket. He held my chin and dried my tears daintily.

"It's normal," he said, dabbing my face with the handkerchief moistened by my tears for cleaning the blood. "It happens to everybody."

"What?" I asked, still furious.

"The refusal of death. The legend says that the holder of Lazarus's medallion must follow the pilgrimage of death. With each step away from your caregiver, your heart will weigh a pound more," he revealed. "The medallion is not a punishment."

Caregiver. Great euphemism. "Then I'm stuck with you."

"For your protection," he said, finishing my cleaning.

"Even if a dog loves his chain, it's still a chain."

"Not all chains have to be shackles," he said and walked around behind me, pushing my swing.

"Wait!" I clung to the cold chains. "Please stop." But he pushed harder, making me fly back and forth, leaving a path in the snow-flakes.

The memory of a long-forgotten sensation became vivid. People who've had a glimpse of the hereafter say they witnessed their entire life recounted before them. That night, below a galaxy of snow, I was transported to the house with the big oaks, where I swung endlessly, staring at the sky. When everything was simpler. Happier.

Little by little, I let go my fear, and a stream of joy replaced it.

"Higher!" I shouted.

He walked in front of me and observed me swinging, arms folded, as if he were genuinely delighted by the fact that I was having fun. This stranger aroused in me more questions than I could possibly even ask. He was fascinatingly terrifying.

"If I'm going to be your slave," I said, "at least I have the right to know your name."

He delighted me with his smile once more, and out of nowhere a black carriage drawn by four ebony horses, with no coachman, appeared in the road, stopping right behind him. The coach's creaking door opened by itself.

"You can call me Sidney." He bowed, extending his hand. "Shall we go?"

Sidney. It was a beautiful name for a kidnapper.

CHAPTER 5

I LOOKED AT SIDNEY'S HAND. My head was packed with doubts. But it was time to stop thinking about me and start thinking about her. Because I would do anything for my grandmother, including tolerating a handsome know-it-all jerk.

I took his hand, and Sidney led me inside the coach. He jumped in after me, and the door closed.

The luxury carriage was worthy of a vampire, upholstered with wine-colored embroidered fabric that covered every surface, including the windows. Only a flickering candelabrum averted the sensation of being buried alive. Sidney sat like a king on his throne. His heel stomped three times, and the horses cantered, carrying us into the unknown. Sidney's fist rested on his cheek, and his gaze focused on me. His eyes blazed, reflecting the candlelight, forcing me to glance away before I blushed.

"A carriage. Odd way to travel to the afterlife, huh?" I said to ease the tension.

"What did you expect? A bright light at the end of a tunnel?" he said, raising his eyebrow. "There are more civilized ways to travel."

"Civilized? For which century?"

"Horses never go out of fashion. They are a representation of elegance and power."

"Elegant? I'll stick with cars."

"More men have conquered the world mounted on a horse than in a car."

"You have a point," I said, remembering Napoleon riding his white horse.

"Then why don't you admire them?" he asked.

"Besides the fact that they are stinky fly magnets that shit all the time?"

He smiled, and the moving coffin stopped.

"Are we there?" I asked.

"No, we have something to do first." The carriage's haunted door unveiled a dense mist that limited visibility beyond ten feet. "Wait here," Sidney said before disappearing. The crickets' chirping was the sole sign that confirmed there was something alive out there, but I didn't dare move.

All of a sudden, a hooded figure appeared at the doorstep, startling me.

"Who—who are you?"

The hood fell, unveiling a fair, crinkly-haired girl with a snub nose and steely blue eyes, a little younger than me, maybe fifteen. She wore a cloak atop a long red dress—very old-fashioned— which contrasted with her cherubic features, making her seem like a grown-up child.

"Miss Niemeyer," said Sidney behind her. "She will accompany us."

She grinned. "Everybody calls me *Pfirsich*," she said with a sharp German accent.

"What?"

"It means Peach." An accurate nickname to describe her pink cheeks.

"Nice to meet you, Peach. I'm Maia Foster." I felt odd, shaking hands with a dead person—if that's what she was. She sat beside Sidney. The coach set in motion, and the creaking wood was the only sound amid the awkward silence.

Is it impolite to ask how she died? I wondered, staring at her. She seemed too young to be dead. Even though I was barely her senior, cancer made me feel like a veteran.

"Is everything ok?" Sidney grabbed Peach's hand intimately.

She nodded, and then he glanced at me, but I looked away.

"We've arrived," Sidney declared as if it were an order, and the carriage suddenly stopped. Trying to figure out how he knew where we were was pointless.

The haunted door opened again, revealing another foggy landscape, but this time I heard the sound of clanging bells instead of crickets. Sidney helped us climb down. An icy wind tugged thick steam away from the chimney of an old steam locomotive that seemed to have been taken out of a Wild West movie. A steam whistle rumbled, and the platform became turmoil. Hasty travelers rushed out of the fog to pack into the train.

"We have to get onboard." Sidney guided us arm in arm through the mob, while I gazed around, wondering if all these lively people were...

"Are they all dead?" Some of them wore old clothes, transmitting a spectral feeling, but I was the only one covered in blood.

"Shhhhhhh. Be quiet, and hide the medallion," he said when we saw a group of soldiers heading our way.

I buttoned up my jacket and ducked my head. We got to the front of the line, where an old man with a long, cottony beard guarded access to the frosty Pullman. He adjusted his gold-laureled captain's cap. Sidney poked me forward.

"Left hand," the captain said, and I obeyed.

His ridgy nails traced the lines of my palm. "Open your mouth," he ordered, just like my dentist, but without a surgical mask to hide his crooked, rusty teeth. His keen eyes looped my mouth clockwise and back, and his beetling eyebrow cambered with surprise when he noticed the chain of the medallion around my neck.

"What is it?" I said with dread.

"Everything is fine." Sidney disgruntledly handed him a small pouch.

The bearded captain nodded slyly. "Careful, girl," he advised.

"Of what?" I asked, but he ignored me, looking Sidney dead in the eye. "What's going on?"

"Pay attention to the whistle," the captain replied, his eyes still trapped in Sidney's gaze.

"Go." Peach pushed me inside.

The Pullman was lined in warm mahogany finishes and leather elbow chairs. It was lit with petrol lamps hung on brass brackets. I found an empty seat next to a tarnished window. A minute later, Sidney arrived, alone.

"What happened? Where is Peach?"

"Don't worry about her." He sat, carefree.

"Who was that scary old man?"

"He is the Ferryman." *Did I miss the boat?* At least that explained the navy suit. "He is in charge of carrying the souls of the newly deceased across the two worlds."

"And what did you give him?"

"I gave him…" He paused. "…what everyone wants."

"Money?"

"That's what you desire most, Maia?"

"I'm not in the mood for mind games."

"It's not a game," he said. "I have to ask the same question to each passing soul."

"Why?"

"Do you decide how everything works at your job?"

I thought of my job with Fred at the music store. What did I desire most? Thoughts scrambled in my head, about my granny, my mother, Jase, cancer, and my friends. But if I dared to set my priorities, what I wanted most was to find true love. "I don't know. There are too many," I finally answered.

"What is it that your heart clings to the most?"

"You first. What is it your heart clings to the most?" I said, passing the heat.

"I'm not allowed to desire," he said with downcast eyes.

"What?" I tried to conceive of the idea of being deprived of desire. The idea of my captor being a prisoner of someone else disconcerted me. "I mean, why?"

"It's forbidden."

"By whom?"

The steam horn of the locomotive whistled, announcing departure. That caused a commotion among the frenzied mob on the platform to board the train.

"I need you to wait here for me, okay?" Sidney said, utterly serious.

"Where are you going?"

"I need to find Peach."

"Oh. I thought you said we didn't need to worry about her," I said as he made his way out. "Wait, but the medallion—"

"Don't worry, just don't move." He headed toward the locomotive, followed by other passengers, leaving the car half empty.

Somehow, even in his absence, the medallion remained lighter than a feather. I tried to pull it over my head, but the chain stiffened around my neck. As soon as I released it, it turned flexible again.

"You are damn clever for a necklace."

I felt the looks of awkwardness from the other passengers who noticed me speaking to my medallion.

"What? We're all dead, you know, so maybe just mind your own business." I shrugged.

There was mayhem on the platform caused by a bunch of men making their way through the crowd. The train chugged off, rocking the car as the locomotive pulled the carriage. Outside, a man dressed as a children's party magician, with a long black cloak, waved his cane and held his black top hat against his head, preventing it from being blown away. Two men in dark suits and shades in FBI fashion were close behind, as if they were chasing him. The flamboyant man scanned the train's windows one by one until he saw me.

"Maia!" the stranger screamed with relief, like he had found a long-missing relative. I looked around, dumbfounded, trying to figure out if he was actually talking to me. All passengers' gazes were on me.

"Don't open the window," an old woman in the adjacent seat advised.

"Maia!" the man repeated. "He is coming!"

"Who is coming? What are you talking about?"

"You have to run!" he yelled, preoccupied with the pursuers on his heels.

I stood and stuck my head out the window. "What do you mean? Who are you? How do you know me?"

"Please!" he said, wheezing, having trouble keeping up with the speeding train. "Please, you have to believe me!"

The train left the stranger and his pursuers behind and entered a tight, rocky tunnel. I tumbled onto my seat, trying to figure out what happened. *I have to run?* Where would I go? And away from who? Sidney had told me to remain in this seat, and I decided I had to trust him.

Two gunshots echoed through the dim tunnel, followed by the howls of passengers in the cars behind.

I jumped off my seat and peeked through the window in the door, but the curious crowd blocked my vision. Another gunshot split the scared mob like Moses with the Red Sea, giving me a glimpse of the caped stranger and his pursuers two cars behind. He must have made it onto the back of the train at the last second.

"Oh God," I sighed, backing away.

Everyone hid beneath their seats, their eyes darting at me. They knew it was me who was causing all this trouble. With no better option at hand, I disobeyed Sidney and hurried to the next car. But my sprint was short—the medallion cast its spell, and it forced me to slow down. I walked into the exterior passageway and found the door of the next car locked.

"Please open the door!" I hammered the door, but everyone cowered beneath their seats.

The train cleared the rocky tunnel, and now we were traveling inside a dark, clouded passage, twisting violently with wind currents and tinted by lightning, as if the train were in the core of a tornado. I couldn't believe my eyes, and the fact that the train was still running on rails suspended in the sky didn't help me to keep my sanity.

"Maia!" the caped stranger said from behind me, scaring me to death.

"Stay back! Don't come any closer!" I flattened against the door.

"Maia, Maia, don't you remember me?"

I shook my head.

"It's me, Frank!" He removed his hat.

Frank? I had never been good with names, but I always remembered faces, and I was certain that I had never seen him before in my entire life.

A bang dazed me, and a bullet pierced the window and hit next to my head, puncturing the metal. I screamed and cowered, covering my ears. Frank used his cane to jam the door and covered the window with his cloak to block the vision of the men in black.

"Run, run, we have to run!" He wrestled the doorway.

"It's jammed. It's useless."

"You have to climb."

"Are you crazy?" I yelled, witnessing the twister around us.

A second shot pierced the window.

"We don't have time for this." Frank offered his hands and pulled me up to the roof. It took a great effort to push myself up, considering the extra weight of the medallion.

On the roof, the threatening whirlwind that engulfed the train appeared infinite. The steam whistle blew, and a blinding yellowish light flashed with a deafening roar, unleashing hurricane winds that swayed the train. A blast of air knocked me off my feet, and I held on to what I could until the winds subsided.

"We have to keep going." Frank helped me to stand, but with the two-ton medallion, I could hardly limp to the end of the car.

"You have to jump," Frank said.

The gap between cars looked wider than the Grand Canyon. "I can't. I'll fall down, it's too heavy."

"Yes, you can," he encouraged me.

"No, you don't understand, the medallion—"

"We'll do it together."

He placed my arm around his neck and twined his arm around my waist. I felt awkward embracing this stranger, but with no better plan at hand, I resigned myself. We moved back to prepare to jump, when the two pursuers broke through the door and made their way to the top of the train, looking unruffled. They buttoned up their jackets, jolting their shoulders and adjusting their aviators in unison. They were like clones. Silk handkerchiefs in the pockets of their jackets were the sole difference: one was crimson and the other indigo. They were dauntless. Professionals. And I could tell they would not stop until they got whatever they wanted—which in this case appeared to be either me or Frank, or maybe both.

"Maia, run!" Frank yelled.

The train's whistle hissed, and we ran—or at least I tried to— and on the last step, he pushed me over the edge. Bluish lightning flashed through the twister as I was in midair, unleashing a heavy rain. I barely landed on the other car, sodden. Frank had lied to me. He hadn't jumped with me. He had stayed on the previous car.

"Frank!"

"Go, Maia!" he commanded as he courageously fought the men in the rain, preventing them from chasing me.

I couldn't leave him behind. I wanted to help, but it was impossible. Frank knocked down the man in crimson with a headbutt and grappled the other to the floor. Mr. Crimson flipped up, back on his feet, and drew a pistol from his suit jacket's pocket, aiming at both men wrestling, waiting to get a clear shot at Frank.

"Frank! Look out!" I cried out. Mr. Indigo did a reversal move, exposing Frank's back to his companion, who pulled the trigger twice.

My hands restrained my screams.

"He shot him, he shot him… He shot him," I whispered,

dumbstruck, watching Frank's body loosening and collapsing between the cars.

Motionless.

Dead.

The murderers adjusted their ties and turned, synchronized, with no trace of remorse. Their shades reflected their true objective: *me*. Self-preservation kicked in, and I fled as fast as the medallion and my tired legs allowed.

I heard the whistle once more, and amid my despair I recalled the words of the Ferryman: "Pay attention to the whistle." So I threw myself down and clung to a roof vent.

Greenish lightning shone and thunder grumbled, delivering an earthquake that rocked the train, nearly derailing it. I lost my grip and slid but managed to grab hold of a crease in the roof. The train landed back on both rails, leaving my kicking feet hanging over the precipice. I wanted to pull myself up, but it was impossible with the weight of the medallion. The men in black had almost fallen off the train as well, but they scrambled back to the top and smiled when they discovered my predicament.

I released my grip before they could catch me and slid over the edge until I caught the roof's rim and swung against the windows. "Open the window, please!" I kicked the window, but the passengers inside cowered.

Mr. Crimson trapped my left forearm and pulled me up. Two tentacles of smoke emerged from the revolving wall of clouds and wrapped around my ankles, pulling strongly in the opposite direction, leaving me dangling over the precipice. A third tentacle emerged and reshaped into a hand that advanced up my body toward my chest. I slapped it with my free hand but passed right through it. I could not stop the smoky hand from reaching for the medallion.

"Please help me!!!" I yelled, thinking naively that someone in the train would come to my aid. I was about to be torn apart by the stretching forces, when my last breath escaped.

Unconsciously, I cried out his name.

"Sidneyyyyyyyyyyyyyyyyyyyyyyyyyy!"

A dark, nebulous torrent penetrated the tornado heading toward us, and suddenly, the burden of the medallion vanished.

The torrent crashed into the metal train roof like a meteorite. Sidney rose from the crater, surrounded by the vanishing dark haze, with his hair swinging and his baleful gaze upon my aggressors.

"Sidney!" I screamed cheerfully.

Mr. Indigo charged against Sidney, who dodged the first blow and counterattacked ferociously. In the confusion, I surprised Mr. Crimson by grabbing his suit and pulling him down. He panicked and released my hand.

I fell into the abyss for a second before Sidney's hand grabbed mine.

"I got you," Sidney said, kneeling beside Mr. Crimson, who removed his glasses to discover there was no sign of his companion. He stared at Sidney in disbelief, his inexpressive face turning to absolute terror. Sidney hauled me up in the air with incredible strength, freeing me of the tentacles. I landed in husky arms that held me tightly against him. Sidney glanced at me with his mesmerizing olive-green eyes, leaving me breathless.

I saw Mr. Crimson escaping from the corner of my eye, heading toward the locomotive.

"He's getting away," I said without taking my eyes off Sidney.

"Not for long," he whispered, getting closer to me.

The whistle blew before we reached a bright red light at the end of the tunnel. The sound broke my trance.

"The whistle!"

Sidney nodded. "Close your eyes and don't open them."

I hesitated.

"Trust me." Sidney turned me around, and we knelt together. He embraced me from behind. I disobeyed him and peeked. His coat expanded, and the fabric morphed into black scales that resembled a dragon's, molding a cocoon around us. The red light outshone my vision when the train penetrated a tunnel of flames. I could barely make out the windy inferno carrying away the burning remains of Mr. Crimson. *What did they want? Maybe the medallion. Why?*

I knew I should be doubtful about the intentions of the dragon that sheltered me, but somehow, feeling his heart pumping against my back and his warm breath on my neck comforted me, even amid this ocean of fire. I shut my eyes and enjoyed the harmony that he aroused in my heart, even though with each passing second, we were closer to my waiting death. I wanted to trust him but forced myself to be skeptical. *Can a predator defend his prey, only to devour it later?*

Sidney returned to normal when the train had cleared the tunnel of flames. Blinking stars infected the night sky. The ground was a limitless sea that perfectly reflected the sky, making it look like we were astronauts traveling through space. The train halted, and we sat on the edge of the roof to behold the humongous crescent moon that emerged over the horizon.

"Where are we?"

"*Mare Serenitatis*," Sidney said. "The Sea of Serenity."

Whoever named it was absolutely right. The place was peace incarnate. A shooting star ripped the sky and collided with its reflection on the thin horizon, like two stars that rendezvoused at the end of their journey.

"It's beautiful," I said, amazed. "What's at the end, where the sky meets the sea?"

"Someone once said there is a beach at the most remote corner of the sky, from where you can contemplate all of creation."

"Have you ever been there?"

"No, but someday I will go," Sidney said, making me wonder if someday, after my passing, my granny would get her cottage at the beach.

Our tranquility was broken by the noises of someone climbing to the train roof. I was afraid Mr. Indigo was still chasing me, but joy overtook me as I saw it was Frank making his way up. I ran to his aid, and as I helped him up, I noticed the holes left by the bullets. But there was no trace of blood.

Could this be because he is already dead? I wondered, while Frank adjusted his top hat and fastened his now holey cloak around his neck.

"You are safe!" He hugged me effusively, which embarrassed me.

"Thanks to you. I'm glad you are ok too."

"Sidney?" Frank saw him behind me. "Sidney, you are alive!" Frank embraced him with childish excitement, but Sidney's expression was no different than mine.

"Alive?" I mumbled. So, was he human after all? Like I needed more puzzles in my troubled head. I pulled Frank's cape to bring him back to me. "Do you know him?" I whispered.

Frank nodded with excitement. "I'm glad that the two of you are finally together!"

"Shhhhhh, keep your voice down." My index finger closed his

lips. "Together? Why would that make you happy?" He was the bringer of death, after all.

"Don't you remember?" Frank scratched the hair beneath his hat.

I shook my head.

"You love him."

CHAPTER 6

LOVE? MY HEART STOPPED, and I forgot how to breathe.

How could I be in love with an arrogant, unabashed jerk with darting eyes and a plummy voice who'd kidnapped me just to abandon me in an outdated train that was sucked into a tornado while I was chased by the dead-people CIA?

I looked at Sidney, who was still stargazing.

He was dapper, I couldn't deny it, but I could not be in love with someone I just met. I was not even sure if he was human… but Frank was glad to find him alive, so maybe he… *Maia, enough!* I chided myself. I was in love with Jase. *Period.*

"Why do you say that?" I shook Frank to ferret out the answers he concealed. "How do you know? Where do you know me from in the first place? And him?"

"You…" His blinking eyes evaded me. "Y-you rescued me, Maia. Don't you remember?"

"What?" That was impossible. I couldn't forget someone so… *peculiar.* Besides, I hadn't ever saved anyone. "No, you just showed up out of nowhere at the station. Remember?"

He nodded slightly. "Yes, yes…" he whispered repeatedly, and his voice escalated to a crisp soprano as he convinced himself. "Yes, I rescued you. I did it!" He extended his cloak and wrapped it around us at the height of his nose, squinting with a frown. "I was marvelous."

Then I understood. It was like he was a boy trapped in the body of a thirty-something man. I sighed, unable to make any sense of what he said.

"Yes, you rescued me, now stop," I said, cheerless, pulling his cloak away.

"Don't take that off. My cape grants immortality."

"Oh, geez. Now I've seen it all. Immortality?" I shook my head. "You can't die because you are already dead, because everyone is dead in this place, and…" *And soon I will be too*, I mentally finished my sentence, feeling the medallion hanging at my neck.

Frank gave me a bewildered look, as if it were crazy to say he was dead.

The locomotive's bell chimed loudly.

"We have arrived," Sidney informed us, but we were surrounded by nothing more than stars for a thousand miles.

"Are you sure?" I asked.

"Quick, hold on to something," Sidney ordered, and I followed his lead, holding tight to a roof vent. He knelt beside me and embraced me again, which made me feel uncomfortable.

The train picked up speed, but after a couple of minutes, nothing changed. It appeared that we were stranded in the same place, as if we had not advanced an inch. We were below the same stars, with nothing else in sight. My leg numbed and my mind considered the possibility that he just wanted an excuse to hold me.

"Are you sure?" I reiterated.

"Look ahead," Sidney said.

At the front, the locomotive had started rotating left, following an askew rail, and it dove into the mirrored lake, splashing and rippling the quiet waters.

"Hold tight," Sidney commanded.

I just had time enough to take a deep breath before the car was engulfed by the sea. The train half looped, and instead of submerging, we surfaced, soaked, into a bright sunny day. The train continued traveling the rails above the blue ocean.

"You can breathe now," Sidney said, smiling, when noticed me still holding my breath in my bulging cheeks like a pufferfish. I blushed but looked away, squeezing my damp hair.

The train pulled parallel to a huge white steamboat with two tall smokestacks and massive paddle wheels. On the deck, hundreds of people waved to us.

"Hey!" Frank yelled, jumping and waving back.

The morning sun rays heating my skin and the magnificent view of the sea infected me with such heartwarming gaiety that I joined Frank, whistling and waving my hands, greeting the passengers.

The horizon was crowded with hundreds of ships coming not just from all directions but from different eras. I recognized sailboats, pirate ships, luxury cruise ships, yachts, Viking boats, battleships, wooden boats, kayaks, and Spartan ships among many.

"Is that the *Titanic*?" I squinted, trying to corroborate from a distance, but Sidney's eyes made me feel ashamed. "What? I just wanted to see if Jack and Rose were on the bow." Sidney buried his face in his hands.

The train and ships all headed toward a humongous island surrounded by rocky cliffs that reached the clouds. Waterfalls sprang from the heights of the mountains, creating an endless rainbow.

"Wow," I said, mesmerized.

The locomotive climbed the cliff's wall through a pass behind the waterfalls. We chugged through above the immense dock, where ships disembarked and people boarded baskets attached to multicolored balloons that worked like elevators, following iron wires anchored to the rocks, to convey them to the top.

"We have to crouch," Sidney said, pointing ahead toward a series of great arches and pillars engraved with different signs and scriptures carved in wood, stone, polished marble, and metal. I felt like I was in history class with Mr. Mankell. After crossing through the arches, we entered a dim tunnel crammed with stalactites and lit by torches illuminating the rocky paintings decorating the cave.

The train cleared the tunnel and circled around the tallest mountain I had ever seen, a snow-crowned volcano belching a vast fumarole as if it were a cloud factory. At the slope of the peak, there was a hidden city with streets inside big rifts and picturesque houses embedded in the wave-shaped volcanic stone, only their facades protruding.

"Welcome to the city of Betheli," Sidney announced.

The place was like nothing I had seen before. "Is this the reason nobody comes back from the dead? It's beautiful," I said, but Sidney gazed at me askance.

The train arrived at the Betheli station, and I felt relieved to set foot on solid ground again, but the platform here was even more insane than the one we had departed.

"Why is everybody always in such a hurry?" I asked Sidney.

"They are late, and we are too." He pointed to a solar clock the size of a fountain at the center of the station's square.

"Late for what?"

"The pilgrimage."

"Hey!" Peach found us in the crowded plaza. "I'm glad to see you are all right."

"Of course we are," Sidney replied.

"Are you?" I asked.

She nodded shyly.

"I'm Frank, madam," Frank said, stepping between us. "Professional wizard at your service." He did a curtsy, waving his cape.

"Thank you, the pleasure is all mine, Mr.—" Peach replied, mimicking the curtsy.

"Mr. Wizard is fine, or just Frank. Or the Midnight Vampire." He did a vampire pose.

"Oh! Not again," I said, pushing Frank ahead as I heard Peach laugh behind me. "We are in a hurry, right?"

"Does 'the Guardian' sound better?" Frank looked back at me, but I frowned at him. "Magic Vampire Guardian of the Midnight, maybe?"

We followed the crowd down the crammed street, and my head went crazy trying to assimilate the mix of people from different eras: a cowboy sheriff with manure-plastered boots, a Pretorian guard polishing a Roman *gladio,* a long-haired knight with a bloodred cross on his chest, and a smoking WWII soldier, all chatting, carefree.

Apparently, the afterlife was a nondiscriminatory, timeless place where everybody arrived at the same time, independent of when you had lived. I searched around for people in space suits or spandex-and-velcro clothes from the future, but the farthest I could go was to a contemporary-looking guy in dreadlocks, with baggy pants and skulled slip-ons, and a cybergoth girl in a corset with PVC skirt and platform boots so unstylish they made my bloodstained attire feel like Valentino.

The houses' facades were also eclectic, ranging from classic Greek to Victorian countryside to postmodern minimalist.

"If everybody is heading to the pilgrimage, who lives in those houses?" I asked, intrigued.

"Sedentary souls," Sidney said. I stared at him, still baffled. "People who refuse to leave," he elaborated.

"Why?"

"They are trapped."

"Trapped? The houses don't look like prisons to me. No bars on the doors and windows."

The river of people guided us to a huge circular area composed of several concentric rings, the inner one step lower than the outer, descending in a spiral. In the center, seven monoliths surrounded a blue fire whirling so tall that the tip was lost in the midday sun. If you stared more than a couple of seconds, it caused light ghosts when you shut your eyes. The full moon shone next to the sun in plain daylight, as if an eclipse were about to occur. But it was not the *same* moon—the craters' patterns didn't match the ones I recognized.

The multitude followed a spiraling line a hundred times longer than the ones for Disneyland attractions. Once pilgrims reached the center, men in long robes gave each pilgrim a lamp lit with the bluish electric fire, and they walked through a subterranean tunnel leading out of the city.

"What are they doing?"

"They receive the eternal fire of the Fountain of Haji," Sidney explained. "It will light their path through the pilgrimage."

"What for?" I felt like a five-year-old on a school trip.

"Protection," Sidney said. "Here, nothing is more dangerous than darkness."

"Maia! Maia!" Someone called my name, and among the crowd I recognized Mrs. Thompson, my gran's best friend, waving to me from two lines ahead. Mrs. Thompson had lived one block down from the big oaks house, and as a kid I'd enjoyed visiting her because she had an amazing library and allowed me to borrow books. She'd introduced me to *Pride and Prejudice*, *Anna Karenina*, *Little Women*, *Alice's Adventures in Wonderland*, and the *Wizard of Oz*, some of my favorite novels.

"Mrs. Thompson!" I slipped through the lines of people until I reached her. "What are you doing here?" I asked stupidly, remembering too late that she had passed last April. I was glad to see a familiar face. She welcomed me with arms wide open but turned her head away to avoid burning me with her cigarette—she'd died of pulmonary cancer and was my ex-chemo partner. She was a legend in the cancer ward because of her strength, surviving over forty years after being diagnosed.

"I'm on vacation," Mrs. Thompson said in a high-pitched voice. "I promised my Ed." Mr. Edward, her late husband, had passed a decade ago.

"I'm glad to hear you two are going to be back together."

Her crinkly eyes turned aqueous. She loved him so much that when doctors treating her terminal cancer had complained about her not quitting her smoking habit, she'd always replied, "Every smoke is a step closer to my Ed." But her tears came accompanied with a smile now that she was so close to seeing her Ed again. I was satisfied too—finding Mrs. Thompson was the proof I needed to embrace the possibility that my mother would be among these people, in this timeless place, even if she'd passed seventeen years ago.

"But what are you doing here, Maia, dear?"

"Emmm…" I didn't dare to say to Mrs. Thompson that her best friend was on the brink of death. "I-I'm looking for my mother. Have you seen her?"

"I'm afraid no. Luvena is not a woman that passes unnoticed. She has your grandmother's eyes, and you have inherited them too." Mrs. Thompson held my chin. "You are so beautiful. The boys at your school must be crazy about you."

I giggled to indulge her. *Yeah, in an alternate dimension in which I am Jennifer Lawrence and Hodgkin is only the name of my dog.*

I yelped when I felt Sidney hooking my arm. "Oh, there you are, Maia. Shall we go?" He became all smiles to greet Mrs. Thompson but shot me a disapproving look before switching back to his fake grin.

Mrs. Thompson squinted. "Is this your boyfriend?"

"He's my…" I gaped, struggling to explain the entanglement.

"Yes, ma'am," Sidney answered pompously, and I turned to him in disbelief. "We are engaged." He clutched me, knocking the wind out of me.

"He is my kidnapper," I mumbled with my remaining breath, too low to be captured by Mrs. Thompson's hearing aid.

"Right, honey?" Sidney nudged me, and a cough erupted from my mouth.

"I'm glad for you, darling," said Mrs. Thompson. "He is a dashing young man. Emma would be proud."

"Thank you, ma'am," Sidney said with his saccharine voice, squeezing her shoulder. "We would like to stay a little longer, but as you may know, *time flies*. So I beg you to excuse us."

Mrs. Thompson laughed. "You still have a full life ahead."

"As you say." Sidney pulled me through the crowd.

"Send my regards to Emma." Mrs. Thompson waved, and I lost sight of her.

"Engaged?" I yelped. "You didn't tell me this medallion was an engagement ring."

"You shouldn't talk to anybody," Sidney said crossly with his hand crushing mine.

"Why?"

"It's too dangerous."

"But why? She is an old friend of my grandmother. She is harmless," I said, frustrated.

"You can't trust appearances here."

We rejoined our spot in the line, where Peach was waiting and Frank was doing his vampire thing again.

"But what can go wrong if everybody is dead?" I asked.

"Dead? Who's dead?" Frank asked naively.

Sidney went silent again, infuriating me even more. I turned to Frank and removed his cloak, showing the bullet holes in his back. "See? He can't die."

"Of course not." Frank snatched the cloak from my hand. "I'm immortal. I'm a vampire."

"Sidney, I have to find my mother," I said, this time with tightness in my chest not caused by the medallion. "You promised."

Peach observed us with concerned eyes.

"Misfortune introduces itself wrapped in fancy paper, ribbon, and topped with a bow," Sidney said, clearly considering the issue settled.

"No." I folded my arms across my chest. "Misfortune introduces itself like fancy boys with cursed medallions."

Sidney stared at me briefly and then averted his eyes.

I guessed I was on my own in finding my mom. So I stood on my tiptoes and craned above the sea of people. We were still at the outer rings, and at the current speed, it would take us the entire day to reach the Fountain of Haji. I wondered what time it was. In the sky, the sun appeared locked at the zenith, and the moon moved closer to completing the eclipse.

I searched around me for more reliable sources. The digital wristwatch of a man next to me displayed 77:77:77. It was pointless.

Everything in this place started becoming confusing. In the vicinity of the square, there was a small alley, and at the end was a house with a Victorian facade of terracotta bricks. I instantly recognized it; it looked just like Mr. Bahiti's store. I snuck out of the line again, trying not to be spotted by Sidney or Frank. I left the boisterous crowd behind and turned into the tranquil alley, even though the medallion's burden increased with each step.

It *was* Bahiti's store, no doubt about it, but the sign above the door was missing, and the curtains were shut. I climbed the steps to the door and twisted the metal handle. The door cracked open, venting an intense odor of damp wood and alcohol. The place was drowned in a dense murkiness, and for the first time, I missed the welcoming old Strauss ringtone.

"Anybody home?" I called, but got no answer. "Mr. Bahiti?"

Inside, the house was unrecognizable. Wooden sticks hung from the ceiling, tied with dried leaves to form odd shapes and symbols. The instruments on the shelves had been replaced by a collection of leather books, pyramids, candles, horns, animal skulls, and small statues of deities covered in a thick film of dust—at least the dust was the same. Another shelf stored dissected animals and fetuses suspended in cloudy jars that were the source of the smell. The biggest jar contained a bunch of what appeared to be eyes… human eyes!

I recoiled.

"Welcome to Bahiti's Cabinet of Curiosities," a hoarse voice said behind me.

A figure loomed out of the shadows. "Mrs. Bahiti?" I recognized Fred's mother. "Are you…" I gulped.

"This is my humble abode."

"But I just saw you a couple of days ago in your son's store." I shook my head. "That means you are…" Chills ran down my spine.

"*Dead?*" Mrs. Bahiti squinted her profound eyes. "Yes, for a long time, I suppose."

"But how do you…" *A ghost coming back*, I answered myself. That explained why I'd never seen her before in almost a year working at the store.

"I visit him often."

"He knows?"

"The living deny many things, my child. They prefer to ignore what they don't understand." Mrs. Bahiti walked to me. "Just like you ignored my warning. Instead of escape from Death, you ran toward it."

"I didn't have a choice."

Mrs. Bahiti glowered. "Didn't you?"

"I wanted to save my grandmother and see my mother, and now I have this…" I uncovered my chest, with the gold medallion buried in my skin.

Mrs. Bahiti's face grew amused. "Who gave it to you?" She reached out to touch it.

"A man, his name is Sidney." Mrs. Bahiti retracted her hand before touching it, as if it were a biting snake.

"The cards were right, but you left before I finished," the old woman said. "I know of whom you speak, but his name is not Sidney, child. He has many names. He is the many-faced." She walked around me, mumbling an endless list of names in languages I didn't recognize. "…*Anpu, Vetalla, Ankou*, or *Vandella*," she finally said in a sepulchral voice.

"Vandella? That's his name?"

"His true nature."

"Who is he?" I asked, afraid to know.

"You should ask *what* instead of who," Mrs. Bahiti said. "He is a creature of the night, a vampire of the soul."

"A vampire?" I laughed, remembering Frank's hammy performances.

"You may laugh all you want, child, but night is falling."

The light that shone through the curtains ceded to a complete darkness.

The eclipse!

"Now it's too late, child." The old lady walked to the shelf and seized something. "It's coming for you."

"Who? Vandella?" I sensed the weight of the medallion, which wasn't getting lighter.

"No." Mrs. Bahiti turned the valve of her antique brass oil lantern, fueling the bluish fire. It was the lantern she'd carried with her when I met her in the basement of the store, the same one distributed at the Fountain of Haji by the men in long robes, only the flame color was different in the world of the living. "The one who walks among snakes, the one who dances on swords."

The old woman chucked a powder inside the oil lantern, invigorating flames that produced images on the glass, recreating scary visions of her words. "It's written that there will come a day when the shadow of Nagelfar the dragon will eclipse the earth, and trembling, the skies will announce the day of night, and thus the beginning of the end. Lock yourself at home, child, because those consumed by the pestilence—both friends and foes—will knock at thy door in screams of agony, but you shall open to none. And when the rattling drums stop at thy house, stare at thy lantern and do not look behind, not even with the corner of the eye, because no door or chain will stop the one who walks among snakes and dances on swords; only the ardent flame will banish him, until the bringer of dawn splits the righteous from the unfaithful."

Mrs. Bahiti closed the lantern's lid, putting an end to the visions. "I cannot offer you protection, child, not from what is coming. You have to go now; you don't have time to waste. The pestilence will not wait," she said, ushering me out.

"No, please, you can't kick me out. I never paid you for the reading. I have your money, here, here!" I said, trying to give her the creased ten-dollar bill.

"Your money has no meaning here."

"But what am I supposed to do?" I said, terrorized.

"Go to the Fountain of Haji to light your lantern, and then seek for the one who gave you that medallion. He is the only one that can protect you now."

"But didn't you say he's dangerous?"

"Sometimes, child, you have to choose between two evils." Mrs. Bahiti swung the door shut after me and ran the deadbolt.

The quiet streets were tinted with an uneven obscurity, with darker shadows and paler lights. It wasn't quite like night—it was still daylight, just robbed of vividness and light. The moon's silhouette eclipsed the sun, and a towering yellowish corona crowned the sky. The tranquility was broken by the blaring of an air-raid siren. I gathered up courage and trudged toward the square, eluding the people evacuating it in panic. In the mayhem, a big man ran over me, and I tumbled flat on my back on the cobbled ground.

A loud clangor, like the growl of an alligator, silenced the screams, and everybody looked up, petrified. A winged shadow crossed the skies, leaving a trail of thick fumes that proliferated in a dense cloud over the square, advancing through the adjacent streets. Everyone fled from the burnt-flesh-odor mist. I guessed it must have been the pestilence that Mrs. Bahiti had told me about. Apparently, the old lady knew what she was talking about.

During the commotion, I found a lit oil lantern that lay forsaken underneath the hopping feet of the frantic evacuees. I crawled until I seized it, but a robust woman in a one-shouldered party dress and pearl necklace fought me for it. "It's mine!" She pulled the lantern, leveraging with her body weight, and my weak arms resisted as much as they could before relinquishing it. The woman rolled over on her back with her slippers flying away. She landed on her bulging belly, and the ashen mist devoured her feet. The hysterical woman cried in agony, trying to reach the lantern just an inch away from her chubby fingers, but in a second, she and the lantern had disappeared, swallowed by the dense pestilence, along with her cries, which bristled my skin.

I didn't think twice. I scuttled back to Mrs. Bahiti's door and pounded on it and begged. My mouth dried with my screams, but the door didn't open. A gloomy figure emerged from the fog, spurring me to squeeze my medallion. It was a bald woman; her withered skin adhered to her bone. Her bare feet hardly limped out of the ashen mist, and a loose party dress hung from one shoulder. Her gnarled hand tore her necklace apart, and the white pearls bounced on the cobblestones. It was her, the woman who'd fought with me for the lantern just moments ago. My hand trembled with the rhythm of my heart.

The woman fell and lurched after me, but I hurried down the sidewalk as fast as the medallion permitted. I pushed each door and twisted each knob along the way until I stumbled against a hefty wood door that was ajar. I entered without hesitation and closed the heavy door behind me. I stepped away, fearing that the pestilence could make it through the wide gap between the door and the frame.

I looked around and saw that I was in a gallery of lofty walls stuffed with cracked sandstone plates, engraved with the names of the inhabitants of the cinerary urns they contained. At the end of the passageway, a door led to a field of crypts and tombstones that extended endlessly over the horizon. I wondered about the purpose of a graveyard in the afterlife.

I liked cemeteries just about as much as I liked hospitals, but I was too scared to stop moving. I hobbled out, stumbling against a headstone. I cursed the stone, caressing my pinky toe over my shoe, when I froze.

It was *mine*. My name was engraved on the headstone, dating my death as yesterday. The epitaph read: *Taken too soon, loved for an eternity.*

Those were Gran's words, I said to myself. I felt an impulse to cry, but I held myself together.

I got back to the entrance, where the moans of the last remnant of people echoed outside. I peeked through the hole of the hinges, witnessing an old man trying to escape the pestilence that engulfed the street. His trembling hand extended, he begged for help with a faint voice. I was about to open the door to help him when I heard the clatter of iron hooves on the cobblestone street. Four coal-black horses pulled a carriage identical to Sidney's and stopped right next to the old man. I lit up with excitement, believing Sidney had come to my aid. But the coach's door gave way to a figure in a hooded cloak that looked like it was carved out of white marble. The figure floated gracefully without touching the ground. When the figure reached the old man, hands came out of the sleeves that morphed like a speeding roulette wheel of shape, size, skin color, and age.

While I stared, rapt, a hand came from behind me, covering my mouth. From the corner of my eye, I recognized my captor with astonishment—it was Mr. Crimson. He must have somehow survived incineration. He pressed his ring against my neck, squeezing my swollen lymph node, but his hand on my mouth prevented me from yelling. I kicked the door, drawing the attention of the cloaked entity.

Mr. Crimson forced me deep into the graveyard. I wrestled him and managed to elbow his liver. He dumped me on the hard ground while regaining composure and then strode after me. I dragged myself through the tombs until my back flattened against a headstone. He snagged my neck with both hands, and I saw my bulging eyes reflected in his shades. I slapped his face, shattering his aviators, exposing his psychotic glare.

Suddenly, the cloaked entity I'd seen outside emerged imposingly from behind Mr. Crimson. The ever-changing hand halted on a man's shape and rested on Mr. Crimson's shoulder, transforming him into a white marble statue. The hand released him and restarted its infinite loop of different hand shapes. The figure advanced toward me, and I knew what it was. It was the grim reaper, the archangel of death. His face was lost in the insoluble blackness inside his hood. Heavy breathing resonated. I was terrified, but my screams were lodged within my throat.

This time, the sinister roulette stopped on a woman's hand that stroked my hair. "Art thou lost, my little one?" The serene voice of an old man slid out from under the hood.

"She is looking for her mother." It was Sidney's voice. I whipped around, and he was sitting on a tombstone like a gargoyle, arms folded—who knows for how long. I was so busy wobbling my head to force the air into my lungs that I hadn't realized the shift in the medallion's weight.

"Poor *wight*," Death said, as if he had been expecting Sidney. "And what is it that she desires the most?"

Sidney took out a small book from his coat pocket and browsed for the last entry in total peacefulness, as if I were not in danger at all. "She wants to find true love," he said, closing the book.

I was in shock. It was like he had read my mind.

"No, my son," Death said. *Son? Sidney was Death's son?* "She was sown in a field of love. No, no, no. She refuses love. But no more, Little One. I will cease thy suffering."

"Not yet, Father." Sidney stood on the tombstone.

"Her life is not in thy hands."

"I need her."

Death studied me. "Is affection what flourishes in thy heart, Son?" Sidney remained silent as I recalled his words on the train about how he was deprived of desire. "Thou wert not named by the *Will* for coveting. Ohhhhhhhh, no, Son of Samael, thou wert named for a different purpose."

"I have a thousand names," Sidney said defiantly.

"Yet thou possessest none," Samael said. "Thou art confused, my son. Thy interest in this mortal girl sparked from curiosity, but she is just another bird that nests in the garden for a season and migrates in winter."

"I need her."

"She has to go back to the flock." Samael extended his changing hand, the wheel of fortune, but I knew what my fortune was. I'd been told by my doctors long before this moment.

Sidney sprang to the sky and waved his hand, releasing drag-on scales that fell around me, piercing Samael's hand. The wounds appeared to smolder from inside, combusting the entire arm into ashes that stacked on the ground.

"Ungrateful," said Samael serenely.

"I told you. She is mine," Sidney said from the tomb where he had landed.

"Then come down and claim her soul. Pay the price for setting foot on this sacred ground and burn alive, if thou consider the soul of this mortal valuable enough."

"I don't have to. The girl has other friends."

Frank appeared behind Samael and swung his cane. "Let her go!"

The floating cloak tangled around the staff like empty cloth. Samael reshaped, trapping the stick inside the murkiness. An arm shot out of the sleeve, hugging Frank's face, and brought him closer to be inspected. "An empty vessel," Samael said before tossing Frank away with ease.

"Now, Little One, come into me." Samael's hands came after me but halted in midair, detained by an unseen barrier.

"My intention was not to harm you but to protect her." Sidney pointed to the dragon scales anchored in the ground, forming an eye circumscribed in a circle around me. "You just got in the way."

"Brilliant, my son," Samael said. "Now thou hast secluded her from even thyself. How dost thou plan to impede me from snatching away her last breath?" Samael clapped three times. "Raphael Hall, son of Jeremy and Gabriella, wake up," he pronounced, and the marbled eyes and hands of Mr. Crimson turned back to flesh. "Press," Samael commanded, squeezing his fist, and the living statue obeyed, choking me with invigorated strength.

But Sidney remained calm on the top of the stone. "Fear not, Maia, you are protected. This breath is not your last."

His words made me feel my breath return, as if there was a force continuously pulling me back to the living. Mr. Crimson uncovered my chest, revealing Lazarus's medallion.

"*Délok*," Samael said. "Poor girl, carrying the burden of an unwanted fate. But thy pain hast come to an end. Maia Foster, daughter of Dario and Luvena, I welcome thee!" Samael extended his arms, and Mr. Crimson tore the medallion apart. The gilded links of the broken chain scattered over the ground and transformed into earthworms. The medallion was absorbed into the bottomless obscurity of Samael's hood. Mr. Crimson tightened his fingers one by one around my neck, squeezing the air out of me, as I resigned to the idea of finally embracing death.

My vision blurred as my life extinguished, and a yellow blaze that seemed divine appeared before me. The radiance grew as it got closer. It was Sidney, shrouded in violent flames that grew with each step he took toward me. He marched diligently in silence, with his immovable eyes resting on me. *Why?* I thought. The insufferable heat subdued Sidney to the ground. The fire had claimed most of his clothes and skin. *Stop, please stop, for God's sake!* I wanted to scream. But he didn't. His charred fingers anchored in the dirt as he pulled himself closer.

"Why is this mortal so important to thee?" Samael asked his burning son. But Sidney didn't reply.

I used the strength of my last heartbeats to extend my numb arm and reach for his hand, but the barrier between us was like invisible glass. *Please save yourself… Goodbye,* I mentally said to him, hoping he could read my mind again.

Samael snapped his fingers, and Mr. Crimson turned back into stone. The pressure on my throat released. I tumbled feebly, coughing. The remaining humanity of Sidney, the unburned left half of his face, relaxed at seeing me safe, and he closed his eyes.

I crawled to him, hitting and scraping the magic barrier, but my efforts were futile. "Don't you feel compassion for your own son?" I yelled at Samael.

"Death is nothing if not compassion," he said, staring at both of us.

The flames melted the dragon scales, breaking the seal. Sidney's hand dropped onto the tombstone, extinguishing the flames. I pulled his burnt body over the tomb, with his face resting on my lap. His skin was leathery and blistered on the surface and looked like glowing coal beneath. My tears evaporated when I touched him.

"Why did you pardon me?" I asked Samael.

"Only the astray can judge both good and wrong, because those that have been hurt know the taste of suffering."

"What?" I said, not truly understanding his words.

"It is coming for thee."

"What?"

"Dost thou not hear the drums rattling, girl?"

CHAPTER 7

DEATH ABANDONED US, leaving a trail of suffering and desolation. The sun and the moon divorced. The sun drifted west, and the moon became a pale sun nesting in the heights as ruler of the skies.

"Why do you cry?" Sidney said with a hollowed voice.

I kept my eyes focused on the sky to avoid seeing his condition. My throat burned with the words I could not say. *If I had stayed in line with him...* His labored breathing incriminated me. Every wheeze was a nail in my chest.

"I don't want you to die." I wiped away my tears.

"Don't be silly. It's convenient to die in a graveyard. Work is half done. You only have to roll me into that hole, no need to shovel the dirt."

"Don't say that. This place is horrible."

"But I could spend eternity by your side." His skinned lips curved with difficulty into a grin.

All this time, we were sitting on the grave that was chiseled with my name. "As a resident, I can tell with certainty, this place totally sucks. I mean, why is there a cemetery in the afterlife, anyway?"

Sidney's finger reached my cheek and caught a tear. "To mourn your departure."

"I don't think that anybody will ever mourn for me."

"Why do you say that?"

"Because I don't deserve it."

Sidney saw one of my teardrops sliding into the creases of his scorched hand and clutched it.

A figure in a dark cloak appeared before us. I rested Sidney's head on the tombstone and stood to confront whatever it was. I had no weapons, but I was prepared to defend him even from the angel of death. But then I noticed the figure carried a bouquet of jasmine, and when it removed its hood, golden frizzles sprouted out.

"Peach!" I said, excited to see her alive, but my thrill was met with a slap to my face. She passed me by, leaving a trail of jasmine fragrance, heading straight to Sidney. My cheek pounded. She was *right*. I deserved to be shunned for putting Sidney through this predicament. I suppressed my tears. I turned away from her nursing him. I could not endure seeing them together. Not after what Sidney had done for me. Although I didn't know *what* he was, I knew for sure he was dangerous. Like Mrs. Bahiti said, he was *Vandella* or whatever. He was evil, and he was… an intruder that had lodged in my ravaged heart, and now didn't I have a clue how to evict him.

And the worst part was that I didn't know if I wanted to.

Could Frank be right about what I felt for him?

Frank? Frank! Where is he?

I roamed around the crypts, searching, and found him on the ground, unconscious, with a stone trapping his leg. I got on top of the debris and pushed the stone aside. "Frank! Frank!" I shook him. "Please, answer me!"

"Are you crying for me?" he said, peeling an eye open.

I hugged him. "Yes. I was scared."

"Do you believe in my immortality now?"

I nodded. "And in your bravery. You are as brave as a knight."

"My mission is to protect you."

"Who gave you that mission?"

A branch cracked. "We need to go," Peach yelled to us.

I helped Frank up, and we returned to Sidney, who stood leaning against the tomb, wearing Peach's cloak and using a long wood branch as a crutch.

"We must march now," Sidney ordered. "Frank, I need your help to make it out of this place."

Peach helped Sidney to climb onto Frank's back.

"Good luck," I said.

"What do you mean?" Frank asked.

"You should go. I'll stay," I answered, though part of me was pleading to go.

"Stay?" Peach turned to Sidney, concerned.

"Yes, my mandate has been delivered. The medallion is now in Samael's hands, along with my soul." I pointed to my headstone. "You will be better off without me."

"Don't you hear the drums rattling?" Sidney said.

I heard nothing beyond the caws of the crows and the howling wind, but I remembered well the spooky prophecy told by Mrs. Bahiti that had been fulfilled exactly so far. "And when the rattling drums stop at thy house, stare at thy lantern and do not look behind, not even with the corner of the eye, because no door or chain will stop the one who walks among snakes and dances on swords."

I could not dare to expose them to whatever was coming. Not in Sidney's condition. So I shook my head.

"Frank, please put me down." Sidney rested on his crutch. "Maia, two souls are needed for the exchange. The substitute shall take the place of the fated wearing the medallion and jump in sacrifice into the magmatic rivers in the entrails of Mt. Touriel at the end of the pilgrimage. At that moment, the substitution will be consummated, and the life of the fated will be forgiven on account of the substitute's soul. And as you might see, your grave is not yet dated." Sidney pointed at the blank space on my headstone.

"But there was a date there just now… I swear it. I saw it. I clearly saw it." But it was empty now. Maybe it was just my imagination.

"You are not dead yet, Maia. You are now in an intermediate state. The transmission between states should be as quick as lightning, as you witnessed on the train on our way here. The dissociation of each element controls a sense in the realm of the living: earth element controls touch sense, water element the taste, air element the smell, and fire element the hearing. The fifth element, space, controls sight." I listened attentively to Sidney, remembering the windblast, the torrential rain, the earthquake, and the raging inferno I'd experienced on the train.

"The medallion bestows safe passage without experiencing death, but now it's gone. Unless you recover it, during the following five days, at the time the moon eclipses the sun, a colored orb in the medallion will turn dark, and you will lose a sense every day."

"What happens on the sixth?"

"You lose your soul. And if by that time the substitution has not been consummated, both souls will perish, and your sacrifice for saving your grandmother's life will be worthless. In other words, if you die here, your grandmother dies with you. Understood?"

"Why didn't you tell me all this from the beginning?" I said, frustrated.

"Because none of this would have happened if you had kept the single rule I gave you: don't step away from your caregiver."

"Why should I believe you about any of this? I mean, I didn't see anybody on the train losing their senses."

Sidney chuckled in pain. "Did you wonder why The Sea of Serenity was so peaceful? Did you dare to peek through the windows to see what the other passengers were experiencing?"

I never considered them. "But what about Frank?" And he did his vampire *thing*. "Oh! Never mind. But what about Mr. Crimson? I don't remember anything about him losing his senses." I pointed to the now marble statue kneeling on my grave holding a bouquet of jasmine.

"I'm pretty sure he has lost them now," Sidney said with sinister humor.

"Anyway, why did Samael turn him to stone?"

"Even angels have hobbies, Maia," Sidney said casually, as if speaking of a friend. "Just like a hunter dissects his prey after killing it to keep it stuffed as a trophy, Samael enjoys creating 'homages to life,' as he calls them."

Homages? I looked around, wondering if all the statues in the graveyard were petrified people. "This is crazy. I just can't. I need time to digest all this."

"Maia, you could spend your days searching in this endless graveyard to find a headstone with the name of your grandmother and wait for a date to be set, or you can come with us and reclaim the medallion and save her."

Peach averted her eyes. I had no idea whether I trusted any of them. But going with them was the only chance I had to save my gran.

"Please, Maia, you have to come with us," Frank persuaded.

"Where do I find Samael to recover my medallion?" I resolved.

"Where all the dead go. The place at the end of the pilgrimage. Touriel."

The town square was still ensconced in the ashen mist, forcing us to leave without a lantern holding the fire of Haji to guide our path through the desolate streets now paved with corpses. Frank and I walked ahead, with Peach behind, helping Sidney, who didn't take his eyes off me. We didn't stop until arriving at a meadow on the outskirts of Betheli.

"The pilgrimage," I said, pointing to an endless line of lamp-lights fading on the horizon on the opposite side of the city. "We can try to catch them."

"No, it's useless. We don't carry lanterns with the eternal fire. That will only draw the attention of the *Flagellants*."

"Flagellants?"

"Religious fanatics you don't want to meet. Trust me. We will go east through the valley, across the highlands. It's a roundabout way, but we will use the forest as cover," Sidney resolved.

"But maybe the pilgrims could lend us a lantern," I said, hoping I could find my mother among the pilgrims.

"During the eclipse," Sidney pondered, "did somebody lend you a lantern?"

I remained silent, remembering how I'd had to fight the woman for one. It was true; no one would help us.

"Besides, pilgrims can't provide aid for what is coming." Sidney pointed at a mountain-sized, anvil-shaped cloud with raging lightning coming from the north. "The *Sheireils*," Sidney said. "The hairy ones."

"Who are they?" I didn't know if I could take another insurmountable obstacle on top of everything else.

"Sheireils." Sidney paused. "You don't talk to them. You don't bargain with them. You don't fight them. If you see them, you run as fast as you can. That's the only thing to know. The only way we can evade them is through the Forest of Pahana, but we must hurry. The drums are getting louder," Sidney said, but the distant thunder was the only thing I could hear.

Soon, we made our way into the forest. As we trekked into the woods, we could not keep track of the advancing storm. The towering oaks and leafy beeches insulated us, creating their own world. Just a few light beams crossed the canopy, captured by the humid fog that settled over the mud. The stifling undergrowth was tight, with no trails, as if we were the first visitors to the forest in years.

It became difficult for Sidney to cross the tangled vegetation. Frank helped Peach assist him while I scouted ahead. It had been a while since the last time I was alone. There were no birds singing, nor crickets chirping; not even the wind dared to resonate. It was totally silent.

I remembered my granny diligently sitting beside my bed, Shelly and the girls bringing flowers and balloons, Darrell and Gary telling their spooky stories. I thought about Jase, so handsome in his letterman jacket. It felt like a decade since I'd last seen them. But I had to let them go. Now they were only inhabitants of my memories.

"Heeeeelppppppppp," I heard the voice of a young girl whispering behind me, and I turned around to find nothing but the foliage.

"Pleaseee heeeeeeelpppp," the sonorous voice reverberated, and I looked around again for the source. "Coooomeee," it repeated, and I caught a glimpse of a person in the fog along a line of trees.

"Who is there?" I asked, but received no answer. I picked up a log and crept in the direction of the cries, which got louder as I approached. But when I got close, I realized it was just a tree trunk covered with moss, creating odd patterns on the bark resembling human features.

"Maia." A hand settled on my shoulder, and I turned, raising the log. It was Peach. "Are you ok?"

I nodded. "Sorry, I heard some voices."

"Ignore them," she said. "This is the forest of the lost souls. If you pay attention, they will never let you leave."

Then there was a grunt, too real to be generated by my mind. Above of us was an unconscious man in military uniform hanging from his parachute, trapped by the branches.

"Oh my God! Is he dead?" I asked.

"He seems wounded," Frank said behind us. "He is bleeding,

but he is breathing!"

"We need to help him," I said, but Peach was in shock. "Please, Frank, give me a hand."

"How?"

"I can climb the tree, but I need something to cut him down."

"Cut, chop, slice, mow," Frank said, rummaging in his pockets and pulling out a small knife.

Tree-climbing had been one of my favorite hobbies as a kid, so I made it to the branch easily. I straddled it and started severing the parachute lines one by one, loosening the puppet soldier. "Frank, this is the last one. Are you ready?" I shouted down. "Please don't die during the fall," I whispered and squeezed my eyes shut before cutting the remaining line, until I heard a slam. Frank toppled, catching the soldier. I climbed down after making sure both were safe and sound.

The soldier was just a boy, barely older than me. I recognized the olive drab uniform of the World War II Allies from movies and photos in history books.

"Jim, Jim," the boy murmured.

"Hey! Are you all right?" I asked as he regained consciousness.

"Who are you?" the intimidated boy asked.

"Relax. Everything is all right. We are friends. I'm Maia."

His breathing eased.

"Who are you?" I asked.

"Bill, Bill Hurlbart of the 508th Infantry Regiment, 82nd Airborne Division."

"You are a long way from home, Corporal," Sidney said.

"I need to search for my unit." Bill stood, dizzy, trying to arrange his gear. "Where's my rifle?" he asked eagerly. "My M1! I must have dropped it during the fall," he said, tramping in circles while pulling his hair.

"Relax."

"You don't understand. It was my prime direction, not to lose my gun."

I joined his search, and fortunately I found a heavy rifle hidden beneath a scrub. He snatched it from me and loaded a clip. Without notice, Sidney pounced on me, taking me down, just in time to evade a burst of bullets coming from some bushes behind us.

"Everybody down!" Bill ordered, hiding behind a tree to respond to the enemy fire.

"Cease fire, cease fire," someone ordered on the other side, quieting the shooting.

"Helmet?" the man shouted, but we remained silent. "Helmet?" the man repeated. "Password, goddamn it, or we will kill you."

"Victory, victory!" Bill answered.

"That was two days ago! Give me today's password, or we will shoot."

"Please don't shoot, its *victory*. I swear it, man! I can't remember the countersign, but we are no *krauts*." Bill was panicked, knocking his head, trying to remember the password, when he was surprised by a knife at his neck.

"It is *throat*. The password is *throat*," the soldier wielding the knife said.

Bill turned, relieved to find the mysterious attacker was a friend. "Duncan, thank God." Duncan sheathed the knife and embraced him. He hissed, and three more soldiers emerged from the shrubbery.

"The fall twisted your brain, Hurlbart," the oldest of the group said, a skew-jawed and blunt-featured man with patches of gray hair above his sideburns.

"Yes, sir," Bill answered with a salute.

"My apologies for the rough introduction," the soldier said, bringing a fat cigar to his mouth. "But we are at war, and friends and foes are easily mistaken. I'm Lieutenant Lovelock, and these are Privates Kerr and Lind," he said, pointing at the two behind him. "And you already know Hurlbart and Duncan. You are lucky that we found you before those *krauts*. We were surprised by enemy fire before our landing. Plane crashed, and our troops got scattered all over the place. We need to get to rendezvous."

War? Krauts? Did they think they were still fighting in WWII? I didn't dare ask, but now, knowing they were friends, I would feel safer walking these woods with them. "Where is rendezvous?"

"At the other side of the valley."

"We are heading the same way."

"Good. We will escort you. This is no place for a girl and a man in his condition," he said, pointing at Sidney. "What happened? Flamethrower?"

"Y-yes," I said, with no better way to explain it.

"We have a medic that could help your friend there," he murmured to me. "But between you and me, I'm not sure he's going to make it."

"He will, don't worry. Thank you, sir."

"So let's move out, people, we are sitting ducks here," Lt. Love-lock commanded.

I was about to walk when a hand on my shoulder halted my advance. It was Sidney's.

"Yes, they are waging war against an unseen enemy," Sidney whispered with his wheezing voice, standing by my side. My eyes searched for Peach, who was a few yards away, squatting in front of some flowers. "The worst prisons are not composed by bars, Maia, but those built by the mind," Sidney continued. "You never know where the cage ends, so freedom becomes just an illusion. And the cruelest illusion of all is death."

"Illusion?" I said, hardly grasping what Sidney was saying.

"Dying is a traumatic experience, but death is a dream so vivid that most believe they are still alive. People who died during slumber don't even recall their demise. Transition for them is seamless."

I turned to the soldiers marching so diligently, wondering if they were unaware of their entrapment. "That's the reason you referred to the world of the living as the *waking* world?" I said, remembering he'd mentioned it back at the hospital. But Sidney remained silent. "But I'm awake; I know about my own death."

"Temporarily, yes, still shielded by the powers granted by the medallion. But once all orbs have faded after the fifth day, you, too, will wander aimless in this realm. You, too, will become a sedentary soul reenacting your past life over and over, craving for what you loved and averting from what made you suffer. Death is no liber-ation from the joy and misery of life. Just a continuation of your reality."

I could not avoid feeling sorry for all these people. "But can they be woken up?"

"Can you bring sanity into a mental asylum?" Sidney turned briefly to Peach, who was caressing the flowers. "Madness is con-tagious, but sanity, on the contrary… I'm afraid nobody can carry you on their shoulders to the ultimate destination." His eyes settled back on me. "It's a path you need to walk by yourself."

"You mean the pilgrimage? Is that its purpose?"

"Purification for the soul and liberation of your mind from the dream of life. But people often refuse to detach themselves from their past experiences; their egos reject the transitory nature of life," Sidney explained. "The eternal fire should enlighten you through the Road of Oblivion. Unfortunately, not even the Fountain of Haji can outshine the temptations of obscurity. Most go astray."

"Liberation from the dream?" I said, puzzled, trying to digest Sidney's words. "Then, I'm just dreaming, and none of this has a meaningful consequence in the *real* world?"

"On the contrary; you can't alter one without affecting the other. Death and life are connected like the two sides of a coin. You just can't see both at the same time."

"But you just said death is an illusion."

"Can you differentiate the moon from its reflection over the water?" Sidney's words made me remember the moon we saw reflected on the Sea of Serenity.

"I'm totally lost, and I need clear answers, no BS attached this time," I said, terribly frustrated. "So please, Sidney, be clear. What is this place?"

Sidney babbled something I could not understand.

"Say that again?"

"You heard nonsense because it's angelic language. The primal language spoken since the creation. Even you used to know it."

"*Me?*"

"Everybody. This language has a seventy-two letter alphabet, which infants can speak but quickly forget when their parents teach them a new, substitute language. Then, for the rest of your life, you remember it only in dreams. Hence, it's also the language of dreams. That explains how people from different countries and eras can understand each other. As you spend time in this place, you will unlearn your language and remember the primal language," Sidney explained. "The words I mentioned can be loosely translated to English as *Becoming*. This place's name, it's the Realm of Becoming. And I regret to inform you that, as when you dream, your logic—your *living* world logic—is of no use in this place."

"Becoming?" I echoed. "Becoming what? If everybody here is dead, what follows after death? What happens after you finish the pilgrimage?"

Sidney remained silent, his deep eyes fixed on mine. "Life," he finally said.

"You mean like reincarnation?"

"Maia!" Frank interrupted us. "We need to hurry up, or we will be left behind."

"You are right, Frank. We have pressing matters to attend to," Sidney said, staring at me. "Please give me a hand."

Frank and Peach assisted him to go faster.

But I stood there for a moment, thinking on everything Sidney had just said, and I started feeling claustrophobic inside the immense forest surrounding me.

I ran after them.

We marched until the last beams of daylight faded and we set up a makeshift camp below a fat oak. I could not drag my feet an inch farther. I remembered my childhood camping days fondly, of sitting by the bonfire, so warming and hypnotizing, stuffed with roasted marshmallows. But soon I realized how romanticized my conception of camping was. The rations that Bill so kindly shared with me consisted of canned stew, hash, or pork and beans. I chose the stew without hesitation; I hated beans and didn't even know what "hash" was. I regretted the decision immediately—the stew was so insipid that it made me feel like the instant soups I'd eaten at work were a delicacy.

"Do you like it?" Bill inquired. I nodded sheepishly but felt terrible about it. I hated when people did that, just from my condition as a cancer patient. Nobody deserves somebody else's pity.

When I'd finished the stew, Bill handed me a chocolate-and-wafer bar. My eyes shone, hoping the dessert could make me forget the flavorless meal, but when I bit in, it made me wonder if the chocolate maker was a Nazi ally—it was unbreakable! It should have been classified as a throwing weapon instead of a meal. I decided to save it for later for the sake of my molars, arguing that I was already full, but honestly, I was waiting until everybody fell asleep to see if the hot flames could melt it.

Bill's generosity extended as he offered to lend me his sleeping bag, but I declined.

"You should offer it to them." I pointed to Sidney, who was sitting propped against a tree while Peach attended to his wounds. "They might need it more than I do," I said, doing my best to avoid sounding sarcastic.

"I did, concerned by her age, but your friend Frank dissuaded me, saying, 'Madam says she doesn't need it, and we vampires don't sleep,' and then he wrapped himself with his cape."

"Oh God," I said, ashamed. "Please forgive him."

"Is he…?"

"Like a kid, sometimes, I know." I chuckled.

"Don't worry, it's ok." Bill smiled. "Here, I insist." He handed me his sleeping bag, and I felt obliged to accept. His gestures didn't pass unnoted by Sidney, who observed us from across the bonfire.

My bones felt heavy and my muscles trembled, but after my chat with Sidney, I could not rest properly. I was afraid of falling asleep. The greenery surrounding us turned into a collection of spindly shapes produced by shadows cast from the fire.

"Looking for monsters?" Lt. Lovelock asked when he saw me uneasy.

"I used to think monsters weren't real," I replied, trying to regain composure.

"War transforms men into monsters. But it also has the power to turn a monster into a man." He drank liquor from his hip flask. "One day, we found a girl in the forest covered in blood. She was a *kraut* pursued by her own kind. She had escaped from a concentration camp, where she had discovered the horrors that hid behind the steel doors. Children with their skin pale as chalk, with numbers tattooed on the backs of their hands, subjected to experiments and the cruelest tortures." His eyes looked lost, as if the bright flames were speaking to him. "In her bravery, she devised a plan to liberate the children, but her plot was exposed. She was able to escape with seven children. Six lucky little boys and a girl for whom a young woman, just like you, stood before a Nazi death squad with open hands, offering her life to protect them as if they were her own."

Lt. Lovelock examined the plated swastika engraved on the empty flask and threw it into the fire. "I have looked many monsters in the eye, girl. And I tell you, you should not fear the dark, but the intentions of those dwelling in darkness."

He stood and picked up his machine gun. Lt. Lovelock disappeared into the blackness of the forest to make his watch. Having him out there provided some comfort. I reclined in my attempt to sleep. Sidney was watching me through the waving flames, restless, with a serene yet eerie gaze. Amid the prevailing darkness, his blistered face looked like the flaked skin of a dragon. Peach wasn't around, so I held his gaze until my eyelids plummeted.

My dreams were not pleasant. My head was heaped with the voice of the girl I heard earlier in the woods, telling me to run, repeating that I was in danger. The fluorescent eyes of a beast lurked in the shadows, but it didn't matter how fast I ran. The soil turned to mud, trapping my feet, leaving me at its mercy. As it came closer, the only thing I could hear was a throbbing drum.

Throbbing drums, getting louder.

"Maia! Wake up!" Frank shook me. I found myself wet from the rain that poured from the leaves. Everybody was shouting frantically. Kerr emerged from the pitch-darkness carrying Duncan over his shoulder with his head wobbling and five bloody slashes of a claw across his face. Kerr dropped him beside me. Duncan's irises were lost in the whiteness of his eyeballs, which reddened with the flowing blood carried by the rain.

"M-make it s-stop, please, it-t hurts," he babbled, convulsing, while I tried to hold him.

"Everybody, alert!" Lt. Lovelock ordered, pointing his machine gun into the gloom of the forest. "Those damn *krauts*."

There was a twinge in the bump on my neck. I touched it—it was feverish. I rummaged in Bill's belongings until I found a hand mirror. The bump palpitated with the incandescent engraving that the ring of Mr. Crimson had marked on me and I had totally forgotten about. It was a sort of skewed cross, with the x-axis slightly tipped down clockwise. I felt like cattle.

A branch cracked in the depths of the forest, and Kerr shot three rounds of his rifle.

"Hold!" Lovelock ordered.

"Bullets are no use against the Sheireils." Sidney stood with difficulty. "Only fire."

Peach and Frank wrapped rags around sticks to make torches. The noises got closer with each passing second. The twinge of my bump infected my ears, throbbing like deafening drums to the beat of my galloping heart.

"Drums," I whispered, and finally understood that the drums Samael and Sidney had warned me about were just a metaphor.

Bill ignited a flare and flung it into the dark woods. The light revealed a small, pale girl in a threadbare dress, shaking and crying with her hands covering her face while the rain dripped from her long, limp black hair.

"It's just a girl," Kerr said. "Come here, girl."

"She is afraid," I said, but the drums in my ears did not yield.

"Give me that." Private Lind snatched the torch from Frank and prowled toward the girl.

"Lind, what are you doing?" Lovelock asked.

Kerr followed Lind five steps behind for cover.

"Come with me, sweetheart," Lind said. "Come on, give me your hand."

An undiluted shadow cast by the darkness itself posed over Lind, asphyxiating the torch. He was pulled into the treetops by an invisible force, writhing like a fish out of water until he vanished in the blackness.

Kerr fell back, shooting randomly until he emptied the magazine. His shaking hand reloaded his rifle and reincorporated to point to the girl, who sobbed out loud. "You bastard! You lured him! You killed him!"

"Kerr! Come here," Lovelock ordered.

"Shut up, you little bastard!" Kerr hollered at the girl. "Are you not going to stop? Then I'm going to make you scream louder!! Look at me!!" He poked her with the muzzle of his rifle.

"He must not kill the girl, or he will open the door for the Sheireils to emerge," Sidney said to me.

"Emerge? From where?"

"From within," Sidney said, and by his worried expression, I knew something terrible would happen, so I ran toward them.

"Kerr, stop!"

"Maia!" Frank tried to hold me.

The girl lowered her hands, revealing her big, bloodshot eyeballs. Her eyelids were mangled, cauterized. Kerr, horrified, shot her.

"Nooooooo!" I fell on all fours, staring at the motionless girl lying in a puddle. "What did you do?"

Kerr dropped his smoky rifle. His breathing relaxed.

"He has opened the door to the hairy ones. Now he is not your friend anymore," Sidney said amid an overwhelming silence. "The Sheireils are here, and he has become one of them."

Kerr unsheathed his knife and clutched it.

"Maia!! Come here!" Sidney instructed.

I tried to stand but slid on the mud. The rhythm of the drums played a song of terror inside me.

Kerr drew the knife up to his face and sliced it. He turned to me, his eyes bleeding, the eyelids chopped off. Behind him, three human figures loomed out of the darkness with dilated pupils and no eyelids as well. Their skin was bone white. Their sharp-nailed hands were long-fingered and short-thumbed, like chimpanzees'. Their feet were wolves' paws. Cords of saliva hung from the several rows of ridged teeth inside their lipless mouths. A line of disheveled butterscotch hairs ran from the head to the backbone, waving as if they were underwater.

I dragged myself back.

"Shoot him," Frank ordered the militia.

They exchanged horrified glances and aimed at their comrade but didn't shoot. Kerr made a twenty-foot leap, landing like an ape in front of Bill. Kerr loomed mighty, terrifying, but Bill didn't pull the trigger. With a powerful backhand stroke, Kerr swatted Bill away.

"No!" I shouted.

Kerr glanced back and sprang toward me. While he was in midair, I heard a blast, and a scintillating silver dot that traveled at incredible speed pierced his chest, crossing the three Sheireils through their hearts, leaving behind a brilliant dust trail. Flames burst out of the holes, and the bodies of the monsters burned in a painful combustion.

The charred remains of Private Kerr fell at my feet.

A loud whinny split the air, and an onyx-black horse galloped out of the woods, ridden by a man in a long raincoat. The horse galloped toward us and stopped right in front of me. The horseman dismounted and shook the mud off his silver-spurred boots. He carried a sniper rifle cradled in his arms, long and sharp as his pointy mustache but better cared for than his scruffy beard. He tipped his hat to me and observed us one by one, taking his time. "I'm following a trail," the horseman said.

"You better keep sniffing somewhere else. No more prey to hunt tonight," Lt. Lovelock said, pointing at the remains of the Sheireils.

But the horseman's eager eyes searched for something else. "Do I look like a friggin' hound, *tovarishch*?"

"Good Lord, just what we needed, a Bolshevik," Lt. Lovelock mumbled.

"I hunt no beast, nor Germans or Americans," the horseman

said. Behind him, the little girl on the ground stirred, rising like a cobra. Her loose head twisted and straightened, baring thin, sharp teeth. She charged after the Russian with drawn claws.

"Sir, look out!" I warned.

Unconcerned, the horseman removed the safety of his rifle. "I hunt demons," he said and pulled the trigger without aiming. In the blast, another scintillating bullet was expelled, traveling toward the woods, but turned back like a boomerang to hit the girl in the back, making her combust like the Sheireils did.

Everyone stayed frozen as the carbonized head of the girl rolled down until the stranger's boot crushed it.

"Tonight I'm hunting a dangerous demon—*Chort*," he said, squinting.

"Never heard of it, Russki cowboy, but it sounds prettier than Stalin's arse." Lt. Lovelock laughed nervously.

The horseman giggled sarcastically and turned deadpan the second after. He pointed his rifle at us, looking through the gold-plated scope. I noticed the stock of the rifle had a chain bolted to it, which was shackled to his right wrist. The man was literally chained to his rifle.

The militia drew their weapons. "Put your gun down!"

"You will never know what the demon looks like until it's too late. It's a shapeshifter. It could be anyone: your foe, your friend, your brother," the horseman said, switching targets until he pointed at me. "Or even your mother." He lowered his rifle. "A mistake committed by all those who disown the true nature of Vandella."

CHAPTER 8

VANDELLA. The horseman's words rang in my ears. The rain had ceded, but that word fell on me like an ice bucket. I panicked. *He is going to kill Sidney.*

"Let me help you." The Russian offered his hand, but I hesitated. *What should I do?* I was unsure about Sidney's true identity, but I cared for him too much to see his heart pierced by the gun of this stranger—and besides, if Sidney died, so did my chances to regain the medallion and save my gran. I needed to make this man leave, and soon, which probably meant being nice to him.

"Thank you," I answered, taking his hand.

"You detoured from the main road." He heaved me to my feet.

"W-we got lost," I said, with my nerves still tingling, removing the patches of mud from my filthy dress.

"A dangerous place to be lost,"

"Thank you for saving us. We are in your debt."

"You misunderstand the situation, girl. I didn't save you. Bastards got in my way," the stranger said, overlooking the remains.

"On your way where? To finding Vandella?"

"Have you seen it? Do you know Vandella?" he asked, interested.

"Nope, I don't even know what that means. You better keep

looking," I said.

The Russian meticulously examined our camp with a rising brow. "Do you have hot food?"

"Errrr… yes."

But he was already moving. He tied up his horse and went straight to the campfire, and I stuck close to him in an attempt to distract him from Sidney. The Russian sniffed all the cans, ruffling his mustache before choosing the pork. He sat on a stone with his gun over his lap and devoured his meal using his fingers while wearing leather gloves, which I found pretty disgusting for a grown man. But I guessed a ration of pork stew was the least we could give him as a reward for saving us from the monsters. And then we could hope he would get back on the road.

Bill was pouring water from his canteen onto Duncan's bloody wounds before stitching, while Lt. Lovelock held him still and injected morphine. The image revolted me. I desperately wanted to help, but I'd never had the stomach for blood. I looked away.

"You'll get used to it," the Russian said, licking the can. "It's the same for everybody's first time on the battlefield."

"I spent years living in hospitals but never got used to them," I said.

"Nothing can prepare you for the horrors of war. Not even hospitals."

"You have a beautiful stallion, Mr.…" I said, trying to change the subject.

"Empress," he said. "She's a mare. Empress is her name. I'm Alek." I was no expert, but the horse was huge for a mare, though her long hair did blow with an air of grace and femininity.

"I'm Maia."

"A mare is a woman's horse," Lt. Lovelock said with blatant displeasure at the newcomer's self-service.

Alek laughed. "Men and gods have committed the mistake of underestimating her."

"Gods?" I asked, thinking it was a jest.

"Achilles was the last fool who dared to challenge her." Alek used his tongue to make two whistles, and Empress pricked her ears and turned to him. He hurled the can with the remaining pork so she could finish it. "Empress beat Balius and Xanthus, Achilles's immortal horses," he said with fatherly pride.

"You raced Achilles?" I asked. "*How?*"

"In Hell," he answered.

I was about to laugh when I remembered where I was and all the crazy and unimaginable things that I had endured so far. I remained silent.

"Then I guess his horses were not as immortal as they said," Lt. Lovelock laughed.

"Achilles was the one in Hell. His horses came after him."

Lt. Lovelock chuckled. "Not so bright, then, maybe," he said to himself, almost inaudible.

Alek turned to him, visibly vexed. "A loyal steed will gallop through the valley of death, will race against the devil, and will descend into the depths of Hell for its master, a gesture of honor and loyalty that not everyone can appreciate."

"Sure, whatever," Lovelock said as he grabbed his gear. "We need to find Lind. Maia, will you be ok on your own?" I assented, and he turned to Alek. "And if you try to do something funny to the girl, I personally will kick your Russki arse so hard you'll land at the Kremlin. Bon appétit, *tovarishch*." He spit tobacco on the dirt, and Alek crooked his head. Lt. Lovelock took Bill and Frank with him on his quest.

"Empress is a racehorse?" I asked, trying to loosen the tension.

"A warhorse."

"And Hell really exists? What's it like?"

"The priest at your church didn't tell you?"

"He did, but honestly, I never believed the part about a pit of flames."

"In Hell, no flames burn hotter than those made of ice."

"What?"

Alek pointed at Sidney, who was leaning languidly against the tree, watching us attentively from across the campfire. "I'm sure he can tell you about flames."

God, I thought he hadn't noticed! I tried to find a way to change the subject.

"Why does he look like that?"

"H-he—there was a flamethrower," I stammered.

"I didn't mean crispy, but angry." He raised his brow. "Maybe it's because I'm talking with you?" He leaned in, and narrowing his eyes, he asked, "Is he your boyfriend?"

"What?—ah—no, no, no. I have a boyfriend, but it's not him," I explained, lowering my voice. "His name is Jase."

"Oh, and where is he?"

"H-he is still alive, thank God." I laughed nervously. "I saw him three days ago, at a party…" I elevated my eyes, following the fire sparks that extinguished in the dark, and sighed, thinking about what Jase would be doing in that moment. How did he remember me? As the nerd girl that helped him pass biology? As Shelly's shy friend? Three days had passed, and I missed him already. I missed Shelly, Lisa, Rachel, and school. Griselda and Fred. I missed gran and her tasty food. I missed my life… except the hospital—and even then, I missed Dr. Wolk, Darrell, and Gary.

"Maybe you are right," Alek acknowledged, twisting his mouth. "Maybe he is not angry but hungry. I'm thoughtless." He took a can out of the fire. "I better take him something to eat."

I jumped from my seat. "It's ok, I'll take it." I snatched the can, only to find it was burning hot—a small price to pay for keeping him away from Sidney.

The brief walk across the camp felt eternal.

"We thought that you might be hungry. You haven't eaten yet." I squatted and gave Sidney the can. He held my hand with the affection of a starving beggar, but it was not food he wanted. His fingers stroked my palm tenderly. I retracted my hand and looked away. Alek observed us with probing eyes. "It's gross, but better than nothing."

"I burned my taste buds off, anyway," Sidney joked.

"Where is Peach? I thought she would bring you food."

He motioned with his eyes toward the scrub where she was kneeling, looking upward, whispering to the sky.

"What is she doing?"

"Asking for forgiveness," Sidney said with gloomy eyes.

"From who?"

"Her children."

I was shocked, imagining Peach having had children so young.

"She has kids? What happened?" I asked, intrigued.

"They died."

"Why?" I prompted, but Sidney remained silent. "Why is she asking for forgiveness?"

"For letting them die… She supplicates for absolution."

She *let* them die? I could not conceive a mother capable of letting her children die. It was unimaginable. A crime. A monstrosity.

"Isn't it sad?" Sidney asked, staring at Peach. "That such a beautiful flower is a prisoner of guilt?"

But I remained silent.

"You just need to look into her eyes to discover who she truly is," Sidney continued. "Delicate but strong. Passionate and devoted. Brave beyond anything I have seen…"

What was so impressive about her? That she was beautiful enough to ignore the fact that she let her children die? I genuinely didn't understand men. *God!* How could they fall for nothing but pretty faces and curvy bodies? She had bewitched him. *Why could he not see it?*

"Are you mad at me?" Sidney asked.

"Why would I be mad at you?" I deadpanned.

He motioned with his eyes toward Peach again.

I was not mad; I was jealous. I was not the beautiful flower, the delicate, or the brave. I was the spoiled brat who thinks she's special. "I'm mad about your secret."

"What secret?"

"That apparently you're Vandella, and everybody knows what that means but me," I finally said.

"What did the Russian say?" he asked, but I remained silent. I was not willing to give ground this time. I needed the truth. I *deserved* the truth.

"Maia, people will tell you things, even awful things, because that is what people do—gossip."

"And gossip exists because people keep secrets."

"There's nothing wrong with secrets," Sidney said, making me remember how I'd hid my disease from my gran and my friends. But this time I was not the one sitting on the stand. This was not my trial.

"If that is what troubles your heart, please do it no more." He rested his hand on his chest. "It's true, I'm Vandella," he said nonchalantly. "I'm also *Chort*, or whatever he wants to call me. I have a thousand names, remember?"

"Please be quiet—" I tried hushing Sidney to prevent Alek from hearing him, but he didn't lower his voice.

"You still don't understand, Maia," Sidney interrupted. "Look at me." He opened his cloak and removed the remains of his carbonized shirt from his skin, revealing his burnt torso. "I have no place to conceal secrets anymore. But the fire didn't rob me of the armor that protected me. It was *you*. You made me vulnerable. You stripped me from my hiding. You found me, and what you see is all

I have for you. No more secrets."

Could it be the truth? I asked myself naively, as my heart fluttered with what he said. *Don't fool yourself, Maia.* I shouldn't believe him.

"You want the truth?" He grabbed my hand by surprise and put it on his chest. "Put your hand through the wounds on my ribs and reach into the depths of my heart. There you will find the truth." My fingers followed his along the contour of his wounds, like windows exhaling the warmth of his interior. Feeling his beating heart transported me to the comfort of his arms, to the black velvet scales and satin in which he had wrapped me to save me from the inferno.

The unburnt side of his face grinned with a crooked smile, and I returned it.

Peach stared at us with tears running from her eyes. She had returned while we chatted. I pulled back my hand and stood, embarrassed.

She embraced me. "Don't worry, my dear, this will end soon." Her tears dampened my cheek while Sidney's warmth still nested in my palm. "Stay away from that man."

I stepped back, bemused, unsure whether she meant Alek or Sidney.

"Thank you for the food, Maia." Peach sat down beside Sidney.

"Are you ok?" Sidney asked her, placing a reassuring hand on her shoulder. She nodded, still weeping.

I returned to Alek angrier with myself. He was hammering a bar of chocolate and wafer with his revolver's butt.

"Shoot it," I said.

"Who?" he asked.

"The chocolate." I sat beside him. "Unless your rifle is not powerful enough to pass through some candy?"

"It's not a rifle, girl, it's a *Dragunov*," he said, caressing the metal frame, following the patterns of the wood overlaying the stock with the fondness of a lover. "Its bullet will travel to the end of the world and back, piercing in its way men and gods alike until it finds its target."

"How does the bullet know where to go?"

"It's commanded by my will."

"Then why hunt for Vandella, if you can just pull the trigger from the comfort of your living room?"

"You don't throw stones at the crows to drive them away from your crops. Crows will never leave, so you must put up a scarecrow. The crows cannot gouge his eyes out, cut his tongue, nor feed from his entrails. A scarecrow is a man that patiently waits below sun and rain, restless from dawn to dusk, just watching. Driving the crows mad. Because what crows fear the most is a man without a soul." He turned to me, dead serious. "I am a patient man, you see."

"Why do you want to kill Vandella so badly?"

"I was hired to."

"Who hired you?"

"It's confidential, sorry—contractual clause." Alek lifted his hand, dangling the chain that kept him attached to the gold-plated scope.

Alek handled the telescopic sight with the care of a priest holding a chalice. "It's called the *Eye of Truth*," he said. Its lustrous golden surface reflected our surroundings in a distorted way, where shadows and lights were inverted, big was small, wide was narrow, and vice versa. "It reveals the true self of a person beyond any façade, uncovering all lies. If it's properly adjusted, it can show both the future and the past."

The golden glint was alluring. An odd desire to touch it grew inside me. Alien ideas to steal it gestated in my mind, to make it mine at all cost and uncover the lies and see my future. "Prove it," I said, fascinated.

"There is no need."

"Why?"

"I already did." Then I remembered him pointing it at us when he arrived at this place, observing each one of us. "Do you truly believe the lieutenant is searching for the lost paratrooper right now?" Alek shook his head. "He shelters in the night because only the shadows can hide the tears he sheds, feeling guilty of abandoning his son. He can't tolerate losing another, because in each boy he packs back home in a coffin, he sees his son's face."

I had no idea if it was true or false, but it was frighteningly convincing. "Is Bill scared too?"

"He is terrified, except when he is close to you." That *was* news.

"What about my friend Frank?"

"Are you worried he is lying to you?" I didn't know why I should be. "Fear not."

"The girl—" Alek said, pointing at Peach.

"She despises me. No Eye of Truth necessary to figure that

out."

"She needs you."

"Why?" I asked, disconcerted.

Alek's finger switched to Sidney. "Ask her companion."

"What about him?"

"What about him, Maia? You lied to my face about him." Alek clutched the handgrip of his *Dragunov*, resting his finger on the trigger with his cunning eyes fixed on me.

My blood descended to my feet. With Frank and the militia away, Duncan badly hurt, and Sidney too vulnerable to fight, we were trapped. We couldn't run or hide. Pulling the trigger would release a bullet that would find and kill us all. I was paralyzed. I thought the *Sheireils* were our biggest threat, but this outsider who saved us from them was even worse.

"Jase is not your boyfriend," he continued. "It's just another lie, like the ones you tell everyone, because you live in terror that they might find what you loathe so much about yourself. And you don't want to be judged. You know well how hard that is, because you are the cruelest judge of yourself. And for what purpose? To gain the sympathy of people that don't give a damn about you? Hoping that one day they may reckon, 'Oh, I misjudged you, how wrong I was,' when it doesn't matter anymore? Well, bad news, girl. You are almost dead, and that day may never come."

I stood up to run away. I could not sustain my facade. I could no longer pretend to be strong.

"Now you have the idea," Alek said, stopping my escape.

"About what?" I gibbered.

"About what Hell is like."

I hurried off through the undergrowth, unable to take anymore, leaving the camp behind, uncertain of what Alek would do. I stopped when I was far enough away to not be heard. I reclined my hand against a tree, and tears sprouted beyond my control.

Was it too much to covet a normal life? To be healthy? To love and be loved with the same degree? Did I not deserve it? And if not, what did I do to be so unworthy?

My feet gave up, and I landed on a bed of jasmine flowers that resembled my gran's greenhouse, providing me a bit of solace. I picked one and brought it close to my nose but smelled nothing, not the flowers, the forest, the dirt, nor my sweaty clothes. I was losing my sense of smell, just like Sidney had predicted.

I pulled all the petals off the jasmine except one and contemplated the plucked flower. It was ugly compared to the others. I placed it gently back on the dirt, feeling guilty. I sprinkled the petals over it, and they fell like snowflakes, whitening the dark soil.

My eyes got tired of shedding tears, and my heart numbed. I knew it was time to go back to the camp.

By the time I returned, Lt. Lovelock and Frank had half carried Lind back into camp. He was covered with scratches, and his right knee was dislocated or possibly broken.

According to Lt. Lovelock, they had found him hanging from the trees. Apparently, he'd stepped on a leg-hold trap that catapulted him into the air. The idea seemed ridiculous to me. That was not what I saw. I vividly remembered the shadows that had descended to claim him.

Was I hallucinating?

I decided not to bother my mind any longer. Lind was alive. That was all that mattered. Besides, there were more important things to worry about now. Correction—*one* more important thing. Alek.

Alek was immersed in grooming Empress's pelage, but the quiet was not peace; it was armistice.

I crawled into the sleeping bag, trying to rest for what remained of the night, but sleep was elusive. Peach was lying down against Sidney's shoulder, sheltered under his cloak.

I looked away.

CHAPTER 9

I WOKE UP, removing the tears that had crusted on my eyelashes. Last night's events seemed so distant. Ashes were the sole remains of the bonfire.

Everyone was in a rush, packing things, so I did my part to help. Sidney seemed in better condition; he was able to walk without support. Alek helped Lind and Duncan to mount Empress. I turned to Bill, alarmed.

"He is coming with us," he explained. "He offered, and there was no other way we could carry them without his horse."

No matter how much I loathed the idea of Alek joining us, Bill was right.

That day, we hiked the steepest ascent of our journey. By the time the forest cleared at the top of the mountain, it was almost midday. Even dead tired, I was pleased to escape the spell of the woods, to see the sun once more. The view of the landscape from the cusp of the mountain was magnificent. It felt like the entire world was at our feet.

"Touriel." Sidney pointed to a volcano at the edge of the horizon. "That's our destination. We must descend the mountain through the forest, following the river to the valley, and cross it to reach the plains. We are three or maybe four days away, depending on our pace."

"That forest is a maze," said Lt. Lovelock. "We should flank it across the grasslands. It would be easier and quicker." What Lovelock said made sense. Sidney's route was hilly, which would cost us more time, and my clock was ticking. Four days was all I had.

"What then?" Sidney pointed to the moon advancing toward the sun, about an hour away from eclipse. "It's nearly the hour of reckoning. How will we elude Nagelfar if he appears? Are you sure you want to deal with the pestilence?"

I shivered, remembering the shadow dragon crossing the sky and the terrors of the pestilence.

"Damn pestilence." Lt. Lovelock was disquieted by the idea. Reluctantly, he turned to Alek for an opinion.

"*Roasty* is right."

"Hurlbart! We need to establish communications with HQ before entering dark territory," Lt. Lovelock ordered, and Bill took out a radio receiver the size of a shoebox. He removed the top lid, unveiling the controllers, and plugged a three-foot-long antenna into a black handset.

"This is Lieutenant Irwin Lovelock, do you copy? Over!" he said, tuning the radio. "Please, somebody respond. We were surprised by enemy fire. My men are all scattered." But only static was received. "If you can hear me, this is Lieutenant Lovelock. I'll see you on the other side. Over." He plonked down the handset with noticeable frustration.

I could not avoid feeling depressed. I knew there was no one at the other end of the line. They were, as Sidney had said, just sedentary souls reenacting their past life. I wondered if all of them had died trying to reach their friends.

"What if they are not at rendezvous, sir?" Bill said, dejected.

"Nonsense, Hurlbart. General Germanicus is waiting for us."

"Germanicus? Like the Roman general, father of Emperor Caligula?" I said, remembering my history classes with Mr. Mankell.

"He is the new commander of the Allied forces," Lt. Lovelock explained, as if that were totally normal.

A Roman general leading WWII's troops? This Realm of Becoming was certainly an eclectic place. I was tempted to ask if Germanicus had truly died poisoned by his own son, like Mr. Mankell said, but guessed my question would not be well received.

"We better move on. We don't have much time," Sidney recommended, and everybody followed his command.

"Are you all right?" I asked Bill, helping him to gather the radio equipment.

"Yes," he said shyly.

"They will come for you, don't worry," I said, convinced that he needed to remain confident as the only way to endure what we might find ahead.

"I told myself that while I was hanging on those trees."

"Were you waiting for Jim?" His expression puzzled. "You called for him when you were unconscious. He was with you?"

"During our landing in Normandy, we were welcomed with antiaircraft fire, and in a matter of seconds, our plane was engulfed in flames. I dove through the thick curtain of smoke after Jim, but once in the air, I lost sight of him. I was able to spread my parachute and suspend in the air to witness the show, the C-47s swooping down like paper planes amid the fireworks." Bill chuckled. "I watched the shining bullets passing through my comrades, their lifeless bodies floating through the searchlights… I saw it. I saw it all." The rims of his eyes turned red.

I hugged him. "I'm sorry to hear that. But thank God you are all right."

"I-I was just lucky. Unlike Jim," Bill said solemnly. His youthful eyes were plagued with the memory of an old man who has seen the horrors of a lifetime. I wondered what he would be doing back at home instead of fighting: going to school, getting drunk with his friends, dating pretty chicks. Instead, he'd jumped from a plane into a slaughterhouse. No boy deserved to be dragged into manhood like that. I imagined them falling, lifeless, like angels cast away from the heavens with their wings torn apart, not knowing if they would fly again.

The descent of the mountain was easier, but the idea of entering another forest was unpleasant. Only Sidney and Peach appeared to take pleasure in the woods. The trees were mostly firs and pines, ranging in hue from celadon to emerald green. They were all teardrop-shaped, almost as if they were cloned—the degree of symmetry extended to their distribution on the field in straight rows as far as we could see. The space between them was so tight it prohibited walking abreast. Each of us picked an alley and advanced in parallel—a military tactic suggested by Lt. Lovelock for spotting potential attackers. "In case of attack, you crawl beneath the firs," he advised, but we lost sight of each other every time we crossed a broad pillar of needles.

At least this woodland was alive—that calmed me a bit. Birds fluttering from twig to twig at the top of the trees, cardinals singing, and woodpeckers pecking. Red deer bounced in the distance, and hares ducked in their burrows as we marched through.

My brain reconstructed the lemony smell of the pines from my memories. It was a shame I could not smell it; it would have been relaxing.

The moon started eclipsing the sun, and our path became dark. The wind changed direction, blowing against us. Flocks of birds followed the currents, as if they were escaping from an imminent cataclysm.

"Don't stop! Keep going! Don't be afraid," Lt. Lovelock shouted from two alleys to my left.

"And no matter what you hear, don't look up," Sidney added.

The wind howled, wiggling the peak of the trees, and suddenly everything went silent, static, and the night's veil fell at midday. The evergreen needles were tinged with a dark gold outline, and the trunks fused with the soil into an enormous shadow that shooed my desire to creep beneath a fir. I resisted my impulse to look up in search of Nagelfar.

I scuttled along, hearing nothing beyond my breathing, watching the outlines of my companions when the trees allowed. A speck appeared in my field of view—it was a milky-white hare with straight ears that stood on its rear legs and looked at me, before disappearing with the same quickness.

I kept my head down and followed my trail until the eclipse came to an end. When I felt the world lighten again, I glanced at the sky, relieved that we'd been spared from the dragon and its pestilence. Then I stopped at the crossroads and turned left and right but saw nobody.

"Bill! Frank! Sidney!" I called but heard nothing besides the wind. I prowled around the broad-pillared trees and knelt to peek beneath them, but I was all alone. There were neither footprints nor marks of their passing. My throat ached, calling for them, as I wandered through the maze of identical trees until I found my own footprints.

Leaves scrunched behind me. It was the white hare, wagging its whiskers. "Wait!" I sprinted after the animal, which left me behind with ease. I stopped, breathless, cursing myself for being out of shape, when I overheard water running in the distance and remembered the brook we'd seen from the heights. I followed the sound down to the banks of a river. The hare was staring at the river, and when I came close, it ran over the water without sinking, as if it were a shallow puddle, and hid in the foliage on the other side.

Could it be possible that I can walk over the water too? I asked myself, extending my foot over the rushing river.

"Don't," Sidney said behind me.

"My God, where have you been?" I said, both upset and relieved to see him.

"I hoped you'd find your way here."

"What? Where is everybody?"

"Wandering around."

"You knew that was going to happen," I said, folding my arms disapprovingly. It was he who had proposed this route, against Lt. Lovelock's advice. "You brought us here. Why?"

"I have a surprise for you."

"What?"

"An amusement park."

CHAPTER 10

I STARED AT SIDNEY, BAFFLED. "Where is everybody?" I insisted.

"Wandering around, like I said. They are trying to find their way out of the mirror's labyrinth, like you did."

"Mirror's labyrinth?" I said, trying to digest how a bunch of trees could become a maze of mirrors… unless it was a single tree reflected a thousand times. That would explain the odd symmetry and uncanny similarity of the trees. But it seemed impossible to believe. *I saw the trees. I touched them*, I told myself. They were not just a plain reflection—they were alive. "How?"

"You rely too much on your sight. Eyes are easily beguiled."

"Like everybody else. And now they're all lost. How can you be so calm? We need to look for them."

"All paths converge on this river eventually," Sidney said, trying to alleviate my concern. "Some may take longer than others to find the exit, but they will. You did it quickly, in fact. I'm impressed."

Crossing the forest was a test? And was that a compliment? I pondered, disconcerted. Sidney was so confusing. Everything he said seemed to have at least a double meaning.

"But what if they are in danger?"

"They are not," he said, convinced.

"How are you so sure?"

"Sheireils can't bear to contemplate their reflection."

"Sheireils are not the only concern," I said, but Sidney remained unflustered. I supposed that Alek wanted Sidney, so maybe he had no intention of harming the others, which gave me enough peace as long as Sidney was by my side. "But if those were mirrors, why didn't I see my reflection?"

"If you expose the trick behind the illusion, it spoils the magic. And magic is created not to be uncovered but to be believed."

Great. I had thought Frank was the magician-wannabe of the group.

"But how?"

"I told you, this is an amusement park," he said, motioning with his hand around him. "The mirror's labyrinth, the Ferris wheel, the enchanted river, and the house of terrors—all of them in one place."

I inspected my surroundings and didn't recognize anything beyond the woods and the river, but I could not deny the aura of mysticism that surrounded the place.

"Do you like amusement parks?" Sidney said, smiling with the unburnt side of his face. "Of course you do, have since you were a toddler," he answered before I could say anything. "There was no happier girl in the world than you riding the white horse on the carousel. Up and down and up, while you swung your hand out to your grandmother, on each spin with greater effusiveness…"

It was as if Sidney had logged inside my mind's library and played the exact memory. I was four years old when my gran took me to the fair for the first time.

"…and you ran to her arms after the ride had finished, saddened by her brief absence," Sidney continued. "And she hugged you, saying, 'My ruddy bear, you galloped all around the world. I'm so proud of you!'"

"H-h-how do you know?" My heart softened as I remembered the face of my grandmother.

"Then you ran from the arms of your grandmother to the Ferris wheel, savoring your pink cotton candy, and bumped into a raised cobble," he continued. "You wanted to cry, but a gentleman picked you up and swung you into his arms to comfort you. 'Don't cry, my dear,' he hushed you, lifting your chin," Sidney said, lifting my chin in the same way. "'Princesses don't cry. Princesses endure, not because they are fearless but because they are brave.'" I remembered vividly how the tears in my eyes had fuzzed the man's face, backlit by the dazzling sun, but I didn't remember him having Sidney's face. But if it was not him, *how was it possible he knew all this?*

"How—" I babbled.

"Magic must be believed." Sidney closed my lips with his index finger. He took my hand and led me to a wooden canoe sitting by the water.

Sidney helped me to get onboard and sat on the plank behind me. The canoe started its travel without the aid of rowing, like it was running on rails. The current delivered us to a cave below a massive pine that devoured the entire river, with a curtain of roots suspended over the entrance. I turned to Sidney, worried, but he pointed ahead, and the roots opened, granting us passage. *How?* Remembering Sidney's words, I quieted my questioning and tried to enjoy the trip. Entering the pebbled cave felt like a cold steam bath. The root curtain covered the entrance again, and we cruised into the cavern in complete darkness until colorful lights started sparkling in the water: translucent fishes that produced wavering flickers when they moved. It was like multicolored fireworks exploding underwater.

"Wow, did you see that?" I asked Sidney, excited.

"Beautiful, isn't it?"

I extended my hand to touch the fish, but they buried themselves in the riverbed's sludge, going dark again.

Suddenly, hundreds of butterflies clustered in the root holes on the ceiling fluttered away, allowing sunrays to percolate inside. The sunlight hit on prismatic formations of crystals that refracted colorful beams, transforming the dull cave into a kaleidoscope. The glistening wings of the butterflies blinked in patterns, decorating the walls like the changing skin of a chameleon. I watched, mesmerized.

The butterflies revolved around us, and suddenly our canoe slid down a cascade and we landed back on the river. The dazzling exit of the cave was an arch of stone held up by two columns. The current pulled our canoe aside, and we descended onto a stone quay. Sidney bowed and extended his hand to help me out. We followed a pathway on the side of the arch and came out through the muzzle of a humongous wolf's head carved into the cliff's stone. We stepped onto a tiny terrace, contemplating the magnificent sculpture from a distance. On its forehead, the wolf had a V-shaped scar. The river cascaded from its tongue into the woods beneath.

"His name is *Apenimon*," Sidney said, staring at the wolf's head. "It means *worthy of trust*."

"The wolf was real?"

"Yes."

Sidney proceeded to tell me an old story about a man who had his sheep herd constantly diminished by wolf attacks. Tired of the situation, one night he decided to set a metal snare. The following morning, he prepared to go and kill the vicious predator. When he arrived, he found a dazed black wolf licking his bloody leg, which was trapped between the sharp metal teeth. The man's wrath softened into compassion for the poor creature. He pondered releasing the wolf, but letting him loose meant condemning his sheep. The man took the wolf to his home anyway, unsure of his decision. The man attended his wounds, fed him, and cared for the wolf for weeks. When the wolf had healed, the man opened the house's door to allow him to leave, but the wolf refused. The man had to throw stones until the wolf was lost on the horizon. From that day, no other sheep were slaughtered. The black wolf was seen by neighbors scaring away other wolves that tried to attack the man's herd.

One night, Death knocked on every door of the town in disguise, snatching everybody's lives like the plague. The grim reaper killed the entire sheep herd, but when it arrived at the man's door, it passed by, leaving the man unhurt. That day, all men and animals in the town died, except him. The man mourned his loss alone, but with time he found peace. After the incident, the man had a long and prosperous life, and when his time came, Death called at his door once again. After welcoming the long-expected visitor, he asked why it had skipped his door years before, and the grim reaper answered, "I did not. I passed by your door to claim a life but found a black wolf guarding it. The wolf offered his life instead of yours." When the man crossed the doors to the hereafter, he found the wolf waiting for him, sitting immovable, just as he had diligently guarded the man's door.

"Why does life have to be like that?" I asked Sidney, who stared at me, bemused. "Bittersweet."

"A man once taught me the phrase *wabi-sabi*. It's a term that refers to the beauty of joy found in sorrow, especially in the evanescence of life. He was a Japanese watchmaker who one day found that his wristwatch had stopped."

"How is it that you, being the son of Death, are not immune to sorrow?"

"My father is immune to both joy and sorrow." Sidney turned away, exposing the unburnt side of his face. "But the legacy of my mother weighs on me."

"Your mother was human?"

He nodded slightly. Staring at him was like contemplating the two faces of the moon. The dark side, even frightening and enigmatic, was equally beautiful. And just like the moon, he exerted a powerful gravitational force that drew me inexorably to him. With my left hand, I caressed the side of his face that had inherited the chaotic nature of his father, scorched by the flames at the graveyard.

"You disobeyed your father…" My right hand touched the soft and polished skin of his mother's side, of wishful and anxious human nature. "…listening to the feelings of the human heart of your mother to save me. Why?"

Sidney's eyes on me were a combination of spine-chilling ice and passionate fire.

"Because you saved me," he said.

I stepped away from him, while my mind struggled to understand. "You talk like we have known each other for a long time, but I had never seen you before that night at the hospital."

"I have known you since your birth."

Impossible, I told myself. "How old are you?"

"For me, it's not about days or years passing by," Sidney explained. "For you, the sun rises and sets. But for me, just like for the sun, day and night has no meaning; tomorrow is yesterday." He stroked my cheek. "I see you in the same way you observed the mirror's labyrinth, where a sole pine reflected in a thousand mirrors became a forest before your eyes. I look at you through the mirrors of time and see a thousand Maias, from your birth to your deathbed, all in the same instant. None more beautiful than the other, all perfect."

I blushed and looked away.

"What?" Sidney said, pulling my chin up to meet my eyes, but I kept silent. "You are beautiful, regardless of what you think." He hugged me, pressing me against his chest. "I was there," he whispered into my ear, and I heard his beating heart. "At the amusement park. I was the uninvited guest to your spoiled seventh birthday party. I was there every time you stared at your bald reflection in the mirror, asking why, until your tears had ceased," he said, caressing the bump on my neck. "I was there every night you looked for a shooting star that could fulfill your desire. I was there every time your heart rushed for a boy."

Sidney's words ignited memories of my whole life, every fragment of memory, of contentment and sorrow, of fear and courage, of love and loneliness. I could not control my tears. "Where were you? Why didn't you tell me you were there?" I slapped his chest, refusing to believe I had never been alone during those moments, that his invisible presence had accompanied me all those years.

Sidney's left eye shed a tear. "I'm here," he said with a broken voice and squeezed me in his arms. "I'm the shooting star." He kissed my forehead.

"What took you so long?"

I hugged him with all my strength. *My shooting star.* My materialized desire. I hoped Sidney's arms could hold me forever.

"*Wabi-sabi*," I said, breaking away from his arms. "Miracles always occur too late for me. I'm *dying* now, Sidney, even before I got to this place, and you know it better than anyone. I came with you to put a quicker end to my misery," I admitted.

"I was also there every time you lied to yourself, telling yourself *I can't.*"

I chuckled, imagining Sidney stalking me through my window. "I'm not lying this time," I said adamantly, my smile evaporating. "I really can't."

"Everything will be all right—"

"Until the moment I take my grandmother's place." I completed his phrase. "Only then will everything be all right."

"You don't believe in what I say?"

How could I? When you've kept so many secrets? I asked myself. "People have told me a thousand times that 'Everything will be all right.' And now look at me. If I'm here, it's unquestionable proof that everything was *not* right."

"Faith is not about believing in what your eyes can see, but what your heart feels."

"My heart? No, no. My heart is an awful decision maker, always hanging on the lost causes."

"Do you trust me, Maia?" Sidney inquired, but I didn't answer.

Sidney stood at the edge of the terrace and held out his hand. "Would you come with me to the end of the world?"

"What?"

I looked over the edge into the murky lake at the bottom of the cliff, at least forty yards down. "What are you thinking? Jumping from this height—we will die, break our necks for sure."

"Is that not what you wanted? To speed things up? To put an end to your misery?" Sidney challenged. "Or are you afraid?"

I flinched. He was *right*. I was a coward.

Sidney opened his arms. "Have you ever wondered how hard it is to release a loved one from this world?"

I shook my head. And he fell from the cliff. My hand flew to my mouth. I cast myself to the ground, peering over the edge in a futile effort to save him, but only managed to terrify myself, spotting how he splashed against the lake surface like a meteorite. In the blink of an eye, he was gone. I counted the elapsed seconds with rushed breathing, waiting for him to emerge alive, but he didn't.

What if he lost consciousness and is drowning? I need to save him! I searched around for a way to descend, but the there was no staircase; the terrace was surrounded by precipice. And even so, it would be too late for Sidney by the time I got down.

There was only one way.

I stood over the edge looking down, and fear possessed me. I closed my eyes and inhaled deeply, convincing myself that I'd either save Sidney, or both of us would die. Then I leaned forward, feeling the air blowing my hair and clothes. I opened my eyes in midair, and before I could think, I hit the water.

The swarm of bubbles dispersed, revealing that I had miraculously survived. It was as if I was floating in nothingness. I could not see Sidney anywhere. The gradient of darkness increased with each descending foot underwater. The sun above me seemed like a fading star, distant, unreachable. Returning to the surface was an impossible journey, and I was determined not to leave without him. So I kept descending.

My eyes recognized moving silhouettes lurking in the shadows. A thick tail of what appeared to be a snake writhed around a stone. The long tentacles of a colossal squid undulated outside a cavern like algae, luring naive visitors. The murky waters were replete with pairs of bright eyes that gazed at me attentively.

My air was running out when, from the depths, a glistening figure emerged, gliding frictionless through the water with the grace of a figure skater. Sidney was naked. His wounds had been magically healed. He circled around me like an eel and stopped when our faces met. He smiled flirtatiously, and my heart bloomed. I grinned, releasing my last breath of air in relief, condemning myself to drowning.

In my last moments of consciousness, I tried to memorize Sidney's face: his fine features, his phosphorescent olive eyes. The way he looked at me, as if I were the only woman on the planet. *It was a perfect last image for taking with me.*

He wrapped his left arm around my waist and passed his right arm around my neck, holding my face from behind, lifting my chin so our lips could meet.

Sidney kissed me.

It was kind but thrilling, smooth but passionate, sudden but endless.

I lost myself in the kiss. He made me forget where I was. I was not underwater. I was high, *so* high, floating in the weightlessness of a crystalline night sky surrounded by stars. His lips provided me not just air for keeping me alive; his breath inside mine ignited the passion concealed in the corners of my heart.

I was brought back to life.

Sidney took my hands and steered me gently, as if we were waltzing across the galaxy. His eyes whispered sweet things to my soul. It was at that moment when, at last, I admitted what I had been denying all this time. What I'd fought to hide.

I was totally under the charm of *Vandella*.

It didn't matter if it was right or wrong. Sidney's mere existence gave meaning to my senseless life. That was what the spell of love did to me.

Frank *was* right.

I loved him.

Sidney carried me to the surface. I caught my breath and dried my dazzled eyes with my palms. He released me, and my feet hit the rocky bottom—we were just waist-deep in the water. I stomped, not understanding how the deep water had transformed into a shallow pond before my eyes. He laughed guiltily.

"Never do that again." I hammered his ripped torso, mad about his suicide prank. "Never, you hear me?"

Sidney caught my hands inside his. "Kiss you?" he whispered with his unblinking eyes, and his lips approached mine but halted an inch before the kiss. "You want me to never kiss you again?" he inquired, savoring the sweet torment.

I was hypnotized, like the prey of a charming cobra.

My lips desperately needed his, but I didn't dare show him that.

What he will think about me if I kiss him? What if Peach finds out? What if he is only playing with me? He is Vandella, a creature of the night, a vampire of the soul... I continued with my endless list of insecurities. Brick by brick, I enclosed myself into the stronghold of distrust.

"What if I refuse?" I retracted, regaining control of myself.

"Even if you forbid me your lips, Maia, I could relive our kiss more times than stars plague the night sky."

"A memory is not reliving," I said. "No matter how hard you try."

"Not memories. Maia, I have to remind you that I can live in all places at once and transcend the boundaries of time. I'm here now, but at the same time, I'm also *there*, taking you out of the water's depths as I kiss your perfect lips"—Sidney stepped closer to me—"that are telling me not to stop..."

He ran his arms around my waist, capturing me again.

"...telling me that we should never be separated," Sidney whispered as the tips of our noses rubbed softly.

"Is that what you want?" My hands held his burly arms, unsure of whether to push or pull.

"If I had to choose to live just an instant of my eternity—it would be kissing you," Sidney said with his velvet voice, and his lips reconnected with mine. His kiss eradicated all doubts sown in my head, and all the voices in me whispered in unison, *It's him, he is the one you have been looking for.*

Sidney's next kiss made me daydream. Wondering about a life by his side, sharing every moment with a man that could relive eternity in a sigh.

Our lips detached, leaving a void that longed for him.

"How does it feel?" I asked, intrigued. "To live eternally?"

Sidney lifted his sight to the sky. "It feels like being born and dying at each instant. Like being a thousand different persons and being no one at the same time." He walked to the waterfall and extended his hand inside the torrent. "It feels like a water stream, in which each drop is an endless possibility."

Sidney's back was scarred, but not from the fire. The deep grooves crossing his back had a different origin. They seemed inflicted with purpose. But it was odd that those wounds hadn't healed, like the rest of his body. It was as if he had deliberately chosen to keep them.

"Why me?" I asked him. "With infinite possibilities at your disposal, why choose me?"

Sidney waded toward me, and his wet hand reached my waist and pulled me close. "Because you—"

A gruff voice interrupted us. "The bastard lied to me."

Startled, I stepped away from Sidney and looked behind me.

It was Alek, standing by the shoreline.

But it was not just him.

It was also Peach, Frank, and the whole of Lovelock's company, enjoying the show for who knows how long.

CHAPTER 11

ALEK'S DARTING EYES SCRUTINIZED US. "The bastard lied to me," he repeated, shaking his head with one hand on his hip and the other resting over his Dragunov, which was propped on the ground.

My blood descended to my feet.

"I thought that boat ride was just another amusement park attraction, but now I see Roasty isn't crisp anymore." Alek squatted and cupped the water with his gloved hand. "'There is a river lost in the woods that carries the water of life,' a man told me once. 'Those who bathe in those waters will be cured of any wound or evil.'" He poured the water out slowly and chuckled. "I didn't believe him."

Phew. My breathing resumed. *So that was the reason why Sidney healed?* I asked myself, contemplating the water. My hands reached for my neck and my navel to corroborate, but my lumps remained with me.

"Where have you been?" Peach said, visibly irritated. "We were looking for you."

I turned to Sidney, expecting he would clarify what had happened. Hoping he would clarify *us* to Peach. He *had* to.

But he remained silent and unexpressive, evading my eyes.

"We—" I started, just to fill the silence.

Sidney interrupted me, "Don't."

That was it? That was all he had to say? All his words and necking and promises had transformed into a *Don't* as soon as Peach appeared? So Sidney truly was playing with me, and all he had said was complete *bullshit*. The water may have not cured my cancer, but it cleaned up my mind enough that I could understand the type of man he was.

The type all women know *too* well.

I pranced out of the water. "We were just enjoying the wading pool," I said sarcastically.

"Let me dry you." Frank extended his ragged cape and caught me as if I were a bird with a broken wing. He wrapped me with comforting arms, warming my hypothermic heart.

"Come on," I said to him, and we sat on a fir trunk away from everybody. I needed to be away from *him*.

Lt. Lovelock and Bill helped Lind and Duncan dismount Empress and shambled them into the water. They swilled their wounds, drank until choking, and replenished their canteens with glee, disregarding Sidney, who plunged into the shallow end and moments later emerged in an impeccable outfit. Bold and dashing.

"So, the miraculous water not only heals wounds but also weaves brand new clothes?" I said, furious.

"What?" Frank asked, bewildered.

"You were right, Frank."

"About what?"

"About my feelings." I sighed.

"I suppose you should be glad about loving someone." He exaggerated his grin.

"I-I don't know what I feel. Maybe you can explain it to me."

"I might be dull, but I know that love can't be explained."

Asking Frank felt like shaking a Magic 8-Ball—you never knew what you would get, but oddly, his words were always charged with truth.

"A lady told me once there were not enough words in the dictionary to explain *Love*. And that's why poets were invented."

I chuckled. "She must have despised the poets."

"To the contrary." Frank stood and started declaiming, acting Shakespearean, "You might know the inception of love, but never its conclusion, because love is wider than the universe but mysterious enough to fit in a heartbeat. Drums, drums are what encourage us into an odyssey of passion, forgetting that it is not of a person but from the hope of getting that person why we fall in love." He concluded his performance with a curtsy.

I clapped. "Wow!"

"She often recited poetry to me," Frank said, his voice charged with nostalgia.

"You loved her?"

His eyes shifted with raised brows, searching for an answer in his head. "*Amare Mora*," he finally said.

"What?"

"It's Latin—belated love," Frank explained. "Sometimes…" He paused hesitantly and started again. "…sometimes the ones in love are the last to find out."

My eyes searched for Sidney, who was explaining himself to Peach. Maybe I was a victim of that—*Amare Mora*—not knowing that you are terribly in love until the day you realize the love has metastasized and the only way to get rid of it is to rip every single cell out of your body.

"Love, the only disease besides cancer that the wonderful waters can't cure." I sighed. "And I have both! I should buy a lottery ticket. My luck is bound to turn around."

"Love surrounds everybody, Maia, especially those who are different." Frank rested his arm around me, and I recognized the loneliness in his eyes. I imagined the bullies making fun of him, abusing him.

"You are no different, Frank." I stroked his hand.

"Yes, I am. I'm not smart. But there is nothing wrong with it."

And there it was. A simple phrase that could change the world.

"Frank, you are far more brilliant than most people that I know."

"Do you think so?"

"Yes, I do. It requires tons of intelligence to realize what you just did. Some of us still don't understand it. It requires courage to recognize it. And you are brave. You saved me."

"I was just fulfilling my mission. To protect you," he repeated.

"Who gave you that mission?"

"Sidney."

That simple word rushed my heartbeat up to sixty miles per hour in less than a second. My eyes unwittingly flicked to him. He was still talking with Peach, away from the group, too far to read their lips.

"When?" I squeezed Frank's arms. "What did he say to you?"

"Before departing, he said to me, 'Frank, you have to protect her from him.'"

"From whom?"

"I don't know his name—if he has one," Frank said, scratching his head. "But they call him the *Ravisseur*."

"*Ravisseur?*"

"It's French, it means kidnapper."

"Is someone trying to kidnap me?" I asked, startled. The closest thing to a kidnapper in my life was Sidney. "But why?"

"I don't know," Frank said, lowering his eyes with an air of disappointment. "Somehow, some people just want to watch others suffer, I think."

A strident laugh drew our attention to the pond, where Duncan could not believe that the cuts on his face had vanished, and Lind's wounds had healed as well, just as Alek said they would.

The soldiers celebrated the event, hugging and singing a military cadence.

"That's the reason why America never beat the Nazis on its own," Alek said, ruining the party. "All you do is brag and complain all the time."

"How dare you! My father fought Bolshevik revolutionaries on Archangel after the armistice of the Great War," Lt. Lovelock confronted Alek. "Russians are just a bunch of drunk wildlings, freebooters of Stalin."

Frank and I hurried over.

"Calm down," I yelled, extending my arms to create distance between them.

"And you, Lovelock, have the guts to say that to me with alcohol stench on your breath?" Alek shouted, being held back by Frank—a fact that I could not corroborate, due to the loss of my smell.

"Please stop!"

"You are rapists! Cowards!" Lt. Lovelock ranted, restrained by his subordinates.

"Enough. Enough!" I shouted. "Jesus, there are things out there trying to kill us, and you behave like this? Do you think that I travel with you because of your lovely company?" I looked into the eyes of everybody, including Sidney and Peach, who had joined the circle. "I just want to finish this stupid pilgrimage, and it ends at the other side of the valley." I pointed at the sky between the mountains. "And the only way of surviving is keeping together. So, either you behave decently, or… or—"

"Or what?" Alek squinted his eye.

"Or—or I will kick your ass!" I exploded, and everybody gazed at me in silence. "That's better. Now you two, shake hands." The brawlers stared at each other for a moment and burst out laughing.

"What? Are we in kindergarten?" Lt. Lovelock asked, and his laughter infected everybody.

"Great," I said sarcastically and paced down the trail parallel to the river, determined to accomplish the journey on my own.

"Maia, wait!" Frank rushed after me.

They called after me, but I ignored them, isolating myself in my imagination, where I could slap everyone to erase their chuckles. *Idiots.*

⚜

A thousand steps later, my thoughts eased. I glanced back and saw a long row behind me: Frank traipsed, penitent, glued to me like my shadow. Later came Alek, inattentively riding Empress, closely followed by the militia, still singing and in high spirits. Sidney and Peach, side by side, straggled at the end.

Empress trotted to my side.

"Get up," Alek said, extending his hand. "I'll take you." I locked my sight ahead on the road. "Stop pretending. Both you and I know that it's not me you're mad at," Alek said pompously. "Ok, as you wish, madam." He tipped his hat and hauled the bridle, making Empress canter until both disappeared on the switchback footpath.

"Stupid Eye of Truth," I grumbled.

The tangerine sun was sinking, turning red like my swollen feet. Exhaustion mocked my rejection of Alek's offer. But I didn't trust him. Alek's motivations for lingering disturbed me. *What did he want?* He could have shot Sidney back in the forest, when he was wounded.

I halted and inspected the trees surrounding us, thinking Alek could be hidden on higher ground, like a kid watching ants through a magnifying glass. The trail disappeared bit by bit, devoured by the imminent darkness. The songs of the militia had extinguished a while ago, along with their enthusiasm. We were just a line of undead trudging into uncharted territory.

A shrill cawing drew my attention to the sky, where a swarm of crows flew above us. They glided to perch atop a brick chimney jutting above the tiled roof of a dilapidated country house. The rocky creek streamed by the side of the house, spinning a big paddle wheel at the side of a cowshed, where Empress was resting, unsaddled. We steered around the three-story property, looking into windows covered by a film of dust.

The timber planks of the portico creaked with the rocking chair, where Alek sat wrapped in a blanket, with his hat over his lap and his Dragunov leaning against the chair's arm.

"It took you centuries," he said.

"Real men march," Lt. Lovelock answered his taunt.

"Men became men because they learned to subdue beasts, otherwise they would still be beasts themselves," Alek replied.

"Men were never beasts," Bill interjected.

"Until they chose to convert themselves into monsters," Sidney pointed out, and Alek glared at him.

"You found quite a house," Frank said, oblivious.

"*Dacha*," Alek said, opening his arms. "What better place to rest than a summer country house? Unless you want to vote for not staying here, of course. Maybe you are fond of sleeping on the dirt."

"It's empty?" Lovelock asked.

"Appears to be abandoned," Alek confirmed.

Everybody scrambled inside. Nobody wanted to sleep in the wilderness after our previous nightmarish evening and the long hike, not even me, but I hesitated to enter. An abandoned house hidden in the woods seemed like an odd coincidence. But it also felt somehow familiar, tempting.

"Go on, girl," Alek said to me. "Make yourself comfortable."

Arguing would only worsen the situation, so I decided to venture inside.

The double-hung windows were covered with empty cobwebs that allowed the last rays of sunlight in but blurred the outside view. The walls were covered on the lower half with wood paneling, and straw-yellow wallpaper ran up the top half to the coffered ceiling. The predominant decoration comprised crucifixes and small holy relief sculptures. The furniture—primarily of leather and cedar—was old as my grandmother, but even buried in dust, it was not worn. It was as if the house had been decorated right before being abandoned. Even the logs in the chimney were unburned, and there was no trace of ashes.

I blew the dust off an old typewriter in front of a leather arm-chair in the living room. It was labeled *Simplex* and was loaded with red ribbon used to type a line of numbers repeatedly across the entire sheet, "*13, 27, 44, 49, 66, 68, 88,*" like someone was trying to memorize a safe combination.

I climbed the staircase, holding the wooden rails while contemplating the gaudy chandelier nested with deserted cobwebs hanging at the top, as if even the spiders had jumped ship.

The first door in the hallway was a large bathroom lined with black-and-white marble tiles and with doors connecting it to two bedrooms. A shattered vanity wall mirror stood out. The shards were piled in the double sink, and a trace of stains—that looked like dried blood—zigzagged to the rusty handle at the top of a white bathtub.

At the end of the corridor, the master bedroom door was ajar. The creaking door revealed my reflection in an ornamented oval mirror hanging above a dressing table that sparked a bizarre sense of familiarity through my spine. It was not déjà vu but a sense of ownership, like arriving home, though I recognized nothing. I ran my fingers over the wool quilt on the bed, trying to stimulate my memory, but no memories were triggered. On the nightstand, a pocket Bible was lying at the feet of a standing crucifix.

A mahogany wardrobe called my attention. I swung the double doors open, revealing it was packed. My curiosity made me shuffle through the clothes, and I froze.

The clothes stored there were mine: my dresses, my jeans, my blouses, everything. I pulled the drawers and found my panties and socks folded in the same way I arrange them. I flinched, trying to digest how my things had appeared here. An urge to run possessed me, when I heard a commotion on the lower floor.

"Maia, Maia!" Frank shouted, and I hurried down. "Maia, we have to leave this place," he said with agitation when I met him at the stairs.

"Why? What's going on?"

"I-I-It's his house," he stammered, overtaken by fear.

"Whose?"

"*Ravisseur!*"

Everybody was gathered in the dining room with perplexed looks. I pushed Frank aside. The dining room walls were tiled with hundreds of photographs of me, from my early childhood to my older days, which I didn't recognize. The photos were all taken without my knowledge or consent. In secret. From a distance. As if the paparazzi had followed me to record my entire life.

I stared at Sidney, who stepped aside, allowing me to see an oil painting at the center. It was my mother lulling me as a baby, with her long, golden hair falling by her side and her eyes fixed on me. My baby hand was grasping the finger of my father, Dario, who was sitting beside my mother, admiring me with such devotion that it seemed unnatural. Surreal.

"It's him! Ravisseur!" said Frank, pointing at Dario.

It was impossible. "No, he is not." It didn't matter how much I despised him, I could not blame him for crimes he didn't commit. "I know him."

"Then who is he?" Lt. Lovelock asked, but I remained silent. "Who is he?" He pulled my arm to make me face him.

"That's Dario. My f-father."

"Why are all these pictures here?" Lt. Lovelock asked.

"I don't know. I have never seen any of these before. That painting is just—impossible."

"Impossible? What are you hiding from us, girl?"

"I'm not hiding anything. My mother died delivering me, and Dario had left us even before that." I observed the painting, yearning for the life that I could have had. How different my life could have been if I'd had a family. "If he had kidnapped me, at least I could have gotten to know him," I said sardonically.

"But—"

"Leave the girl alone," Alek interjected from the doorjamb. "She doesn't want to talk about it."

"But this house—"

"We are not leaving this house. Not at nighttime," Alek interrupted Lt. Lovelock again as he approached him. "Or is it that you are afraid of a photo album?" he said mockingly.

"Nonsense." Lt. Lovelock spat tobacco out of his Habano.

"Then we stay," Alek declared, and everyone looked at me, waiting for my decision.

Maybe it was the idealized homesickness from the thought that this could have been my family's home that made me forget the danger of staying. I was fearful but curious to discover clues that could reveal more about my mother and her troubled relationship with Dario, since my grandmother had been very closed-mouthed about the subject.

I nodded.

CHAPTER 12

EVERYBODY SETTLED INTO THEIR OWN BEDROOM in the spacious house. Tempers relaxed. The idea of billeting in a comfortable house was pleasing to the soldiers, even in a situation like this, I guessed.

Bill cooked the rations in the kitchen, and all praised him for what they called their "best meal in months." Even Lt. Lovelock joked about promoting Bill to official chef of the division and toasted with a jaundiced wine Bill had found in the cupboard.

"It's tasty," I feigned when Bill asked my opinion, but for me the food tasted almost like nothing. I took the salt and shook it over my stew until Peach, who was sitting across from me, halted my hand.

"Too much salt," she said, and the idea that my taste was the second sense I was losing struck me like lightning. I gave up the hunt for flavor and surrendered to the idea. *It was gross anyway*, I told myself, eating a few more spoonfuls of stew. But the sound of them munching, their lousy jokes, and the fact of being surrounded by walls garnished with my pictures soon made the dinner intolerable. "Excuse me." I stood up and went to the portico. I held the banister and devoured a mouthful of fresh air that soothed my claustrophobic thoughts.

"You lost your appetite?" Alek said, rocking in his chair, still wrapped in his blanket like an old man, with his eyes lost on the dim fields. "I hate their gabble too. I prefer the chirping crickets."

"Yes," though I couldn't hear any crickets. Even the crows on the roof were quiet. Everything was awfully quiet.

"You are like me."

"Pardon me?"

"Yes, you and I don't ignore the fact that we are dead. We are not troglodytes desperately trying to satiate our emptiness."

I felt glad someone else was aware of our condition, but I couldn't help but feel offended by his comment. "You ate like a troglodyte last night."

"I did it consciously, knowing that trying to relive my experiences when I was alive, it's just a placebo for this incurable disease we call death. But them…" Alek pointed backward with his thumb and chuckled. "They still pray at night to return home."

"There is nothing wrong with praying."

"Every seven eclipses, I witness men and women walking into their graves with a flash of consciousness in their eyes, some rejecting their demise, others crying a river the night long and rising with the sun to continue their journey in searching for purpose, just to end up back in tears at the cemetery. No, girl, praying has never solved a damn thing."

"If everybody is so displeasing to you, why don't you leave?" I said, upset. "If you feel so clever, why don't you finish the pilgrimage and free yourself from this 'disease,' as you call it?"

"Told you."

"Vandella?" I said, and he averted his eyes. "Why do you care so much about him?"

Alek continued admiring the insoluble darkness that fought the pale light of the oil lamp hanging from the ceiling.

"I had a farm just like this, away from people, far from their egoism and ambition. My sole concerns were to harvest my fields, pasture my goats, and milk my cows to provide for my wife and children. I sat on my porch every afternoon, just like this, until twilight, watching our two boys playing." His eyes moved like he was seeing them.

Alek remained silent for a few seconds.

"Then my firstborn was taken from me." He paused and took a deep breath. It was the first time I saw him losing his even-tempered attitude. "I did everything to save him. But my efforts were in vain. I arrived to witness his execution. My son glanced at me a last time, just like he did after making mischief when he was a youngster." Alek chuckled. "What a naughty boy, what a naughty boy." He shook his head. "And then his eyelids shut forever." Alek's eyes dampened.

I walked to him, jaw stiffened, and held his bony hand.

"I'm very sorry for your loss. But—I should ask, what does that have to do with *Vandella?*" I refused to acknowledge that Sidney could perpetrate such a monstrosity.

"It was a shadow darker than the night, hugging my son from behind. I can never forget those mesmerizing eyes that lit up before robbing his soul," Alek said, with his hands clenching the chair's arms. "He was just a boy—my boy."

"Why didn't you shoot?"

"I did." He chuckled. "And I missed." He tried to shield his face with his quivering hand but slammed it on the chair's arm with determination. "But I promised myself to never miss again, regardless of the price." He clattered the chain attached to the fetter around his wrist. "And I've happily paid it."

"Is it worth it?"

"No regrets." He squinted. "No regrets."

I tilted my head up to the starless sky, hoping to hear a cricket bold enough to chirp, but there were none.

"You and I aren't the same." I paused. "But sometimes I wish I could stop feeling regret."

Alek stared at me in silence.

I walked sure-footed inside the house and overheard the loud chatter in the dining room, so I shot straight toward the stairs.

"I missed you at the table," I heard Sidney say when I passed the dark living room. He was buried in the armchair in front of the typewriter.

I leaned against the doorframe. "Alek was telling me a story."

"Fables." Sidney stood and walked to me. "No one cares."

"You should. It was about *Vandella.*"

"All I care about is you, Maia, don't you understand?" He ran his hand through my hair. "You are my sustenance." His lips darted for mine, but I veered my head away.

"You should go back to Peach." I gently pushed him away.

"Are you jealous?"

"Oh, did you notice?"

I stared at him, saying in my thoughts the feelings my lips didn't dare pronounce, hoping he could say the words my heart clamored for desperately. But he gazed at me in an endless silence, imprisoning me in his cage of dread and fascination with those unforgettable eyes.

"I can't," Sidney whispered.

I fled to my room, mad at him for teasing me like a hunter of prey locked in a zoo's cage. But I was angrier at myself, for once more not being able to say everything I felt.

That night, not everything turned out to be a misfortune. Even considering the condition of the house, Bill drew a hot bath for me that after two days on the road was more than revitalizing, and getting rid of that bloodstained dress was a total relief. It helped me to unravel the cobwebs of my mind.

In the end, the unsettling fact of having an exact copy of my wardrobe became a blessing. Fitting into clean underwear and the cozy pajamas my granny gave me last Christmas was heartwarming. Close to faint from tiredness, I checked that the bedsheets below the quilt were clean, and I prepared to go to sleep, brushing my hair at the dressing table.

"Maia, Maia." I heard a vague whispery voice outside my room.

Hesitant, I removed the lock and opened the creaking door to find the corridor empty. I closed the door and was about to sit at the dressing table when I heard it again. It was a female voice, which meant it had to be Peach. I stepped into the corridor, hoping she would show herself, but there was no one in sight. Frustrated, I decided to leave the door open and went back to brush my hair, observing the reflection of the dim corridor in the mirror, waiting for Peach to appear.

The bathroom door swung open, lighting up the corridor. I turned around, waiting for her, but she didn't come out.

"Maia," the voice called again.

Vexed, I glanced toward the mirror, not paying attention to her childish game, when I saw a figure emerging from the bathroom. I swiveled on the stool, but again the corridor was deserted. *I'm so tired that I must be imagining things*, I told myself, but as I brushed my hair, a feminine figure framed in the mirror walked toward me.

As the image came into focus, I recognized the woman.

It was not Peach.

It was my mother.

CHAPTER 13

THE REFLECTION OF MY MOTHER stood at the door with the passionate smile that I had memorized from her photographs, her long golden hair curling at the tips, which fell over her white nightgown.

"Maia."

"Mom?" I said with a constricted heart, overflowing with excitement. I was finally going to meet her.

I revolved on my stool to meet her, but the doorway was empty.

"Maia." I heard her whispering over my left shoulder again and found her vivid image in the mirror. "I'm here, my darling," she said, closing the door. My mouth gaped, witnessing in awe how it swung shut on its own.

"Shhhhhh, it's ok, my dear, don't be afraid."

It didn't matter where I turned; her voice sounded like it originated from the farthest corner of the room, and I always heard it over my left shoulder, as though she was glued to my back.

"Mommy is here now. Mommy is here." I felt her comforting hands on my shoulders and saw my pajamas sagging with the invisible pressure of her fingers. I saw her reflection snatch the brush from my hand and continue brushing my hair. She hummed a lullaby, while I watched the brush floating in the air, still battling to understand what was going on.

"Since the doctor told me you were going to be a girl, I imagined myself brushing your hair, undoing the knots while you recounted your day: your jubilance, your problems, heartbreaks and loves." My mother paused, biting her lower lip, and stared at me with a bittersweet grin. "Now, seeing you a young woman, I realize how much I missed."

"Why?" My red-rimmed eyes started to release tears. "Why did you have to go?"

Her fingers wiped my tears with a gentle touch.

"I don't know," she said serenely. "But you made it so far, my dear. I'm proud of you. We are together now. And we always will be."

I longed to hug her above anything else in this world, but the space behind me was empty. "It hurts. It always has."

"I feel your pain, my dear. Not having you by my side has been torturous."

"But where are you, Mom? Why can I only see you in the mirror? I'm tired of caressing you through a glass, of having you living inside picture frames."

"I'm trapped," she said, and with her fingertip she touched the mirror, creating waves on it as if it were liquid. "I'm held captive in a prison made of mirrors, living disembodied as a reflection."

"How—?"

"By the work of a spell."

"Why? What happened?"

"It was the price I had to pay."

"You had to pay a price? Why?"

"I loved too much." Her lips tried to curve into a smile but failed. "You are too young, my dear, naive and reliant. You have much to learn about deception. That is the reason why I'm here…" She bowed, placing her face beside mine. "…to open your eyes."

"Open my eyes to what?"

"The truth."

My mother's reflection walked away, and the doors of the wardrobe sprang open, exposing a passageway that ran into the thick walls. The candelabrum resting on the dressing table floated across the room, carried by her invisible hand, until she handed it to me.

"Go, my dear." I saw my mother's dim reflection on the candelabrum's plate. "Go and uncover the truth."

I ventured inside the tight passageway without hesitation, not scared of the darkness or the cobwebs. I arrived at a window that looked into Bill's room. It was like looking into the house from outside. But somehow, I was not outside; I was *in* the window. I had become a part of the reflection, just like my mother.

I wondered if anyone could see me, but fortunately Bill was kneeling with his elbows resting on the bed and fingers intertwined, praying with eyes shut.

"Lord, I'm not worthy of your mercy, 'cause I have sinned," Bill whispered. "But you are righteous. So, I beg you… keep her safe. Take care of her for me until I'm able to see her again… and I can tell her everything I was too coward to say," he said. He was probably referring to the girlfriend that was waiting for him to return from the war.

Bill finished his prayer and took a deteriorated teddy bear patched with red thread and held it against his chest for going to sleep with the candles alight.

I looked at Bill until he fell asleep, feeling sad about him, but mad about *them*. He was a kid forced to fight the nightmarish war of men—egoist, brutal, and fiendish men.

The sound of shackles and chains rattling echoed against the walls in the quiet night. The clanging of the chains stopped at Bill's room, and the door opened gently, as if carried by the wind. I hid aside, with my back against the wall, and peeked.

The shadows inhabiting the corridor watched Bill sleep.

Then a figure loomed from the murkiness.

It was Alek.

I was about to yell to wake Bill up when I felt a hand restraining my scream.

"Shhhhhhhhh," hushed my mother. "Don't. You can't let him hear you."

Alek stood beside the bed. His gloomy eyes observed the boy, unmoved by the teddy bear. He reached for Bill's belongings, extracted the radio, and removed the lid. He then drew a small radio from his belt and adjusted the knobs of both instruments. Once he finished, he carefully put everything back as it was and walked out with the secrecy of an assassin.

I followed the passageway to the window showing the next room—it was Lovelock's. He was sitting in a chair. His trembling hand held a bottle of whisky, with his sight lost in the quivering flame of the candle.

"Harvey… my son. I hope you are now a brilliant scientist," Lt. Lovelock said in a toast. It was just like Alek foretold back in the forest, when he'd proved to me the powers of the Eye of Truth.

In the adjacent room, Alek was sitting on the bed with his back to the window. He placed the radio on the nightstand and unfastened his belt, which was empty of bullets. He unsheathed his revolver, emptied the chamber on the couch, and searched his pockets for more, picking up the empty shells. He placed the belt inside his mouth and bit down on it. He then opened his leather raincoat and from his boot withdrew a shining knife with a serrated edge. He turned it to his chest and thrust it into himself, then started sawing, back and forth, with the chilling sound of the metal hitting the bone. He tossed his head back violently, with muffled groans and an expression of unbearable suffering. After finishing the nauseating task, he spat out the belt and gasped. I noticed the marks embossed on the leather of his belt were not made by the awl of a tanner, but the cumulative work of his teeth.

Awed, I watched how Alek cupped the bloody pieces of flesh in his hands and started fitting them inside the empty shells' casings.

The magic silver dots that traveled in whimsical patterns to kill their targets were Alek's own flesh and blood. Alek consumed himself with each bullet shot in his vindictive and self-destructive crusade.

Alek was a desperate monster, and we were all locked up in this haunted house with him.

I overheard a discussion unfolding in the next room, so I snooped. Inside were Peach and Sidney, facing each other at the center of the room.

"I'm tired of pretending. I can't continue with this farce anymore," Peach complained.

"You have to."

"I know, I know." She rubbed her face. "But you know how hard it is to look at Maia, and…" She buried her face in Sidney's chest.

He caressed her hair affectionately. "You knew this would happen, but you still accepted."

"Yes, yes, but for how long?" She tilted her head up, searching for his eyes.

"Until we recover the medallion. Then it will be all yours."

"But what if she refuses at the end? And tries to stop us?" Peach asked, but Sidney remained speechless. "You promised me." She shook him.

"She suspects nothing, and I will make sure it stays that way." Sidney hugged her. "I'll fulfill my promise."

My hands covered my mouth, and I cowered below the window, feeling his words thrusting into my heart like Alek's knife.

All this had been a game.

I had been deceived.

Betrayed.

Again.

Sidney was using me. Both were using me.

It's not fair. Why? Why?

I bit my finger to restrain my crying. My disappointment. My rage.

I could not bear it any longer. I crawled out of the passageway, glancing into Alek's window on the way. He was honing his knife—dutifully.

Then I understood why he was that way. He had been wounded to the point that mutilating himself was not painful anymore. Sorrow had converted to determination. Satisfaction had displaced the suffering and numbness. My fear of him faded into compassion, maybe sympathy.

I crept out of the wardrobe and broke into uncontrollable tears.

"My poor, poor child." I heard the voice of my mother and felt her shallow embrace. "Now you know the truth. His honeyed words are just a trick to delude you. Now you see that all this is just a scheme perpetrated by Vandella to exchange your life for the frizzle-haired girl. A plan to give back life to his beloved one using a sacrificial lamb."

It didn't matter how much I wanted to deny it. I had perceived the signs and ignored them all. I was a fool. I was furious with myself for believing in him—once again.

"But I-I have to save Gran," I said, wiping my tears.

"Yes, you have to save us both." Her invisible hand caressed my cheek. "Only you can."

"How can I save you?"

"I live trapped in this ethereal prison because of him, because of Vandella."

"What do I have to do to set you free?"

"First, we need to break the spell he cast on you."

Sidney had cast a spell on me? I thought about how strong my love for him had felt, how intense. Was that the spell? "How?"

"First, you have to take two of your hairs and tie them around his wrists," my mother said, handing me the brush. "You have to count to three and then whisper, *Oge ido, Sov Ido* as you do it."

"*Oge ido, Sov Ido?*" I repeated, trying to digest my mission. Was this angelic language? I wondered.

"You must act now, while he is asleep. I'll go and make sure he doesn't wake up. I'll open his room, letting you know when you can come in and perform your task," she said. Her reassuring presence abandoned me.

The door of my room opened as she made her way into the corridor. I stood at the doorway with my loose hairs in hand, looking back into the mirror at the reflection of my mother advancing to Sidney's room, not walking nor flying, but something in between, like gracefully ice-skating on the air. When she arrived at his door, she trespassed like a ghost. After a minute, Sidney's room's door opened. But my mother didn't come out.

I skulked through the corridor and entered the room on my tiptoes. Peach was snoring on the bed, facing the wall. Sidney slumbered on a chair, immobile, with his head hanging from his shoulders, eyes hidden. Luckily for me, his hands hung over the armrests. There were no mirrors in the room and no sign of my mother in the window's reflection. I couldn't feel her presence either.

I extended the first hair and rolled it around Sidney's wrist. "One, two, three," I whispered and tied a knot. "*Oge ido, Sov Ido.*"

The desire to hold his hand possessed me, and I could not resist, but a sound behind me scared me and I jerked back. It was Peach, flipping on the bed. I held my breath for a couple of seconds, fearing Sidney might wake up, but he remained unconscious.

I observed them, plagued with guilt, still refusing to believe what I had heard. Peach slept placidly, like a little girl, harmless, even tender. Sidney looked like a diligent father, protective and dutiful. But I would not allow my eyes to fool me again. I could not let them prevent me from fulfilling my mission. I had to save my mother and my granny, so I hurried and tied the second hair.

"One, two, three," I counted and finished the enchantment. "*Oge ido, Sov Ido.*"

I fled the room without looking back. The reflection of my

mother was expecting me in my room, seated at the dressing table.

"It's done," I said, closing the door. "Now what?"

"Maia, my dear," she said with a comforting smile. "Now there is one more thing for you to do. Tomorrow you will continue your journey with them."

"No. I don't want to see them."

"Vandella feeds from you, my dear, from your words, your thoughts about him. He is drawing your energy, your soul."

Sidney's words were vivid on my mind: *"You are my sustenance."*

"To break the bondage between you and Vandella, first we need to debilitate him so the enchantment can work. Tomorrow, all you must do is remain silent. He will speak to you, but you shall not reply. Then he will question you, but you shall not answer. After the third unanswered question, the spell will dissolve."

"Then you will be free?" I asked.

"Then we will be together for eternity." My mother stood and walked me to my bed. "Now, you have to rest. Tomorrow will be a long day." I lay on my bed, and she tucked me in and sat on the edge of the bed.

"Would you stay with me?" I said to the hollow air where she was supposed to be.

I felt her hand caressing my forehead and descending to my cheek.

"*Forever*," she said, and comforted me by crooning a lullaby.

My eyelids turned heavy and plummeted.

My dream was flooded with forgotten memories, going back into my past until I found myself inside my mother's womb, suspended in space and time, wrapped by the warmth of her love as I was lulled by her singing from the outside. I was tranquilized by the sound of her heart pumping, giving life to mine. The heavy burden on my shoulders disappeared, and for the first time in a long time, I felt secure and at peace.

CHAPTER 14

I HEARD THREE KNOCKS ON THE DOOR.

"Maia, are you ok? It's getting late."

"Yes, yes!" I waved my hand, trying to slam the snooze button on my alarm like I did at home, but instead I hit the crucifix on the nightstand, knocking it to the floor.

"Maia, is everything ok? Please open up!"

I went to the door, still feeling disoriented. It was Bill.

"Are you okay?" he asked, concerned.

I nodded.

"You better come down. We are having breakfast before leaving."

"I'm not hungry, but I'll be down in a minute."

"Okay."

I closed the door and leaned against it, staring at my reflection in the mirror and remembering the night's events, still uncertain whether it had been a dream. I walked around the mirror, examining all the corners of the room in search of my mother. But I was alone. I rushed to the wardrobe and swung the doors open. I rummaged through the clothes, looking for the passageway behind, but my hands smashed against the timber plank at the back. The wardrobe weighed too much for me to move.

"Maia!" Bill shouted from the stairs.

"I'm coming!"

I gave up the idea of finding the passage and chose an outfit: jeans, knee-high leather boots, a long-sleeved shirt, and cozy jacket felt like the best option for hiking through this terrain.

When I came down, everybody was packing in a rush. Sidney was sitting in the armchair in the living room, oblivious, looking at the typewriter as if it were a TV set. I tried to see if the hairs were still tied around his wrists, but it was impossible from this distance, and I was not getting near him.

Before leaving, I went to the dining room and admired my collection of photos hanging on the walls. One called my attention above all. The picture had captured the exact moment Sidney recounted back in the woods. My gran was pacing after me with the merry-go-round in the background, and I—four years old, wearing a denim overall dress—was safe in the arms of a stranger. The frame of the picture had cropped his head above his nose. *How convenient*, I said to myself, remembering the frustration I'd felt during my golden velvet dream. But this time, the photo exhibited enough to recognize the man's smile. It was Sidney, without a doubt.

I picked up the photo and dropped it on the floor. The glass shattered, and I removed the photo in an attempt to reveal the stranger's identity hidden beneath the frame, but there was no more. I folded it and put it inside my bra. I contemplated the portrait of my family for the last time.

On the porch, Lovelock's company was ready to march, waiting for Bill to collect the food. I walked out and gave a last look to the idyllic house that I could have inhabited in a different time, a different reality, one in which I had a family.

I noticed that the roof was clear. Not a single crow was perched atop it.

Empress cantered gallantly, ridden by Alek. She stopped in front of me. Alek bowed, offering his hand to take me. His open raincoat made his bullet-studded belt visible. The image of the bullets reignited the hideous memories of the night before. But even considering the terror that Alek provoked, like Mrs. Bahiti had predicted, I had to choose between two evils. Alek seemed like a less painful option than Sidney.

I took his hand with no second thoughts.

Alek pulled me up to Empress with ease, and I sat ahead of

him. He hauled the bridle and tapped the horse with his heels, making her rear and neigh before shooting off at a speed I had believed impossible to reach by a living creature.

Behind us, everybody yelled, concerned about me but unable to do a thing. Their guns were hanging from their shoulders, and by the time they were readied to shoot, we were out of their range. I was riding with the sole person of the group who could have hit a moving target in such conditions.

"What are you doing? Where are you taking me?" I cried. I felt powerless. "Stop the horse, now!"

But Alek kept hauling the bridle, and Empress sped up.

"I told you to stop!! We are leaving them behind." I struggled, trying to jump off the moving horse.

"Be quiet, girl," he said. "I'm not the kidnapper. There is just one way out of this place, through the valley, and we are all heading that way. I'm just speeding things up."

"Why?"

But arguing was not an option at this point. "You ought to be grateful. I'm saving you from the painful blisters of your feet."

I sighed, trying to relax. After all, Alek was helping me keep away from Sidney.

Empress left the woods behind in minutes—a journey that would take at least an hour for the group—and made it into a rocky landscape with sporadic patches of grass scorched by the burning sun. After her frenzy, the horse slowed down. *A terrible place to get lazy*, I thought as the unbearable sunbeams forced me to put my jacket over my head.

"Drink," Alek said, handing me his canteen.

"I hope it's not liquor."

His forehead puckered. "We left the drunkard fifty miles behind."

I sipped, and when I tilted my head up, I noticed the moon crossing the sky, aiming for the sun.

"Thank you." I gave him back the water. "I was parched."

"I always wanted to live in a place like this."

"Why? I mean, are not you Russian? Isn't it cold there?"

"Precisely," Alek explained. "When I was a child growing up near the arctic, the arid landscapes seemed so alien to me, but also intriguing and fascinating. I fell in love with the Wild West the first time I saw *The Magnificent Seven*. After I had finished it, I promised myself I would watch all Wild West films I could, something particularly challenging, considering only a few arrived legally to the Soviet Union during the Cold War. *The Good, the Bad and the Ugly* was my favorite. I grew up dreaming to become an outlaw. I was able to get my first smuggled Colt when I joined the *Spetsnaz* Commandoes." Alek unsheathed his revolver and twirled it around his trigger finger with a skill rarely seen even in movies. "My comrades nicknamed me *Sentenza*."

"What?"

"Sentenza, it's the original name of *the Bad* character in the Italian version of the film." I guess that explained Alek's fascination with cowboy gunslinger outfits. "It means Sentence. They used to say once I had aimed at a target, it was a death sentence." Quite appropriate, considering what I had witnessed.

"I never really got the big deal about the Wild West. I mean, no disrespect. But there was nothing besides stinky horses and hot sun," I said, experiencing desert heat firsthand.

"Honor," Alek replied as quick as if the word were hanging at the tip of his tongue.

"But you said it yourself, the Wild West was full of outlaws."

"Not all laws are honorable."

Empress cantered for hours, and it was almost midday when we arrived at the entrance of the valley where the mountains converged. I could tell the eclipse was approaching.

"The Valley of the *Grigori*," Alek said.

"What?"

"The Watchers." He pointed at the mountains.

It was a rocky gorge, where huge human figures with sharpened features were carved into the stone. They ran along both sides of the canyon, facing each other. Each giant, the size of the Statue of Liberty, was holding something in its hands: a sword and shield, a depiction of the sun, another of the moon, a pen and parchment, a block engraved with unrecognizable script, a pentagram, and so on.

"It has been said that long ago, before the dawn of civilization, the Watchers descended from the heavens," Alek explained. "They shared their secrets with the primitive humans. They taught our forefathers the arts of war, astrology, the art of writing, the knowledge of the earth and clouds, and even the secrets of magic. They devoted themselves to mankind so much that soon they fell in love with women and conceived offspring of beings that enraged God, who sent his angels to punish the Fallen. They were condemned to eternal imprisonment in the rock until the heart of the last of the cursed descendants had ceased to beat. Now they watch over mankind day and night, waiting for the moment they can be freed to return to the heavens."

I glanced up to the giant statues, which indeed appeared to stare at us as we made our way through the canyon. "Can they really see us?"

"People refer to them as *those who are awake*. The twenty leaders of the two hundred fallen."

The statues had plaques at their feet with markings I didn't recognize, but the number of markings increased with each statue, which made me guess that maybe they were numbers in the angelic language Sidney had spoken about.

"Some are missing," I noticed. "Where are those? They escaped imprisonment?" I pointed out the scattered rocky debris of what once was the sculpture.

"Legends say that some escaped, and others were needed by God, so He freed them from their stone entrapment but assigned them to tasks equally mundane as penance."

"Are they alive? I mean, for real?" I asked, unable to believe the inert rocks could harbor life.

"Wait and see."

Alek's eyes were drawn to the sky, where the moon started eclipsing the sun. He halted Empress, and we observed how the shadow of the moon advanced through the canyon, and as it passed, the stone statues became translucent, revealing the fluorescent forms of the giants trapped inside. Their hearts pumped red light that irrigated their humongous bodies. The eclipse also revealed baleful pupils that were scrutinizing us.

"Oh my God!" I said, astonished, wanting to hide. "Can they hear us?"

"Indeed."

The eclipse reached totality with a red corona. "Nagelfar!" I cried. "Oh my God, we need to take shelter, the dragon is coming!"

"Don't worry, girl. Nobody dares to cross this valley during the eclipse. Not even dragons."

"Why?"

"They fear the eyes of the Watchers."

"Then what are we doing here? We need to go!"

"We wait."

"For what?"

Alek pointed ahead, where a dark figure walked down the road in our direction. Alek hauled the bridle, and Empress cantered and stopped in front of a tight road that forked where the seventeenth Watcher had once stood.

As the figure came closer, I recognized Sidney.

It was evident that Alek knew Sidney was the sole person from the group capable of reaching us. He had planned this.

The Watchers' eyes aimed at Sidney, and their hearts galloped as he made his way into the canyon.

Sidney stopped thirty yards away from us.

"You are bold, coming here at this time of the day," Alek said indulgently.

"I know the game you are playing," Sidney replied.

"I don't know what you are talking about."

"You certainly do," Sidney said fiercely, staring at Alek with the same enraged look he'd given to my pursuers back on the train.

"My intentions are peaceful," Alek said, unfastening his belt containing his revolver. He presented it and dropped it to the ground under the skeptical look of Sidney. "What?" Alek asked. "My Dragunov?" He unsheathed the rifle from the saddle and released it, but it swung, hanging from the chain attached to his wrist. Sidney frowned. "Not much I can do about it." Alek chuckled.

"I have some ideas." Sidney narrowed his eyes, erasing Alek's grin.

"You better get down, girl," Alek whispered, and I slid off Empress.

I strode five steps ahead and halted.

"Come with me, Maia," Sidney beckoned. "Together we will go to Touriel. Just the two of us. I promise." I remained unresponsive, as my mother had instructed me.

Impatient with my lack of response, Sidney stepped forward, but I stepped backward.

"Maia, what is going on?"

I stayed silent. He closed his eyes and dropped his chin to his chest.

"I know what you saw, what you heard. I know you visited us at the darkest hour of the night."

My whole body stiffened, and my eyes sank, unable to meet

Sidney's gaze.

The eclipse concluded, allowing the midday sun to eradicate the somberness that had settled in the valley, converting the Watchers back to lifeless statues.

"Last night, I experienced something I had never felt before. I was having a dream. Or at least, I think so. It felt the way people describe them." Sidney chuckled. "We were sitting on a swing at a beach of glowing sand so shiny it appeared to be formed by stardust. Before us was the endless sky of the Sea of Serenity, with the immenseness of stars twinkling like fireflies. You rested your head on my chest and transferred a warmth that appeased my restless heart with an absolute certainty that I have found my whole. I kissed you until a million shooting stars fell from the sky. You took my hand, but your hand was cold—colder than mine—and we ran along the beach, tinting the sand with multicolored lights with each footprint. Then you counted to three and released my hand. You were so close, Maia, but your heart felt so distant. Then you turned into sand and vanished before my eyes, leaving an unfillable abyss."

Doubts entangled my thoughts like ivy. But once again, I kept silent, to uphold the promise made to my mother.

"Maia, does love feel like my dream?" Sidney asked like a toddler that has started to uncover the world. "If so, I wish I could be forever asleep."

I wanted to exclaim the feelings that were buried in my chest, but my hand locked my quivering lips.

Sidney spread out his hand. "Maia, I want to ask you: do you want to sail with me for an eternity to the beach made of stars?"

I squeezed my eyes, trying to stop my torrential tears, but it was futile.

Sidney's hands magnetized against each other, and a thick skein of hair grew out of thin air, handcuffing his wrists. A mouth-shaped fissure broke at his feet, and ravenous hands with torn fingernails emerged from the depths, dragging him into the entrails of earth.

Watching him suffer, I was overcome with guilt and quickly repented of what I'd done. "No!" I bawled, terrified, and ran to his aid, kicking the hands and pulling at Sidney. "Alek! Help me, please," I cried, but Alek gazed at us, unmoved.

"Maia, you have to go," Sidney said, buried chest-deep in the ground.

"No, no, no," I said, pulling as hard as I could.

"Maia, you have to run. Go!"

Sidney's hands slipped through mine, and I fell flat on my back.

"Maia, listen to me, please, you have to go."

"I-I-I will not—I can't," I babbled.

"It's okay." Sidney smiled. "I forgive you," he said, and his head was devoured by the hungry rocks.

I dug at the ground like an anxious hound, my tears moisturizing the arid earth. "Yes, yes," I whimpered. "I want to sail with you to the sea of stars." But my words came too late.

"It's pointless; he won't hear you," Alek said, fastening his belt.

"Wha—"

"What have you done?" Alek asked indifferently.

I wanted to cry, sucking in a breath through my clenched teeth.

It was me who did it. It was my revenge for him still loving Peach.

Now do you feel satisfied, Maia? I punished myself relentlessly.

"Now you truly know what—"

"What Hell feels like," I interrupted. "I know."

Alek leaned his rifle over his shoulder, and he left, driving Empress on the way back until disappearing within the mirage of the road below the radiant sun.

Inconsolable amid my desolation, I glanced up and saw the incriminatory looks of the Watchers on me. They made me feel minuscule, insignificant, and wishful of cutting my heart out and feeling nothing ever again.

CHAPTER 15

"HUSH, HUSH, MY BABY," I heard a voice over my left shoulder. "Don't cry, my dear. Mommy is here and always will be."

A slim full-length mirror with gold-plated frame hovered out of the road that forked into the valley where the statue of the seventeenth Watcher had once stood. It floated smoothly a foot above the ground, as if it were mounted on a rail. My mother was wearing a dark gown, tight on top but layered below her hips, like an inverted black rose.

"My poor, poor child," she said, looking at me with compassionate eyes through a veil that hung from her headdress. "Weep no more. Now you are free from his entrapment."

"You never told me he would die."

"My dear." My mother floated away from the looking glass, and I felt her hand caressing my jaw from my chin up to my nape, and she hugged me. Shivering, I watched the action in the reflection. The mirror framed all her movements like the work of a professional cameraman. "He is alive," she whispered.

I stared skeptically at where she was supposed to be.

"Don't you believe me?" she said, reassuring.

"Where is he?"

She passed her hand over the mirror. The reflection rippled and showed a trail on the mountain's ridge, where a crestfallen Sidney was escorted by four men. They wore full-length dark robes, their faces covered by white beaked masks gathered at the necks, with glass eyes, leather hats, and long-cuff gauntlets. I had seen their spooky attire before in books—they were plague doctors. They prodded Sidney with long wooden sticks, hauling him by ropes around his neck, as if he were a bearer of a contagious disease.

Maybe it was an illusion, but the image felt real. So real that it produced in me a mixture of emotions: glee to see Sidney alive, sadness at seeing him bound and secluded, but above all, guilt, knowing I was the one responsible for his current condition. With every second I looked at the scene, my torment grew.

"Where are they taking him?" I cried, and the mirror reverted to my mother.

"Back home, where he belongs."

Where is Sidney's home? I never asked him.

"Rejoice that it was your fortitude that accomplished the deed." I felt her caressing my bloody and dirty fingernails, which surprisingly didn't hurt. "Now you and I shall be together."

"But if I truly broke the enchantment, why are you still inside the mirror?"

"Fear not, my child. Tonight you'll be by my side to witness a new dawn." She extended her hand, smiling. "Together at last, mother and daughter. As always should have been."

Like I always wanted, I thought, and held her hand.

She heaved me to my feet and led me into the forking road, with the looking glass hovering three steps ahead so I could see her reflection by my side.

As we continued down the road, it became surprisingly foggy and marshy, considering we had just stepped out of an arid valley. We were surrounded by lofty elms covered by golden, dog-sized larvae with spiny blue protuberances that slithered up. Huge cocoons that looked like Egyptian sarcophagi hung from the treetops with silk threads, from which—I presumed—emerged the condor-sized moths that flew around us like hungry vultures. My mother was unconcerned with the scenery. She started collecting bunches of red elderberries in a wicker basket that materialized in her hand. The mirror floated from shrub to shrub while she sang in a beautiful voice. The footpath took us to the gate of a long fence formed by intricate thorns and crowned with red flowers.

"Where are we?"

"Home," my mother replied. "Don't you remember?"

"No," I answered, disconcerted.

As we got closer to the gate, the thorns retracted, creating a hole that entwined back after we crossed. Inside, we found ourselves surrounded by robust and perfectly geometric walls of shrubs that formed a magnificent hedge maze.

"Wow," I said, amazed.

We made our way through the maze, but the walls were so identical that it was impossible to determine where we had been, and so tall that I couldn't get any point of reference.

"I think we are lost," I said as we traveled, following a spiral that felt infinite.

"Nobody gets lost. Not even the sheep that abandon the flock. For some, the freedom to commit mistakes is more seductive than the toll of the bell."

The mirror leaned so I could observe a trail of red berries that my mother had left behind.

"Oh, good thinking, the old Hansel and Gretel trick."

"They are not for us, but for our trackers. They are poisonous when not cooked," she explained, while I stared in shock. "We don't want a lost sheep following our steps—*unwise*."

"You mean real sheep?" I said, confused.

"They are men in sheep's clothing. Men are astute, my dear. They want to use you, and like the rattlesnake, they know well when to ring the bell."

My mother waved her hands, and the curved walls straightened before us. The path led to a castle that ran along the horizon, with as many windows as a beehive and its walls tinged vibrant tangerine from the dying sun. "You are nothing but a princess, my dear, and you shall not fall for any man."

I gazed openmouthed at the magnificent fountain surrounded by four bronze seraphim squirting water from their mouths, following intricate patterns that seemed to defy the laws of physics.

The tall double doors of the main entrance swiveled open, and a tiny, plump man scurried out. He was dressed as the Jack of Clubs, with a funny hat and a wig of curly blond hair.

"*Heer* Queenliness." The man did a curtsy to the vacant space where my mother was and then did the same to me. "Princess."

Dumbstruck, I returned his bow.

"Welcome home. We had been expecting you—"

"Why did you take so long?" interrupted a muffled voice.

The man's head rotated like a puppet, and a crying face came out from beneath the wig. "We were so worried for you, and we didn't know what to do."

"Shut up, Brutus." The head rotated again, revealing a third, more belligerent face. "Can't you be quiet for a moment?"

The face switched to the crying one, which now sobbed uncontrollably. "Why can't you understand me—"

"Shut up!" retorted the hostile one, and it used the club in his left hand to hit the crying face until the right hand interposed and the head turned back to the "normal" face.

"Apologies, my lady, please understand," the man said. He seemed terribly ashamed, but I could not hide my laugh, so he showed our way inside the castle in an attempt to hide his embarrassment.

"Who is he?" I asked.

"The butler," answered my mother.

As we promenaded through the endless empty corridors, I had a feeling of déjà vu. I remembered the finery, the granite walls, the seraphim on the columns and the paintings of lush people. *This was my dream. My golden velvet heaven.*

"I remember. I remember this."

Exhilaration kidnapped my heart as I imagined myself waltzing through the ballroom, guided by handsome gentlemen. *This is real, it's happening,* I told myself. The claps of the butler crashed me back to reality. I was waltzing—alone.

"Sorry," I said, my cheeks hot.

"You will look beautiful tonight, my child," my mom said, with the look of a parent attending her child's school play.

"Tonight?"

"Yes, tonight. We are having a gala. We celebrate that you are finally here to take the place you deserve, by my side, as the princess you are."

A princess? I asked myself, dubious. *A true princess?*

"Make the preparations," my mother ordered.

"*Heer* Queenliness." The butler clicked his heels and minced away in urgency, trying to settle another argument between his three personalities.

My mother hooked my arm and took me upstairs, through a

panoramic spiral staircase of engraved granite, with oil paintings embellishing the wall at each step. The last one was the portrait of my family, the same idyllic image I'd seen at the cabin in the woods.

"It's beautiful, isn't it?" my mother said.

I started to respond, but the words went sour in my mouth. The questions that had plagued me my entire life surfaced.

"Why? Why did you have to leave so early? Why did he abandon us?"

"To prove who you really are. You are strong. You not only overcame a mother parting in the early hours of your life but also survived the abandonment of your father."

"I never asked to be challenged that way. I just wanted a normal life. A living mom, a loving dad—was that too much to ask?"

"A coward should never be called Father, nor Husband, and that was what he was, a coward who played a love tune. Convincing, enchanting, lying… and then he threw the deadly blow." My mother clapped her hands. "But he failed. And a wounded sheep never forgets. A wounded sheep never forgives. Don't you see, Maia? You *survived*. You triumphed over the demons that lurk inside men. You proved yourself as the princess you are, and now you deserve nothing less than a kingdom," she said, waving her arms up to the magnificent vault. "Nothing and nobody in this world is more important than you. You belong above them all. Now no one will hurt you, my darling. And if someone dares, you will never forget and never forgive." She pointed at the painting. "Just as you never forgot what he stole from you."

"My family," I said.

She smiled. "Tonight, you'll see Vandella again." She must have noticed a change in my expression upon hearing his name. "No, mourn no more for a man that is unworthy of your tears, my child. You need nobody; it is they who need you. He will kneel before you, humiliated, asking for forgiveness."

I could not imagine Sidney begging for anything.

"And you will stare at him with the cold sympathy of vengeance. Because now, my girl, you are the one who will toll the bell."

My mother closed my hand and opened it again, and a small, gilded bell with a bloodred ribbon had materialized inside. I looked at her, doubtful, but she nodded reassuringly. I held it between my fingers and shook it. The clapper produced no sound, but the whole building quivered. Then the bells in the bell tower resounded throughout the entire castle. The oil painting of my family cracked and flaked, vanishing into the air, revealing a new painting beneath. It showed my mother crowned as a queen and me holding a small scepter that supplanted Dario's finger, with his place now vacant.

An army of gleaming knights marched up the stairs, their armor clattering. The company knelt before me, presenting their swords and lowering their helmeted heads.

"All men at your feet, my dear. As you wished. As you deserve."

The central lines stepped aside, allowing four knights carrying a palanquin on their shoulders to pass through. They rested the poles on the floor and knelt similarly.

"Sit," my mother commanded.

"Me?"

"Take your place on the throne," she ordered.

I tiptoed to the padded throne, and they pulled me up with tremendous synchronicity. Two knights opened the doors, revealing an endless hallway.

"Clean up, my child. This is the most important night of your life. Tonight is your debut." She grinned, and the palanquin launched across the hallway, leaving her image behind.

My transport passed uncountable identical doors. It felt just like the maze garden, making me wonder how we made it through. But one thing was completely certain: having these gentlemen take me wherever we were going was essential; there was no way I could make it this far by myself.

They finally halted and lowered the palanquin. A door opened, and the butler shot out.

"At last!" he said, tossing his head back and spreading his hands like a peacock. He scurried to the step of my moving throne and helped me down. "I'm glad to finally have you here, Princess."

"Thank you," I said, flattered.

"We missed you for ages," said the sad personality, on the brink of tears.

"Get out!" The belligerent one brushed the knights off.

"Missed me? Have I been here before?"

"Of course!" The butler ushered me into the room.

The bedchamber was majestic. It was like entering a cathedral. At the center was a tall four-posted bed covered with canopies embroidered with Arabic patterns. Oil paintings embedded in the gold-plated walls portrayed me at various ages, telling of a life of lushness and refinement.

"Here you are riding your gallant white steed that was the gift of your mother on your seventh birthday," he explained, like a tour guide of a museum. "Over here you are winning the polo competition."

"But I don't even like horses," I said, and he looked at me, astounded.

It was quite different from the modest life I'd really had. But it was not the luxury that drew my attention, it was my beaming smile that remained constant in all of them, luminous and ravishing, never dull and darkened by the shadow of cancer.

"When did I leave?"

"Pardon me?"

"Yes, you said you missed me when I left this place. When was it?"

"Mmmmmmmm, three or four…" He deliberated, twisting his mustache.

"Four years?" I said, forcing my mind to recall events from when I was thirteen.

"Oh no, no, no, no. Days, child. Four days."

"Four days? And you missed me for *ages*?"

Four days ago, I was chained to my hospital bed, having dreams about this place… *Could it have been true that I was here?*

"This way, Princess." The butler guided me to a tub in front of a picture window framing the sun setting over the garden, a scene worthy of being captured in a painting by a Renaissance master. "Your bath is ready," he said, pouring steaming water and essences into a foamy pool that would outshine any spa.

"Thank you."

He extended his hand, and I shook it, but he raised his eyebrow. "What?"

"Your—*dirty*—clothes."

"What?!" *You pervert!* "I'm not going to undress before you."

"Please, Princess, don't be alarmed." His head rotated until he revealed his hairy nape, hiding all three faces below the wig. "I'm blind. You can put me to the test."

"How many fingers am I holding up?" I walked around him, making silly faces instead.

"Four!" "Six!" "Two!" The three all made different guesses.

"No, you idiot, it's not six."

"How it could be two? Moron."

"Shut up, the both of you." The face revealed itself. "How many did you have?"

"Emmm—none." I shrugged.

The faces hid again and continued their argument while I undressed. I kept the childhood photo from the fair with me and handed the butler my clothes before getting inside the hot tub.

"Not that way, you idiot!" said the butler's angry personality as he stumbled blindly off.

"Shut up and walk." He tottered through the room, colliding against furniture, before finding the door.

I chuckled.

I slipped under, overflowing the water. It was so relaxing. I surfaced, feeling invigorated. I rubbed myself, contemplating the breathtaking scenery. The solar disc tinted the clouds with such extravagant colors that they appeared to be candy floss. Surreal.

It made me wonder where everybody might be. Frank, Bill, Lt. Lovelock… they were probably better without me. *I'm trouble.* Now they were safe from all threats, away from Alek, from Sidney. I still couldn't believe that Sidney had lied to me. Part of me still believed there should be an explanation for his behavior. That he was innocent. And with every passing moment I thought about him, that part of me grew uncontrollably. Like a tumor. It had been just a couple of days since I met him, and I felt like he had invaded me.

"*Wabi-sabi,*" I said, feeling the combination of joy and sorrow he had taught me.

I admired the photo again, caressing his cropped face, his beautiful lips. It offered comfort to my troubled soul. Even if I was just a toddler and didn't remember precisely, the idea of being in his arms goaded at my heart.

Maia, stop! I scolded myself. *You love Jase, don't you remember?*

Jase, Jase, Jase, I repeated, retrieving his image from my memory: so gallant and dashing in his football jacket, snatching my sighs with his beautiful eyes, making me shudder as he wrapped his left arm around my waist and passed his right arm around my neck to hold my face from behind, lifting my chin so our lips could meet… *Oh, Sidney.*

I shook the fantasy out of my brain.

Why? Why do you feel this even after knowing he fooled you?

Then I admitted that it was too late. It didn't matter if it destroyed me. This love had metastasized in my whole being, and now it was inoperable.

What am I going to do when I see him? I thought, lamenting the absence of Shelly's advice. The support of my best friend, my counselor. Without her help, I had no idea what to do.

It was dark by the time the butler returned, carrying a mannequin bearing the beautiful scarlet silk gown with crinoline skirt from my dreams. I could not conceal my happiness.

"Princess, you will look *belle, belle.*"

I blushed at the thought of seeing Sidney again like my mother had promised, so I dressed for him—my Mr. Darcy.

The uncanny being more dream than man.

My golden velvet dream.

My Sidney.

The butler arranged my hair with the voluptuous headdress, placing plaited trimmings. He helped me to fit into the bodice—with all his heads hidden behind his wig, of course, even when I was wearing my underwear—and fastened my corset, which accentuated the curves of my body. I crowned my attire with a pearl necklace and bracelet. Finally, the butler inserted my feet in the exquisitely embroidered satin shoes.

"Perfect," I said, contemplating my apparel.

"*Belle*, simply *belle.*" The butler clapped vigorously.

"Thank you," I said, practicing my curtsy.

Outside my bedchamber, my transport was already waiting for me, with the four knights kneeling meekly. I climbed to my throne, and the knights rode off down the endless corridor like racing stallions.

"Stop, stop!" I yelled as soon as we arrived outside the main hall. "I will walk from this point, thank you."

Two guards opened the doors leading to the stairs with reverence. I took a quick glimpse at the family painting before descending. Even with it embellished, I liked the previous one more. Although both were a lie, some lies are sweeter than others.

I followed the sound of the music through the corridors until I found the ballroom. The wooden doors opened before me, revealing a masquerade ball. The whole hall hushed at my entrance, and I stopped, completely thunderstruck. I felt like I was crashing a stranger's party.

A gentleman in outlandish vestments and aureate mask welcomed me with a bow. "Princess," he said, extending his hand.

I performed my curtsy unconsciously and held his hand. He directed me through the crowd. The women were dressed in full gowns; richly colored, extensive jewelry; and turbans with flamboyant feathers. The men were wearing garish medieval outfits, long cloaks, and pointy hats. Courtiers wore colorful masks shaped like birds, pigs, dogs, sea creatures, and harlequins and jesters. Only their eyes stood out, profound and piercing. I searched for the familiar faces I had seen in my dream—Shelly, Lisa, Rachel, or even the gossiping, smug witches—but could not find them. I was the only person among the thousand attendees exposing my face.

Everybody greeted me on my way to the heart of the ballroom, where—just like in my dream—the magnificent dome displayed the full moon among the dangling chandeliers.

An assembly of chords and flutes flooded the place, playing Mr. Bahiti's sonata.

My companion held my waist, and we spun on the sleek marble floor, carried by the music. My eyes were away from him, busily scanning the attendees in pursuit of Sidney, but I couldn't spot him.

"Your hunt is in vain," said my dancing partner in a jester mask with a voice that reminded me of Jase.

I flinched, alarmed, releasing myself from his grasp.

Before he could say anything else, a tall clock chimed, bonging ominously. The music stopped, and in silence, the courtiers divided at the two sides of the room, leaving a long passage that ran from the entrance to a throne in the heights of a podium. I stood alone in the middle, surrounded by inquisitive eyes.

The clock counted to twelve, and then the main door opened. The entire crowd bent their heads as the reflection of my mother in the mirror floated over the lustrous floor's tiles to me. She was wearing an ivory gown, embroidered with gold thread. An off-white, rigid tunic, more armor than cloth, rested on her shoulders, rising to her ears. Her crown reminded me of the Pope's hat and appeared to be merged to her head. Gold details that started at the point of her nose formed a mask around the top half of her eyes. Gold needles emerged from above her eyebrows like the intricate horns of a deer and continued behind her ears, descending with a pattern of beautiful diamond earrings.

"Mother," I greeted her.

"My darling." She followed the outline of my face with the tip of her long, golden nails. "You look astonishingly beautiful."

"Thank you. You look beautiful too."

"Come," she said, and we ambled, arm in arm, to the throne. "Have you enjoyed the celebration in your honor?"

"Ye-yes, it's great," I stuttered, as all terrible liars do.

"I'm delighted to hear that," my mother said. "Now, it's time." She released my hand.

She floated the stairs up the podium and rested like a feather on the golden throne, and the hovering mirror stood by her side, reflecting her outline. Her bare feet rested on a padded stool, and I realized that the soles were covered in scars—bizarre, considering her feet never touched the ground.

She clapped twice, and everybody turned to her like disciplined soldiers.

"My dearest, my children," she addressed the audience with a seductive voice. "We are gathered tonight to rejoice at the return of Maia, my beloved daughter, by whose sacrifice we stand this night, just one step away from freedom." I was surrounded by a deafening applause.

I blushed.

"Don't be shy, my dear. You earned it. Make pride yours."

"Thank you," I replied uncertainly.

"Now, my child, it's time to fulfill your duty." My mother snapped her fingers, and a void opened at my feet. I stepped backward. The courtiers gathered around to see.

I realized the void was only a projection, like the one she'd showed me in the mirror back in the valley. The image showed an endless throng of waving torches, all looking to the center, where a huge, cross-shaped stone platform rose above the crowd. At each end of the cross, there was a wooden chair facing inward, in which four elder women waited impatiently. At the intersection of the cross, there was a concentric circular platform, and in the center a bottomless pit of flames.

"Bring the accused," one of the old ladies ordered.

The horde pushed forward a man in torn clothes. He stumbled, climbing the stone stairs to the center of the platform.

"Sidney!" His name came out of my mouth unconsciously. He could hardly stand, still handcuffed by my bewitched hair.

CHAPTER 16

"WHERE IS THE PROSECUTOR?" one elder called.

Prosecutor?

Out of thin air, a mirror materialized in front of Sidney. It appeared floating in the air, as if all this time it had been hidden in plain sight by its hair-thin depth. I recognized the gold-plated frame. My mother appeared on it, as if she were broadcasting live from the ballroom.

"Four Mothers, I salute you from beyond on this heavenly night." My mother waved her hand, and the mirror rotated so the four elders could see her. "I bring to you the many-named, son of the claimer of souls, last of the cursed offspring of the Fallen—"

The oldest-looking of the four women interrupted my mother. "Introduction is not required. We all know who he is." She glanced at Sidney, even though the iris and pupil of her eyes were fused with the snowy layer of the sclera—she must have been blind. The wrinkles on her face were pronounced like tree bark, making her look older than the mountains, but her hair was black as the feathers of a crow. Her clothes were made of the skin and fur of wolves and bears tied around her body. Her hand played with the flames of the bonfire at her feet, creating figures of men and beasts that vanished in the air, the only thing that her eyes appeared to recognize besides Sidney. "What is the accusation?"

"First Mother of the North, the crime perpetuated by the accused is *Defiance*." My mother pointed at Sidney, who stared at her, unmoved. "Disobedience to carry the oath to which he was named by the *Will*."

"How do you declare against the accusation?" the First Mother asked, looking back at Sidney.

Sidney closed his eyes briefly and answered, "Is it not truth that a mother can see into the heart of her son?"

Mother? Son? Could this really be Sidney's mother? I gave a second glimpse to the old woman, trying to find a resemblance.

"A mother can be judge and jury, but never executioner. And it's to an executioner you need to prove yourself innocent, because a feather weighs a mountain when not carried by the wind." In the bonfire, a firebird formed, and she squeezed it in her hand and released the ashes. "Continue," the First Mother ordered, nodding to the mirror.

"The accused has as many sins as names, most based on deceit and delusion, and in its lowest form—*seduction*." My mother stared at me with darting eyes. "The accused has lured victims, young human girls, with romance and promises of love and then deceived them."

"Do you have witnesses to sustain such bold claims?" one of the elders said with a needle and thread at her hands, sewing a garment. Her face was inked with red in a strip across her eyes and another coming down from the lips down to her neck, which was saturated with beaded necklaces. Her gray hair was arranged with multicolored flowers like her gown, with the same flowers continuing in tattoos covering her forearms.

"Indeed, Second Mother of the South."

My mother clicked her fingers, and the mirror unfolded itself, creating another mirror that detached. The reflection warped and presented the first witness.

It was Peach.

I wasn't delighted to see her, but it gladdened me to know she was safe.

"Sidney! A-are you ok?" Peach asked anxiously, and a smile fluttered across her face.

"It's evident that you two are more than acquaintances," my mother said derisively. "The reason you have been summoned here is to testify," she said, addressing Peach. "Do you know the reason why the accused is here?"

Peach nodded.

"Good. Do you swear to speak nothing but the truth?"

She paused for a moment and answered timidly, "Yes, I do."

My mother's mirror moved around the room, as if she were there giving her speech. "Are you aware of the punishment for those that give false testimony?"

Peach shook her head.

The mirror flipped suddenly to face Peach. "Believe me when I say that you don't want to find out."

"Proceed," the Second Mother said.

"Can you please describe how you reached this place?"

"H-he helped me cross."

"For what purpose?"

"To trade a life."

"Ohhhhhh, I see, the pagan rite in which a person takes owner-ship of the deeds of a sinner—*entertaining*." My mother raised her brow. "And whose life were you trading?"

Peach's eyes lowered and searched for Sidney, who nodded sub-tly. "M-Maia's," she mumbled.

"Who? I could not hear you?" my mother demanded.

Peach closed her eyes hesitatingly.

"Who?"

"Maia. Maia Foster!" Peach confessed.

"Did she know?"

"What—"

"Was she informed of your intentions?"

Peach shook her head.

"Then, she was tricked into coming here?"

"Yes."

Peach finally admitted it. Everything was a farce. Just a plot contrived by the two to use me. All Sidney wanted was to save her, even at the expense of my sacrifice. *Why? What did I do?*

"And were you also fooled in similar fashion by the accused?"

"No," Peach refuted emphatically. "It was me." Her voice soft-ened. "It was me who proposed it to him."

Sidney observed stoically.

My mother's reflection floated closer to Peach. "Are you con-fessing authorship of the plot?" she asked, squinting.

"Yes."

"Did you know that it is forbidden for him to alter the course of a human life? That he was breaking the primeval law of coexistence by bringing you here?"

Peach nodded, clearly suffering.

"Did you know that he, as a timeless being, can witness cause and consequence all together, meaning that he already knew your entire plot was predestined to be a fiasco?"

Peach continued nodding with her eyes closed, like a scared child.

"Then what was the motive that persuaded him to commit such a crime, already knowing that he would be punished here?"

Tears ran down Peach's cheeks. "Love," she babbled.

"Ohhhhhhhhh, *flesh* affairs," my mother said with disgust. "You must know that even if you came up with the plan, it changes nothing. Everyone here knows well that he is the culprit of the sins, either by act or by omission." My mother addressed the audience, "So, I ask you, righteous *Flagellants*, the Thirsty for Justice, how should he be found?"

So, these people were the religious fanatics Sidney had warned me about at the outskirts of the city of Betheli.

"Guilty!" The men and women of the audience roared in emotion, with heinous faces, waving a scourge with three tails. They were wrapped in white tunics; some had their torsos exposed, with their backs still bleeding from the flogging, hence their nickname.

"Noooooooo! You can't do this, he is innocent!" Peach cried. "I'm the one who did it! Punish me!"

"Silence!" One of the old women hit a gong with a gavel, silencing everyone with a loud, metallic din. Her eyes were covered with beaded yarns that hung from a tiara, and her hair was arranged in a similar fashion in thin braids. She wore an orange tunic with golden finishes that shone like the setting sun. "This court judges no humans. He is the one solely responsible for his actions."

"Thank you, Fourth Mother and mother of the West," my mother said.

"I'm sorry, Sidney. I'm so sorry," Peach whimpered.

"Don't be." Sidney extended the palms of his cuffed hands toward her. "There is nothing to forgive about love."

Love.

Passionate love.

Requited love.

An alien concept to me, even though it had felt so close. It was her all along, not me.

All my life, I had seen couples falling in love in the same way a dog watches from the pet shop the contented dogs parading by the hand of an owner. I always asked myself, *When? When would it be me?* Day in, day out, without an answer.

Maybe I'm defective.

"Witness dismissed," my mother said, and Peach's mirror flipped, and her image disappeared.

The projection on the ballroom floor also vanished, and I was back in the castle, cut off from the courtroom.

"Now it is your turn to testify, my dear," my mother said to me.

"What?" I answered, stupefied, seeing everybody's eyes were on me. "N-no, I mean, I can't." I was not prepared to point my finger at Sidney—even after hearing Peach admit their love—but I could not lie either. It was hard enough for me witnessing the drama to be part of it.

I just couldn't.

"This is not about your wishes, Maia. It's about responsibility. About making things right. Did not your grandmother teach you about that?"

I sighed, remembering my gran and all I had come through. I was still so far from saving her. "Responsibility is about fulfilling promises," I said, quoting her words.

"That's right," my mother said with a melodious voice. "Don't you want to free me? Or is it that you don't long for a reunion? Imagine it, you, your grandmother, and myself, living here, blissful—forever."

"I came this far just to save her."

"And this is how you accomplish it—by testifying. This is the *right* thing to do."

"I can't." I closed my eyes and lowered my head.

My mother descended from her throne and pulled my chin up. "I know what you feel for him." I stepped back, dumbfounded. "It's okay, my dear, nothing to be ashamed of. I'm not asking you to lie. Only the truth shall be spoken."

"But what if what I say condemns him? I could not live knowing—"

"Do you believe a mother capable of condemning her own

son?"

So, the First Mother was Sidney's mother, his human half. My stomach revolted at the idea of Sidney being judged by his own mother.

"But she mentioned an executioner."

"Have you seen one waiting in the wings? Punishment never comes if the accused is found innocent."

"Will he be?"

"That is not for us to decide, my dear. Our job is only to bring truth and justice. And nothing will make me prouder than having a righteous daughter."

"Okay," I said, unconvinced.

A rectangular hole opened before me like a door, a portal that materialized as a mirror in the court, just as with Peach, taking me back into the courtroom, this time staring out of my own mirror. Sidney's mesmerizing green eyes contemplated me again. Even in his deplorable condition, his wry smile was the silver lining that made me sigh.

"You look lovely in that dress," Sidney said with a velvet voice.

I felt guilty. "Thank you," I said, evading his eyes, clamping down my left fingers on my right elbow to release my tension.

"Do you know what is missing?"

"The medallion?" I answered, mimicking our discussion back at the park outside the hospital, where all this had started.

"No, your breathtaking smile," he said.

"Maia Foster," interrupted my mother. "Do you swear to speak nothing but the truth?"

I stared at Sidney and replied, "Yes, I do."

"Do you know who this man is?"

"Yes, his name is Sidney."

"I mean his *nature*," she amended.

"I think so. He is some sort of messenger of Death."

"Do you consider *messenger* the right word to describe him?"

Vandella, Vetala, Chort, creature of the night, vampire of the soul... he had been described as so many things, yet for me all resumed in only one—*love*. "I'm not sure," I finally said.

"Did he explain his true nature to you?"

"Somewhat," I said, trying to be as vague as possible.

"Were you aware of his heartless intentions to exchange your life for hers?"

"No."

"How did you learn about it?"

I evaded Sidney's sight. "I spied on them."

"What did they say?"

"They said…" I hesitated, but my mother glowered persuasively. "They said that they were lying to me until I recovered the medallion so they could seize it from me."

"What else?"

"They mentioned that I might refuse and try to stop them, but he promised to do everything to impede that possibility." Anger possessed me as I remembered Sidney's words.

"A clear act of collusion," said my mother, addressing the Flagellants, who howled in response. "The accused acted treacherously, with premeditation."

"Silence!" The Fourth Mother hit the gong with her gavel.

"It's time for the reaping of the sooth," said the Third Mother and mother of the East, turning an hourglass upside down. There was no ordinary sand inside—it shone like stardust, projecting chromatic light fractals onto her white tunic. Her creased face was inked with the stripes of a tiger, and her battered hands were exposed. "Concede voice to the accused."

My mother addressed Sidney. "Do you swear to speak nothing but the truth?"

"Yes," he answered confidently.

"Do you admit that you brought Maia here with the sole purpose of exchanging her life, and by doing so, you broke the universal oath that you swore to uphold?"

"I willingly and consciously broke all the existing laws with the goal of exchanging a life."

The Flagellants buzzed.

"Do you admit to deceiving her to do so?"

"It was the only way," Sidney answered, unmoved, sassy, nailing a stake through my chest. His eyes exhibited not a pinch of remorse. *It was true.* He'd protected me through the entire odyssey, but he did it only to use me.

"Do you see, my dear?" my mother whispered in my ear. "All men are the same." And she was *right*.

"So, what we had was a lie?" I confronted him.

Sidney remained speechless.

"Why?" I asked, disheartened.

He broke his silence. "I promised her."

I felt stupid. *How could I have believed him?* Sidney was in love with her and always had been. I was just a diversion for him, a step to climb to a higher end.

I was the fool who'd thought that, somehow, he could really love me.

"After acknowledging all testimonies, how do you declare yourself of the charges imputed on this tribunal?" my mother asked Sidney incisively.

"Guilty," he said.

Perhaps Sidney was confident that his mother would rule in his favor. But the Flagellants ignited with thirst—not for justice, but for violence. "Punishment!" the throng echoed.

"Silence!" the Fourth Mother commanded.

"As you might see, Mothers, little is left to be shown." My mother's mirror floated around, reaching the elders. "Tonight, the truth has been exposed. The accused, using the powers conferred by the *Will*, intervened in mortal affairs by interchanging the lives of the victims, breaking the laws of coexistence and universal balance. But what can we expect from the offshoot of sin?" She contemptuously looked at Sidney. "Sadly, we have attested that his incentive in fooling a young girl with fiddling romance was the most mundane objective of impregnating her with a scion and—by doing it—perpetuating the sinfulness of his kind."

I turned to my mother, flabbergasted by her angry speech, but more by Sidney's callousness, even against such accusations. Was that indeed his true purpose?

"The Children of the Damned. The bearers of original sin," my mother continued. "The sin of falling in love with mortal women committed by the Fallen, now incarcerated in an everlasting sarcophagus in the Valley of the Grigori until their lineage—carried since Cain—perishes." My mother's mirror floated back, and she pointed at Sidney, almost at his nose. "And *he*, son of Samael and the First Mother, he is the last one." The Flagellants responded, clamoring at her words.

Sidney was a Child of the Damned, a son of Samael, a Grigori who'd fallen in love with a mortal woman, the First Mother. Sidney was the last remnant of the cursed offspring, and as Alek had explained, his mere existence kept the resentful Watchers imprisoned in wombs of rock, until his heart ceased to beat and they'd be freed to return to the heavens.

"Silence, silence!" The Fourth Mother battled to regain order.

"And Mothers, I tell you." My mother floated around, addressing them with the same accusing finger. "Condemn him and enjoy a silent night. Exonerate him…" She looked deep into their eyes. "…and you will witness a rouged dawn."

Hands rose all over the gloomy horizon, supporting her claims.

"Prosecution ends," my mother said, extending her arms in a bow.

"Silence! Time for deliberation has come." The Third Mother spun her hourglass upside down.

The eyes of the three others turned white like those of the First Mother. They extended their hands and entered a trance. The quartet hummed a melody and sung a hymn in a tongue not composed by man; I guessed it was angelic language. The flames of the bonfire excited with the canticles, producing whimsical forms that gave life to a remembrance of the bygone events, with Sidney, Peach, and me as the protagonists. Sidney's flame appeared halved in the visions—his left side, his human side. The three flames floated in different directions, with Peach's extinguishing first, then Sidney's, and finally mine. The Mothers closed their eyes, putting an end to their hymn, and opened them back up, looking normal once again.

"The jury has reached a verdict," announced the Second Mother.

"Kneel," my mother instructed, and Sidney obeyed.

He was prostrate before me, vulnerable, just as my mother foretold. But even after knowing his scam, I could not be happy to see him that way. It made me feel miserable. Yet I still wished this to be different, to be better.

"I forgive you," I said to Sidney under the glare of my mother.

He repeated the same words he'd said to Peach. "There is nothing to forgive about love."

Then the verdict was heralded.

"Under the crimes of breaking the sacred vows and intervening in the cause of a mortal life, we hereby declare the accused…"

Silence extended across the entire crowd.

"Guilty," the four declared in unison, and the Fourth Mother hit the gong.

"There is only one punishment for those who act against the *Will*," said the First Mother, glancing at Sidney with narrowed eyes.

"*Death.*"

"What?" I refused to believe what I'd heard. Sidney's life was being taken by his own mother?

It didn't matter how mad I could be with him. My mind rejected an existence in which Sidney did not exist. Even if I tried to fool myself, the truth was that my heart was still not prepared to beat if it was not for him. But it didn't matter how I felt. The crowd in the castle and at the tribunal roared euphorically.

My mother's lips curled into the smug grin of victory.

I stepped aside from the portal.

"You *knew*," I said, addressing the empty throne. "You knew from the beginning this was going to happen, and you used me. You convinced me that his mother would forgive him… but you *knew* this was just a kangaroo court."

"The trial was not a farce, my dear. Only truth was spoken. He is a confessed sinner, Maia, and death is the only way to guarantee that no other woman suffers what he did to you. He deserves no less. Rejoice, my righteous daughter."

"Silence!" The gong of the Fourth Mother restrained the chatter.

The First Mother enlivened the bonfire with her hands, shaping flames that depicted her words. "But it was in the epoch of great turmoil that the *Will* extended the arms of forgiveness around the sinners with eternal compassion," she continued. "And by that reason, tonight we honor the mercifulness of the *Will*, and humbly follow the example. We sentence the accused to the *White Death*, in which he will be exiled from creation, and there he will wait for eons in the cruelest isolation, until all his names have been forgotten and his deeds never pronounced. Then he will disappear. Drown in the silence of the nothingness."

The smile of my mother transformed into a scowl. "A rabid dog that has bitten is not taken away from the victim—it's killed. Eradication is the only way to avoid spreading this disease. The crimes of a sinner should not be forgotten, they should be obliterated!" she proclaimed, and the masses screamed their agreement.

"Mother, what are you doing? Stop!" I exclaimed, but my voice got lost amid the ruckus.

A disturbance in the distance grabbed the attention of the Flagellants, who cringed like scared dogs, creating a circle around an unwelcome visitor. Amid the sepulchral silence, only the thunderous clang of horse hooves could be heard, like the steps of the devil.

A black steed ridden by a man in a long raincoat made its way gallantly through the horde. As they got closer, I could see that the horse was Empress, and the horseman was no other than Alek, nonchalant, with his rifle in his arms.

Empress climbed the stone stairs of the court, and Alek dismounted, shaking the mud off his silver-spurred boots.

"Ma'am." He tipped his hat to me and made his way into the center, turning around to see the Four.

"Who are you?" the second Mother asked.

"I'm the one who frightens the night," Alek said.

"What business brings you here, outsider?" the First Mother asked.

Alek extended his arm, pointing to Sidney.

"I'm here to offer my life in exchange for his."

CHAPTER 17

ALL EYES RESTED ON ALEK. All ears heard his words, but no mouth dared to break the silence.

"I'm afraid your journey has been pointless, outsider," the Third Mother said. "The destiny of the accused has been decided."

Alek chuckled. "You misunderstand me, my ladies. I'm not here to dispute the sentence." He stepped closer to Sidney and looked him in the eye. "He is certainly guilty—*irrevocably.*"

Alek removed his hat.

"Tonight, I come before you Mothers as the father of a son who was snatched too soon by Vandella. I come before you, humble, with an entreaty for you to grant the final wish of a doomed man." Alek opened his raincoat and unbuttoned his shirt, then removed handfuls of straw until he revealed his heart, pumping inside his rib cage, dangling like a withered fruit in a leafless tree.

His entire flesh had been consumed by his desire for revenge. Bullet by bullet. Bit by bit.

"What is it you want?" the Fourth asked.

Alek pulled the tip of his glove to reveal his skeletal hand and pointed at Sidney's chest.

"I want to carry out the sentence," Alek said.

"We appreciate your helpfulness, but silence is the sole executioner during the White Death," the Mother explained.

"That's why I come offering my soul in exchange for the right of donning the hood." Alek hammered his ribs with his fist. "Allow me, and with my gun, I will ease his pain—*forever.*"

"This is not open for discussion, outsider. No mortal soul could outweigh a Fallen in the balance—not even a half-blood like this one," the Second Mother clarified.

"Mine is no ordinary soul. I'm the bearer of the *Eye of Truth,*" Alek said, taking his Dragunov from his shoulder and raising the gold-plated scope. "And wielder of the powers of the *Spear of Destiny* to kill humans and gods alike," he said, uncovering his belt, holding the bullets stuffed with his flesh. "I was entrusted with both with the sole purpose of carrying out my mission."

"Hmmmmm, unusual, yet a powerful patron you have found for backing your crusade, outsider," the First said, caressing the flames. "But more unusual is your willingness to die."

"Vengeance is my engine. Vengeance is my ally."

"Your perseverance amuses me, outsider," said the Mother, taking a handful of flames into her palm. "But I'm afraid you will go back empty-handed."

The multitude howled at her words.

"Fate has been laid," she reassured.

The crowd booed and flung torches that scattered over the platform. The Flagellants had been waiting for blood to be shed. The throng shoved against the platform like an angry sea colliding against a dock. It was an incessant tide of hands trying to drag everything into their dark depths.

"I'm afraid you are not aware of your position in this situation," Alek said with faint displeasure. In the blink of an eye, he drew his revolver and shot at the First Mother before any of us could react. The shining bullet traveled in her direction but deviated and hit a Flagellant waving a spiky flog behind her. In the wake of the bullet, a gust of air blew her hair and extinguished the fire in her hand.

The Flagellants quieted. Not even the Mothers could hide their trepidation. Alek's skeleton hand spun his revolver and sheathed it.

"Dead means dead," Alek said, putting back on his glove. "But for a timeless being, death makes no difference if it's carried out tonight or in one million nights." He tilted his head in Sidney's direction. "For him, both nights are tonight."

Even hearing it previously from Sidney's mouth, it was hard for me to understand how all time was condensed in one instant for him. *Could he be living his death at this moment?*

"But if you refuse, and I walk away empty-handed…" Alek walked to edge of the platform and glared down on the Flagellants, who crawled back, yelping like beasts, afraid of him. "You should be aware that if you don't throw flesh to the wolves, none of you will see the sunrise. Not even your precious son."

The First Mother's eyes looked at Sidney, and even though they were clouded in white, a glimpse of sorrow emerged.

I had been harsh in judging her. It was clear that the sentence of life in isolation was the only way for a mother to protect her child. Knowing that somewhere her son continued existing was her way of saving him, at the expense of her own suffering.

No words were needed between the two. She already had accepted silence for grief. And Sidney assented discreetly.

The First closed her eyes, and the other Mothers did so after her. They hummed a hymn that felt like a funeral march, and the bonfire grew like a pyre.

But it was no funeral. It was a sacrifice.

Sidney was going to be sacrificed to indulge a capricious mob, and I felt like everything was my fault. Like I should sacrifice myself instead of him.

The deafening gong resounded, and the Mothers opened their eyes.

"It has been decided," the Second announced.

"Outsider," the First Mother said with reluctant voice, "your offer has been accepted."

The Flagellants rejoiced with the news, their lust for blood sated.

"No! You can't do this," I shouted, trying to force them into reason. "He doesn't deserve this. You are wrong!"

"Silence, girl!" the Fourth ordered. "He was found guilty independent of how the execution is carried out."

I turned to Sidney, on the brink of tears.

"You can take his life in exchange for your soul," Sidney's mother said, disheartened, and lowered her grim face.

Alek wore his hat and tipped the brim to her as a gesture of gratitude.

"Alek, please, don't do it, please," I begged.

"Maia, enough!" my mother berated me.

"Please!"

"Be silent, girl," the Fourth said.

"Please, Mothers, there must be a way—"

Sidney finally broke his silence. "No, there is not a way."

His eyes rested on mine.

Alek whistled, and Empress climbed the last steps. He grabbed a rope from the saddlebag, fastened one end to the saddle, and with the other end tied a knot around Sidney's wrists. Alek hopped on the horse.

"Get moving," he ordered Sidney. "The journey is long."

"Halt," the Second Mother ordered. "Where are you going? The sentence must be consummated and payment retrieved."

"The lion that conquers a chained beast cannot proclaim to be King himself. I'm a hunter, not an entertainer. This is my prey, and I'm going to hunt him."

"The court demands a guarantee," the Mother said, clearly concerned by the rage of the crowd.

"I'm a scarecrow." Alek threw a handful of straw over the ground. "I don't have a pound of flesh more. The bullets I carry are the last. Once the last has been fired, you can come to claim your pledge."

"And if you fail?" asked the Second.

Alek stared at her impassively. "I won't," he said and hauled the bridle. Empress cantered down the stairs, pulling Sidney after her.

Not even the Mothers would dare to stand up against Alek.

Sidney looked back at me as he was pulled away.

Ephemeral.

Like the last passing second of an eternity.

CHAPTER 18

"SIDNEY!" I RAN AFTER HIM, but the image vanished before I could reach it, leaving me standing among the faceless courtiers in the ballroom.

The reflection of my mother descended from her throne, and I felt her invisible hand slapping my cheek. "What are you trying to accomplish? Do you want to ruin everything we have fought for?"

I caressed my sore cheek, abashed by everybody staring at me. I jostled them away and scurried out of the ballroom.

"Why? Why?" I vented furiously once alone.

The windows in the hallway were dark, the moon clouded. There was no scenery to help me regain my calm.

The door to the ballroom opened, allowing a fringe of light to filter out.

"I'm so sorry, my dear," my mother whispered, and I eyed her reflection in the window, embracing me from behind. "But you must understand who he *really* is. He is not Prince Charming. It's just a mirage. He is a demon, a vampire, a wicked being that is trying to fool you again."

"But it's unfair. H-he doesn't deserve to die."

"Was he fair when he lied to you?" I went mute. "Those that lie once cheat twice. The first time for telling the lie, the second time for pledging not to do it again."

It was true, but I still chose to believe in him. "He will not lie again," I said adamantly.

I held my mother's hollow hand over my shoulder. "You have to help him," I begged. "Please, Mother. He did wrong, but I know he has changed."

"Changed?" My mother removed my hand from hers, visibly upset. "You are so naive." The anger in her voice turned into remorse. "And so was I at your age. I loved the wrong man too. 'It's normal,' I said to myself, over and over again. 'Everybody has ups and downs, good and bad moments,' I tried to convince myself. I cherished the good times and ignored the bad. I tried to build my dreams around the man I thought he was. The man I loved. The man that was everything to me." She collapsed in my arms, and tears ran down from her eyes, moistening my dress. "But I wasn't everything to him." She sighed and glanced toward the window. "Time digs up everything that we thought forgotten and reminds us that if we tried to bury something in the past, it's because it was already dead."

My jaw stiffened, listening to her. She caressed the window, which framed a rain of tree leaves carried by the autumn wind.

"No, my girl, nobody changes. We fool ourselves with stories to hide our incapability to say, *Enough.*"

"Sidney is not my father."

"Believe that, and one day you will find yourself alone, carrying an innocent in your womb with no place to go. Then you can ask yourself if he was not like the others. Then you can ask yourself what *unfairness* really means."

Maybe I was inexperienced in love, but I knew perfectly what unfairness was. Since I was a child, I'd been familiar with the feeling of impotence, of despair, of abandonment.

"Don't make the same mistakes as your mother. You have the power to say enough is enough."

"I-I don't know—"

"You have to. The time has come for you to choose between the people that truly love you and the empty promises of a scoundrel."

"He—"

"Look at me, Maia." My mother forced me to face the empty space where she was. "I'm a shadow of what I once was. But the enchantment that keeps me prisoner will last until his last breath extinguishes."

"*What?*"

"He has to die for you and me to finally be together."

"I-I—" I stepped backward.

"Who are you going to save, Maia, your mother, or—*him?*"

"Why does it always have to be like this?" I said, frustrated. My entire life had been a torturous tradeoff.

"Because that's what adulthood is, Maia. You can't have everything you want. And now you are about to choose who you are going to lose."

"Why? I don't want everything, I just—"

"You can ask *why* all you want. It changes nothing. Choices are made both by your action and by your indifference."

"But what you are asking is—"

"*Unfair?*" my mother said with squinting eyes. "I had to choose between the man I loved and my right to bring my child into the world."

"Wha—" My stomach tingled, and my chest tightened as my brain refused to conceive the idea of my father pressuring my mother to get rid of me.

"But I chose you, Maia. I lost the man I loved and even my own life because I chose you." She extended her hand. "Who are you going to save?"

Was Sidney's life really in my hands? The truth was I could not save him even if I chose him. He had been sentenced and was on his way to confront execution. His life was solely in the hands of Alek. *There was nothing else I could do*, I said to myself, trying to numb my guilt.

Then I saw her.

The reflection on the window projected the image of my mother, pregnant, standing before the mirror in the seclusion of the bathroom. I knew it was a memory of her past, but it hurt me just as if I were her. Maybe I was. Both were one in that moment. All we had was each other. At least for the moment that pregnancy lasted, we were together. My breath condensed on the window, blurring her image. I extended my hand to reach her, but my fingers drew the bars of the prison that impeded me from caressing her, and the projection faded.

I was selfish, setting my feelings before the sacrifice of my mother.

"I-I-I'm sorry, Mother." I broke into tears and threw myself into her arms. "Please forgive me."

"Hush, hush, my princess. Worry no more. You are with your mother now, and nothing will be wrong."

The clock inside the hall chimed with three reverberating clangs.

"It's time to return to the ball," she said, wiping my tears. "You can't show frailty, my dear, or they will trample you."

I nodded.

We went back to the ballroom and walked across the hall amid cheers and applause.

"Finally, the moment has come," she proclaimed when her reflection rested on her throne. "For us to witness a new dawn!"

The masked courtiers cheered for her.

A new projection appeared on the floor before me. It was a forest of tall, leafless birches, striped like zebras, soaked by the bluish light of a radiant full moon. The pastures at the base were dusky ochre, outlined by white trails formed by snow.

The quiet of the image was broken by Alek riding Empress. Sidney appeared behind, battling to keep their pace on foot. His agitated breath condensed in the air.

I closed my eyes.

It still hurt.

"Look at him, Maia," my mother ordered.

"Please, Mother," I said, looking away. "I don't want to watch it."

"Maia, you have to. Witnessing his suffering is the sole way to heal your wounded heart. You must savor his pain. Find delight in his misery. You will find victory only in his defeat. Because it's in defeat that he will taste the bitterness of remorse. When he will regret exchanging you for another."

Empress halted at the top of a hill, and Sidney fell to his knees. Alek dismounted, carrying a torch, with his rifle hanging from his shoulder. He shook the snow off his silver-spurred boots and walked to Sidney.

"Drink," he said, handing him a canteen.

Sidney drank with the thirst of someone stranded in the Sahara.

After quenching his thirst, he returned the canteen, and Alek drank a big gulp before packing it in Empress's saddlebags.

"I would prefer to toast with vodka," Alek said. "But I want to avoid stories about how you lost because I had intoxicated you."

"How considerate," Sidney said sarcastically, catching his breath.

Alek anchored the torch in the snow and knelt before Sidney.

"The same thing my father told me when he found his vodka replaced." Alek unsheathed his revolver and emptied the chamber. The bloody, spent shells stained the purity of the snow. "He was a hardworking laborer during the day to hardly sustain a family of six, but at night, alcohol converted him to his true self. He was as good at hiding his vices and perversions inside the bedroom as my mother was at hiding her scars and bruises before going outside the house."

Alek reloaded his revolver with the delicacy and precision of a watchmaker.

"'Bring me my bottle, boy,' my father told me one night, and so I did. He got drunk before staggering to the bedroom where my baby sister was sleeping. I wept outside the door, hearing her cries as I stared at the lamenting look of my mother. I prayed to God to stop it and clung to the bottle of rat poison until he came out of the room, vomiting and kicking the shit out of me. 'How considerate, little son of a bitch,' he said, strangling me on the floor until I reached for the bottle of poison and struck him with it. I hit and hit and hit, smashing his face. The bottle was dyed in red but never broke."

Alek chuckled. "But why do I waste my time telling this to you when you know it already?" He stomped his boot on the empty shells, burying them in the snow, and funneled his weight on his knee to stand and stroll away from Sidney.

"You were present that night—*Vandella*," Alek said, his sight lost, contemplating the icy landscape. "You were outside the house, watching through the window as my little fingers fought to reach the poison bottle before my father choked me." He paused and turned to Sidney, clutching his revolver. "*Yes*, you waited for me to complete the job. A job not suited for an eleven-year-old. Remember?" Alek asked, tilting up Sidney's chin with the barrel of the revolver, but he remained silent.

"Oh! I forgot. You are living it right now. We—humans—are the forgetful, not your kind. But I remember well. I forced myself to remember. I visited the graveyard daily, to spit on the tomb of my father, to never forget that he was my first and last victim, because every time I aim my rifle, he is the only person I see."

Sidney stared at him, unresponsive.

"Do you remember my petition when you brought me here? Or will you pretend you forgot that as well?"

"You asked me to take you to the shores of Hell," Sidney finally spoke.

"That's right. That was the only way to stare into my father's eyes again and tell him that I was not a child anymore. That he could not abuse me or my family any longer. I came to reassure him that every minute of the suffering of my beloved sister was going be heaven compared to the place I would turn Hell for him."

"And so, you did," Sidney said grimly. "And now you fulfilled your word of coming back from Hell after me."

A smile popped on Alek's face. "That's it, my sweet friend. I'm back, and you know well why."

The two stared at each other for a moment, measuring the size of each other.

"It's time." Alek kicked the torch into the ground and pulled Sidney up.

"It was suicide."

"What did you say?" Alek answered, taken aback.

"Your son." Sidney paused, looking into the impatient eyes of Alek. "He took his own life."

"Shut up!" Alek pointed at Sidney's temple. "How dare you!"

My hand flew to my mouth to conceal my scream.

The sound of a branch crunching captured the attention of both men.

"Come out," Alek shouted to the trees without removing his eyes from Sidney. "I know Vandella told you where he would be, where to search. He is timeless, after all. But thanks to the Eye of Truth, I can also peek into the future. So come out."

Frank stepped out from behind a birch.

"Frank!" I called out, unable to hide my enthusiasm under the scowl of my mother.

"You are lost, son," Alek said, still aiming at Sidney. "This is a battlefield now. Now go!"

"I-I will not allow you to murder him!" Frank shambled toward them with arms wide open.

"Your mission was to protect *her*, Frank, not me. You should stay out of this," Sidney said, annoyed.

I couldn't believe that Sidney could still think about me in such condition, even after what had occurred.

"I'm sorry, Sidney. But I can't save her. Only you can."

"You moron. I said go!" Alek said, pissed. "Don't you hear the drums rattling?"

Drums? My hand reached for the knob at my neck, and I remembered the *Sheireils* that attacked us during the night at Pahana Forest.

Frank stared, not moving.

Alek lowered his revolver slowly as his breathing relaxed. He pulled the trigger, and the bullet ripped off Sidney's handcuffs. The spell broke, and strands of my hair dispersed over the snowy soil.

"Now the duel begins," Alek said solemnly and strode away, adjusting the scope on his Dragunov. "You have until the count of ten, so you better make the most of it."

It didn't matter. He could count to one thousand, and the bullet would reach Sidney even at the world's end. He would never miss.

"Run!" Sidney pulled Frank down the hillside, and both slid to the bottom.

"One, two, three..." Alek started the count, reloading the chamber of his rifle.

"Come on!" Sidney hurried with Frank through the forest.

"...ten," Alek finally said, and in complete calmness, he came close to the cliff and raised his left foot over a bulging rock. He rested his left elbow on his knee to support his rifle. Alek aimed downhill, with his right eye on the scope, observing Sidney through the eye that could reveal the truth and lies harbored in the hearts of men.

"Keep going, and don't stop no matter what," Sidney ordered, looking behind as he pushed Frank in front of him, to cover him from the eyesight of Alek.

"*Uvidimsya*," Alek whispered and closed his left eye and held his breath.

The cold snow extinguished the torch on the ground beside him.

Then Alek pulled the trigger.

CHAPTER 19

IN THE INSTANT THE BULLET LEFT THE BARREL, everything paused. My heart froze, my lungs contracted, my body went rigid, the thoughts in my restless mind disconnected—all the vital functions of my being ceased. Every organ, every cell, every atom in me was focused on what was going to happen. I was watching the show in slow motion.

It's like in the movies, I thought naively, awed by the sensation I was experiencing. But then I saw her laughing. It wasn't my mind slowing the scene down; it was *her* doing. My mother was so intent on wanting me to watch Sidney's execution that she would make it last for an eternity.

Suddenly I felt claustrophobic. Being physically trapped, living the fractions of seconds as if they were minutes, was physically painful. Living the frustration of wanting to act, to scream, to cry in vain, when all you can do is watch as the life of the man you love is snatched away before your eyes is indescribable.

The bullet traveled over the static background, zigzagging through the trees. Sidney turned to meet his destiny like a convict before a firing squad. His arm, covered in dark dragon scales that grew out of the pores of his skin like plants, stretched until it shaped into a shield he held before him. His armor that had endured the fierce fires did little to protect him this time. The bullet pierced his plating effortlessly.

The corners of my mother's mouth slowly rose to her cheekbones as the bullet approached its ultimate destination.

One inch before reaching his heart, the bullet veered upward, flying toward his head.

My mother gasped in surprise as the bullet skimmed Sidney's face, blowing his hair back, before shooting straight into the night sky like a star.

Time resumed to normal speed, and my scream finally came out of my lungs.

"Sidneyyyyyy!"

Flabbergasted, Sidney glanced up the mountain, where Alek stood with his rifle across his shoulder. The northern wind carrying snowflakes blew his raincoat open, revealing his skeleton and his heart pumping inside. Solemn and victorious, Alek wore his hat, staring at Sidney with the eyes of a lion who pardons the life of a lamb.

Alek saved him? Why? Which truth about Sidney did Alek see through his scope that made him change his mind, even despite having to pay for his failure with his own soul? Could Sidney really be innocent?

Maybe that was the reason why the Four Mothers accepted the deal. The words of the First Mother came to my mind, "A mother can be judge and jury, but never executioner. And it's to an executioner that you need to prove yourself innocent."

Sidney needed to prove himself to Alek.

Then I remembered the last words of Sidney's father, Samael. "Only the astray can judge both good and wrong, because those that have been hurt know the taste of suffering."

Alek was Sidney's true judge.

But why would he let him live? Even with his heart exposed, the dark horseman was an enigma.

Amid such uncertainty, of something I was completely sure: I felt grateful to Alek for forgiving Sidney, even if that meant my mother would not be free.

My mother's right eyelid quivered unceasingly. "Only a fool tries to hide from darkness, because nobody can outrun his own shadow," she said with a gruff voice, and her features transformed into a vicious smile.

"S-Sidney!" Frank warned back in the projection, pointing with a trembling hand to the gloomy woods.

A hundred pairs of lidless, bloodshot eyes shone in the darkness. Cords of saliva hung from the teeth jutting out of their lipless mouths. From the bleached birches emerged the bone-white figures with sharp-nailed hands and wolves' paws. The creatures' howls reverberated as if they were underwater. A throb in the bump on my neck matched the rhythm of the rumbling drums in my ears. The Sheireils had awakened once again.

The nightmarish creatures pounced like chimpanzees after Frank, who watched, terrified.

Dragon scales covered Sidney's fist, forming a gauntlet with which he punched the muzzle of the leader of the pack.

"Run!" Sidney pushed Frank down the hill.

The wounded Sheireil carefully held his broken, dangling mandible between its sharp claws, but instead of nursing his wound, it pulled until its jaw tore apart. The bloody beast stared at Sidney and bellowed with rage-fueled pleasure. His flaky tongue came out, wiggling like a snake before attacking. The whole pack followed his lead.

Frank loped down the slope while Sidney deflected the blows of the beasts that surrounded him in an attempt to buy time for Frank to escape, but a clump of Sheireils defected from the herd after Frank. Even for Sidney, it was useless to try to fight a dauntless enemy when he was clearly outnumbered. Sidney dodged his adversaries and hurried through the woods after the beasts chasing Frank like rabid dogs. Sidney raced at top speed, but he could not catch them. Without stopping, he tore apart his rags, exposing his torso, where raven-black fur had grown, covering his entire body. His jaw deformed into a pointy snout. His extremities transformed into paws, and he growled and gnashed his jaws as a bear-sized wolf.

I saw that he had a V-shaped scar on his forehead. It was the same wolf of that marvelous sculpture back at the cascade. The wolf from the story that Sidney had told me.

Sidney was *Apenimon,* the *worthy of trust.*

With powerful strides, the wolf overran the Sheireils and nudged Frank from behind, swinging him up in the air with his snout. Frank flipped backward and landed on the wolf's back. He held onto the wolf's neck as they descended the mountain, eluding the trees.

"Good!" my mother said enthusiastically. "No true war was ever won by infantry, but by cavalry." She raised her hand, and the butler appeared from behind the throne, holding a small bugle that hardly fit his chubby fingers.

"*Heer* Queenliness has spoken!" the butler declared and played a military call.

The wolf galloped into a frosted canyon with ample advantage and veered right at full speed but halted abruptly, sliding on the frozen brook.

"What is happening?" Frank glanced back at the Sheireils up the hill, now far behind them.

The wolf growled with squinting eyes and bared his white fangs.

A faint quivering in the soil quickly escalated into a tremor. The tops of the birches before the sinuous canyon were tumbling down, one by one, an ominous force that advanced in a rampage.

It was the cavalry, but these were no horses.

They were centaurs, but not the dashing kind from fantasy novels. Hundreds of white centaurs, half horse, half Sheireil, rampaged down the valley, fully armed with sharp spears, longbows, and unsheathed swords.

The wolf turned around and withdrew from the rain of arrows, following the canyon, barely escaping the herd of chimpanzee-like Sheireils that descended the peak in hot pursuit, joining the ferocious stampede, climbing on the centaurs' backs like skilled riders.

"Run, you cowards!" my mother said, and the masked courtiers laughed, as if the feast of horrors were a comedy show.

"Mother, you can't do this! Stop!"

"I'll be the justice that the law couldn't deliver."

"But—"

"Have you really forgiven him? Have you forgotten his deceit? The humiliation that he chose another?"

The wound still hurt.

"Maia, this is the moment you reclaim what he stole from you: your confidence, your dignity, your pride. I'll make him repent for betraying you. I will make him crawl at your feet, begging for pardon."

The centaurs threw spears, which the wolf zigzagged to elude. The spears anchored on the ground, and Frank managed to snag one.

"Sidney, they are coming!" Frank turned around, riding the wolf backward to confront the enemy.

The Sheireils riding the centaurs swiftly got in range. The first beast jumped after the wolf with claws unleashed but was deflected by a swing of Frank's spear. The creature rolled over the soil and was crushed by the hooves of the centaurs, as if it were caught in a hungry garbage disposal.

A second Sheireil leaped after them, and Frank extended his spear, impaling the beast. The creature slid down the pole, snapping its mandibles like a wild piranha, trying to bite him. Frank screamed, fighting to divert the jaws, but the relentless monster sunk its claws in his shoulder.

"Frank!" I bawled, powerless.

All my life I had ached to have my mother with me, but I never imagined what she would be like.

I closed my eyes, and for the first time in years, I prayed to that mute God that had always ignored my call. I begged. Not for me this time, but for the people I loved.

I expected daunting silence, but thunder crashed.

I opened my eyes and saw a bright beam of light cross through the centaurs until it reached the Sheireil fighting Frank and blew it away into dust.

A whistle echoed through the canyon, and from the gloomy forest emerged a black steed that galloped over the canyon's shoulder.

It was Alek, riding Empress.

Our cavalry has arrived. My heart rejoiced.

Alek was welcomed by the arrows of the Sheireils, and he retaliated with his Dragunov. The shining bullets followed convoluted paths, killing at least a hundred Sheireils, which turned immediately into ashes. Two centaurs lined up alongside the wolf and lashed out against Frank, knocking him off. Before Sidney could react, the beasts plunged their spears into his flanks.

"No!" I cried, seeing the wolf yowling in pain.

Sidney was trapped between the two, caught by their spears, forcing him to keep pace, or his entrails would be sliced open.

Frank rolled amid the hooves of the violent stampede. Alek noticed him in distress through his scope and pulled the trigger, but the rifle's chamber was empty, and there was no time for reloading.

Alek hauled the bridle. "Come on, girl!"

Empress descended the slope of the canyon and clashed with

the stream of centaurs. Alek forced his way through them, using his Dragunov to parry the attack of their swords, and drew his knife to cut limbs and throats. He aligned Empress's trajectory to intercept Frank a hundred yards ahead.

A centaur attacked Alek's right flank with a powerful blow of its sword, but he contained the hit, trapping the blade between his rifle and knife. Alek tussled back and forth with the ugly beast, balancing on Empress, keeping an eye ahead.

A centaur rammed into Frank, who vanished from Alek's sight.

A Sheireil riding on a centaur approached Empress's left flank and exploited Alek's distraction to thrust a pike into his side, across his ribcage.

Alek released a cry that competed with the uproarious laughter of my mother.

The Sheireil pulled the pike, and the spearhead hooked between Alek's ribs, almost knocking him off of Empress. He could not counterattack; his arms were still trapped in the struggle with the centaur at the other side.

There was no time. I could see that they were about to pass Frank at any second.

In a spout of rage, Alek rear-kicked the centaur, burying his sharp spur in its leg, and then knocked it down with the rifle's butt. Frank became visible yards ahead, ducking on the ground. Alek elbowed the wooden pike, breaking it in two. He pulled the spearhead out of his rib cage and threw it against the Sheireil.

"Frank!" Alek leaned over the horse's side with arm extended. Frank grabbed his hand, and Alek pulled him onto Empress.

"Sidney is in trouble!" Frank said.

"I know, I know." Alek drove Empress out of the stampede and up through a small ridge to overtake the lead with a clear path.

"Brave and clever," my mother said, raising her hand. "Yet stupid in the end—if there is something that the night has in abundance, it's wings."

"*Heer* Queenliness has spoken!" The butler played his bugle.

Frank yelled as a Sheireil with demonic wings hooked its claws in his shoulders and pulled him high into the air with powerful wingbeats.

Alek tried to react but was surprised by the attack of another flying demon that grabbed his Dragunov and tugged, extending the chain and Alek's arm. Alek clung to the saddle's pommel to avoid being carried away.

The projection shifted back to Sidney. Despite his pain, the wolf charged against the legs of his captors, causing a major collision. The wounded wolf rose from the ground, searching with his pointy ears and glowing green eyes for Frank. Sidney scuttled against the unstoppable stampede, sidestepping between the centaurs, eluding their attacks. His paws climbed the stepped wall, and he reverted to his human shape. Sidney strode the last steps to the rim and jumped. His arms covered with scales, transforming into dragon wings, which he waved to propel himself up in pursuit of the demon carrying Frank.

Sidney maneuvered toward the Sheireil, aiming with the serrated edge of his wing. The Sheireil lunged with its spear. Both figures clashed in the face of the full moon. The Sheireil was split in half, but his spear managed to rip the part of Sidney's flank not covered in scales.

The three tumbled down.

Sidney maneuvered his wings and intercepted Frank, who held to his shoulders. They glided above the infested canyon of Sheireils furiously flinging spears and arrows. Sidney tried to elude the projectiles as he descended.

The canyon emptied into a frozen ocean. The agitated sea had been locked in an endless plain of ice. Broken masts and smashed prows bulging from the ice recounted the tragedies of wrecked ships.

Sidney landed on the solid sea waves and reshaped into a wolf, with Frank riding on his back. But the wolf was moving slower than before. Frank looked horrified as he saw his hands covered in Sidney's blood.

The shrieks of laughter brought me back to the ballroom. I was surrounded by derision, laughter behind the comfort of their masks. I could not watch a second more of my friends suffering for morbid entertainment. I had to do something.

"Please stop this carnage, Mother," I raised my dry voice, hoping to appease her anger. "I'm sorry. I failed you. I can't abide your wishes. I want to be with you, but not at the expense of their sacrifice. Please, please—*stop*."

Her grin vanished. "You promised me."

"Yes, and it kills me that I can't keep that promise."

"You have betrayed me. *You* above all—*my daughter*," she said despotically. "You are just like him. Just like your father."

"No, Mother, please. I love you and would do anything to take back the mistakes. But please, spare their lives!"

"There is only one thing for you to do, my dear," she said serenely. "Watch them suffer. Unleash all the teeth of darkness!"

The butler stepped forward to conjure a new monstrosity. I lurched forward, running to stop him from blowing his horn.

"Hold her!" my mother ordered, and two masked men restrained me.

"Let me go!" I kicked.

"Silence!" my mother proclaimed. "Maia, you are most ungrateful. But now you will learn to obey me." She pointed to the projection, and the shadow cast by the wolf on the frozen sea darkened and reshaped into a feminine figure with long hair, wielding what appeared to be a slim sword.

No, it was no shadow. It was a blurred specter that floated gracefully inside the thick ice like a hologram. The features sharpened, revealing its identity. It was her.

"How?" I asked in disbelief, seeing her unbound from the world of mirrors.

"How naive, my dear," my mother said. "The crystalline frozen sea acts as glass and the silver-stoned sea bottom as reflective coating, creating a humongous mirror, in which I can freely move. Your friends were not naive but stupid by choosing this place as battleground."

"Sidney, look down!" Frank warned him.

My mother grinned viciously and slashed with her blade, and a sharp stake of ice protruded through the floor in the path of the wolf. Sidney dodged it and sped up with great effort. She brandished her sword and pierced through the ice with the violent velocity of a machine gun. The wolf danced, evading the ice stakes that emerged at his feet until one finally hit on the target. The wolf howled as the stake pierced his stomach. Both Frank and Sidney fell to the ground and slid over the ice before crashing against the prow of a ship.

"Sidney!" I yelled in despair.

Frank rushed after the wolf, who was breathing heavily, with eyes closed.

"No, no, no, Sidney," Frank said in panic, pressing the wolf's stomach to stop the bleeding. "Please, you can't give up now," he said, bursting into tears.

The wolf licked Frank's hand and opened his eyes.

"Thank God." Frank hugged the wolf.

The hard ice trembled. The horizon was filled with the ravenous stampede of bawling creatures.

"Pl-please, you have to get up and escape!" Frank helped him up.

The fur retracted, and the wolf morphed back into Sidney. "I'm not leaving you here," Sidney answered hardly.

Frank shook his head. "I'm slowing you down."

"They will—" Sidney frowned.

"I cannot die, remember?" Frank pointed to the bullet holes in his cloak, which he'd received when he defended me on the train. "I have no soul. I'm just the empty shell of a man that craves to have the dreams of a human."

"But if you're here, that means you have a soul."

"No," Frank interrupted. "That just means that I was here to do my job. And I failed. You don't have to sacrifice for me anymore. I'm expendable. You must leave—it's the only way to save her."

"You are wrong. A soul is merely kindness. And you are—above all—*kind*, my friend." Sidney held Frank's head, and then he stood with difficulty.

"Now go."

Sidney assented and departed.

Frank glanced back to the horizon covered by Sheireils.

"Lo-love is bigger than the universe b-but magical enough to fit in a heartbeat," he said, squeezing his fists before charging against the stampede.

Stoic.

Heroic.

But above all—*kind.*

I closed my eyes and lowered my head, unable to watch Frank's suffering amid the shrieks of laughter infesting the ballroom.

"Watch," my mother ordered, and the masked men forced my eyes to witness the reflection.

There was a trail of bloody footprints on the ice. A host of trapped sailors illuminated by the moonlight were suspended under it. Their bodies had been preserved so splendidly that they seemed alive inside their ice coffin. The whole sea was a cemetery, but instead of crosses, each tomb was marked by emerging hands.

"You cannot run forever," my mother said to Sidney, floating around the sailors' corpses.

"I'll run until the end of the world if I have to."

"I'm afraid this is the end of the world." She fondled the face of a bearded seaman. "It's useless to resist the inevitable. Cease now, or you will only prolong your suffering."

Sidney plodded with his eyes set on the horizon, still radiating hope. "Never."

The hand of one of the sailors caught Sidney's foot, making him fall to the ground, face-to-face with a long-dead mariner. Suddenly, the eyes of the man moved inside the ice. Sidney knelt, startled.

"This frozen sea is no graveyard, but a prison," my mother explained to me. "Its prisoners were buried alive in a cage of translucent bars that torture them with the illusion of liberty within their sight. Men and women are kept awake to witness the sun rise and set, but the incoming second is equal to the previous. Their screams of suffering are eternally drowned in the petrified water. Screams not for freedom, but clamoring for an end. Any end would be kinder than being imprisoned in the *Mute Sea*."

"The Mute Sea," I repeated, with chills. The idea of being buried alive for an eternity was horrifying.

The sailor hadn't meant to attack Sidney. His hand signaled for help, compulsively tapping with his index finger on the ice. The eyes of the man silently pleaded to Sidney.

Alek was right.

These were the shores of Hell, and no flames burned hotter than those of the ice.

The figure of my mother emerged from the depths beneath the mariner. The eyes of the man contorted with despair, seeing her arms wrapping around him like an octopus, leaning her face against his.

"Poor, poor boy," she said, staring at Sidney. "Fight no more. Surrender to the unavoidable. Close your eyes and sleep deeply, then I will wake you on the sunrise of the third day."

Sidney gasped, with his hand suppressing the hemorrhage in his belly.

My mother extended her arms to him.

"I'll stop your suffering. All you have to do is call my name."

"My life is not in your hands," Sidney said with labored breathing. "It is only in my father's."

"Then… so be it," she said with a sepulchral voice.

An ice stake shaped like the tail of a scorpion rose behind Sidney and pierced his back.

"Noooooooooooooooooooooo!" I cried.

"Fear not, my child, he is right," my mother said, trying to comfort me. "I can't kill him. It's a pleasure denied to me."

The ice stake shoved Sidney down until his arms gave up and smashed his head against the ice.

"It is in my power to fulfill your deepest desires, and I will do it," she said, caressing Sidney's face. "Not because you deserve it. On the contrary, I'll give to you what you desire the most with the sole purpose of snatching it away later in the most painful way you can imagine, so torturous that you will implore your father to come and take your life."

My mother kissed Sidney's lips. She extended her arms, which turned into ice when they emerged on the surface, and twined them around Sidney's neck, pulling him down gently. Sidney submerged through the ice as if it were liquid. They sank into the depths of the Mute Sea until the darkness devoured both.

CHAPTER 20

I JERKED VIGOROUSLY, struggling to release my arms from my captors.

"H-how could you?" I demanded. My heart pumped wrath into my bloodstream. I ached to climb the steps up to that throne and… and… and… weep over my misfortune.

What else could I do?

"Release her," my mother ordered.

As soon as I was free, I broke down. I crawled to caress the marble tiles that had shown Sidney's face in the projection.

"How could you?" I sniffed. "Why is it that you hate me that much?"

"Hate?" My mother stood, shocked, and descended from the throne, followed by the floating mirror. "One day you'll understand that everything a mother does for her children is for love. And I love you, despite everything, Maia. Not being able to draw you away from him before he hurt you, it breaks my heart. Maia, I failed you. I'm deeply sorry."

"No. No. You are a liar. You conjured the Sheireils. You are evil!"

My mother looked at me abashed. "I have no control over them."

"You told the butler to call them!"

"Maia, when somebody knocks at your door and you choose to open, they are not intruders if you invite them in. Tonight, darkness knocked at your friends' doors, but only they are responsible for letting it in. Or is it that you already forgot?"

Forgot?

"Did you forget what happened back in Pahana Forest? Don't you remember your trooper friend shooting at the girl?"

"How do you know about that?" I said, remembering Kerr aiming at the crying girl in that stormy night, consumed with hate after the sudden disappearance of Private Lind. Sidney had warned me, "He must not kill the girl."

"Why do you ask questions you already have the answer to?" *The mirror*, I realized. My mother had observed me all this time using her power to visualize any place, like I had witnessed my friends through the projections on the reflections. "Maia, have you ever wondered what would have happened if instead of shooting the girl, your friend had cared for her?"

"But the girl was evil."

"Why?" my mother inquired, glowering. "For desperately crying for help during the rainy night? For bearing the scars of her suffering? For being of a different kind? What decides who is friend or foe, Maia? Good or bad?"

My iron-solid reasoning cracked.

"To offer a hand to someone in need is an act of kindness, even if it's a demon," my mother explained. "On the other hand, accepting the help of a demon in a moment of need is…"

"What?"

"Maia, when you arrived in this place, did you witness any demon dragging a chained soul to Hell?" I could remember nothing of the sort, and even Alek mentioned he had requested Sidney to take him to Hell. "The pilgrimage is a straight path for the righteous. No harm can happen to those who walk the path with lantern in hand. But for most, darkness is too alluring, and they go astray."

"But that is unfair. They are not entirely conscious, they are not awake," I said, trying to explain the dreamlike state of this place as described by Sidney.

"You are so naive, Maia." My mother laughed. "How do you think your paratrooper friend Kerr lost his life? In a trench in Normandy, fighting beside Lt. Lovelock? Let me reassure you, Kerr survived the war, but your friend Lind was not so lucky. During the bloody battle of Okinawa, Lind died consumed in an explosion before Kerr's eyes. Kerr had spared the life of a Japanese woman who turned out to be a suicide bomber. Kerr swore over Lind's body to kill them all, and the next time he faced a Japanese person, it was a little girl, crying for her mother below the rain, and—"

"Kerr killed that innocent girl." I completed my mother's phrase. "He shot her as he did in Pahana Forest."

"As it is above, so it is below," my mother said, making me remember Sidney's analogy of the interconnected worlds as the two sides of a coin. "Your friend felt hurt, and it was easier to respond with hate than with compassion. That night, darkness knocked, and he chose to open his heart to hatred and became a Sheireil. Poor children," she said with compassion. "They have to mutilate their eyelids to avoid slumber. They prefer to wander in a perpetual vigil, for their dreams are more frightening than their days, which they spend feeding from the sins of the sinners, because their own are not aliment enough. Those zombies are just scavenging for sanity in a world of madness."

"But then why did the Sheireils attack Sidney and Frank? They are not—"

"*Sinful?*" My mother's laugh erupted. "An infant could cross unharmed through an army of monsters. Innocents don't fear obscurity. And if they do, it's because they already know what dwells in the shadows, and they are innocents no more."

"How do you know everything about them? How do you know what Kerr and Lind did in life and how they died?" *Could her mirror also allow her to peek into the waking world?*

"I listen to the whispers from the graveyard," my mother said. "Every time Kerr digs himself out of his grave, feeling remorseful, he departs from the city of Betheli in search of his friend and wanders through Pahana Forest until he finds him. *Pahana* means Lost White Brother, and that is what those soldiers find in that place. A lost brother."

I remembered my experience in the forest, and it made me shudder—all those whispers.

"But no matter which path your friend Kerr takes, he will invariably face the girl, and every time, he makes the same choice and dies as you witnessed. Then, seven eclipses after, he will rise again from his grave, asphyxiated by the remorse, and will cry endlessly for forgiveness at his friend's tomb, over and over again."

So that was the reason I'd found Mr. Crimson again in the graveyard, even after I saw him die. Apparently, everybody came back to life in the cemetery—if I could call it *life*, what they experienced here. This place was an endless cycle of punishment, a—

"*Purgatory*. It's the word you seek," my mother said, trespassing into my thoughts. "But on the road for atonement, everyone is their own punisher. No, Maia, I don't control the Sheireils. But I know who is responsible for bringing them here." She extended her finger and started drawing the silhouette of a man on the floor, creating a black-and-white animated impression of her words. "Who wanders the night, leaving a trail of flesh-crumbs as bait for luring the monsters? Who has hoisted high the flag of vengeance against your loved one? Who, above all, needs sanity to atone for his own sins?"

The drawing slowly became clear.

"Alek." I had nearly forgotten about him. "No! He forgave Sidney."

"He is a schemer, Maia. You know he wanted this from the very beginning."

"You are lying!"

"Why would I lie?" The mirror floated around me, scrutinizing me with piercing eyes. "Or tell me, who led you into the cabin in the woods? Who kidnapped you and brought you before the Watchers? Who led your beloved to the doorstep of Hell, abandoning him to his fate, when he had the power to save him from such agony?"

I could not answer her questions without feeling overwhelmed by asphyxiating doubts.

"Yes, he connived against us," my mother said with a euphonious voice. "Alek is the one to blame. He is the traitor. And now he flees through the fireflies' forest, believing that his rapid horse will help him escape judgment. But fear not, my dear, he shall face punishment."

The drawing on the floor came alive, displaying Empress escaping through the brightened woods. The birches' foliage was composed of millions of fireflies that twinkled like stars. The snow had melted into an inch-deep pool of water that covered the entire field like an enormous mirror. It was as if Empress were galloping through the constellations. After them, the Sheireils were in hot pursuit, bobbing like monkeys from branch to branch at the top of the birches. Alek took the opportunity to reload his Dragunov with the remaining bullets on his belt.

He aimed his rifle ahead and squeezed the trigger three times. The bullets turned back, maneuvering through the woods and cutting down the beasts behind.

"Come on, girl," Alek ordered, and Empress galloped faster.

The shallow waters of the pond wavered. The surface tension broke, and a gleaming blade emerged like the dorsal fin of a shark, chasing Empress. It was a slim sword wielded by a hand made from water. The hand released a powerful blow aiming at Empress's legs, but a silver dot came out from the depths of the woods toward the attacker. The hand recoiled and swung the blade, cutting Alek's bullet in half.

"Did you think it would be that easy?" Alek said, halting the horse and looking back. "Two bullets got rid of the minions. The remaining was just promenading, killing time, expecting you."

On the reflection of the blade, a section of my mother's face grinned. "I'm flattered." The sword submerged, and the image of my mother appeared on the water's surface, floating beside Empress. "But it's getting dark, and soon you will be devoured by a night that will see no dawn."

Behind them, the fireflies turned off, leaving behind total darkness.

"You forget that I'm he who frightens the night!" Alek said imperiously and tipped the brim of his hat. "Now, come get me!" He clenched Empress with his heels.

"You fool."

The steed galloped with the speed of a cheetah, leaving my mother's image behind.

Alek aimed his Dragunov, using the scope to track her reflection. When he pulled the trigger, the shining bullet traveled, furrowing on the water's surface and around the field like a missile chasing a jet fighter. The bullet continued until it reached my mother, who deflected it with a swing of her sword.

She waved her hand, and from the birches, a swarm of fireflies descended and attacked Alek, who crossed his arms in front of him to shield himself. My mother seized the opportunity, disappearing and reappearing in their path, and retaliated with a blow of her sword.

Empress jumped in time to evade the sharp blade. Alek fired aimlessly in midair, but my mother vanished before the bullet could reach her, smashing on the empty ground.

"What a mare," she said, floating gracefully beside the two. "It would be a shame if something terrible happened to her."

"Don't you dare," Alek threatened, adjusting the scope. "You can't hide from me."

"We'll see." My mother laughed viciously before disappearing.

Alek tracked her movements around the horizon using his scope. His index finger fastened on the trigger and prepared to shoot, but then he froze. He pulled his pale, astonished face away from the scope as if he had seen a ghost. From the reflection in Empress's right eye, the sword popped up like a jack-in-the-box and stabbed Alek in the chest.

"No!" I bawled.

My mother had used the reflective surface of Empress's eye to materialize the sword. She could literally transform any reflective surface into a portal. Shooting at her would mean blowing Empress's eye out.

"You prefer to lose your soul rather than sacrifice the eye of your horse?" my mother asked, stirring the blade inside his rib cage while Alek's hand squeezed the blade, trying to stop it. "What a shame to see how love has made you predictable."

My mother pulled out the bloodstained sword. Threaded at the tip of the blade was a creased family photo. It portrayed Alek embracing his two children in the cornfields of the farm he had described to me. "And this was your pathetic attempt to save him? *Mediocre.*"

"I'm not your puppet," Alek said, snatching the photo from the sword.

"No, you are my hound, and in the same way I released your chain, I can pull it back." My mother's reflection appeared on his Dragunov and pulled the rifle to the ground, with Alek chained to it. He fell off the saddle but hung with his boot hooked in the stirrup, scuffing over the ground, splashing on the water. But Empress continued galloping—it was more dangerous to stop, with my mother's reflection tailing him.

"There is only one punishment for a dog that bites the hand that feeds him," my mother said. "But fear not. I'm merciful, and your cage of woe misses you." Everybody in the ballroom laughed.

Alek's bony left hand clung to the girth of the saddle, and he started climbing back up with superhuman effort. He tugged his shackle, curling his right arm against the thumping force tensing the chain. His other hand attempted to reach the revolver at his waist, but it was just off of his fingertips.

His fingers fastening the girth unrolled, revealing the creased photo of his family. Then, finally, I understood that it was not revenge that fueled him—it was devotion.

It didn't matter how hopeless his situation could be, Alek would never give up.

Alek's desire to avenge his son had been harnessed by the evil interests of someone who took him from Tartarus, chaining him to the Eye of Truth and bestowing the powers of the Spear of Destiny in exchange for killing Sidney. *"I was entrusted with both with the sole purpose of carrying out my mission,"* Alek had said to the First Mother during the trial.

Someone incapable of doing it by herself. *"I can't kill him. It's a pleasure denied to me,"* my mother said when I begged for Sidney's life.

Someone who would benefit from eradicating the last vestige of a curse that kept the Watchers imprisoned. *"I live trapped in this ethereal prison because of him, because of Vandella,"* she'd said back at the cabin in the woods.

Someone who was an accuser, a persecutor, and a seducer.

The evidence was conclusive. And as hard as it was, I had to admit it.

I had been fooled once again.

Then I dared to do the unimaginable.

If she could come out, maybe I could go in. I submerged my hand inside the projection, warping the reality like water, and my hand materialized on the other side under the astonished looks of the partygoers. I unsheathed Alek's revolver and deposited it in his hand. He pulled the trigger, and the bullet traveled across the portal to the ballroom and went straight to the vacant throne.

Blood sprinkled out of thin air.

In the reflection on the floor, I saw my mother's cheek cut from the corner of her lip to her ear. She looked appalled as she held up her trembling fingers, stained in crimson.

She bawled, but no sound was heard.

Then the sky thundered.

I glanced through the dome, where a maelstrom stretched its

nebulous tentacles across the sky, releasing gusts of wind that broke all the windows, carrying the screams of my mother, flooding the entire place with strident howling.

I ducked to shield myself from the shattered glass and covered my ears from the deafening sound of the *Banshee*. But chips of glass didn't fall; they floated before hitting the ground and then blew back up, pulled by the maelstrom in the sky.

"How could you, after all I have done for you?" she asked, nursing her wound.

I stood up. "What have you done? All this?" I waved my hands, signalizing my surroundings, my golden velvet dream. "You have done nothing." I pulled my jewels off, undid my headdress, and tore off the hoop skirt of my dress, dumping everything to the floor. "I don't want any of this. You can have it."

"How dare you say that to your mother!"

"No—no. You are not my mother. My *mother* is sitting beside my bed at the hospital."

"Watching you die, one sense at a time."

"I don't care if I die tomorrow, as long as I use my last breath fighting for who I love."

Her expression turned severe. She uncovered her cheek, and sticking out her flimsy forked tongue like a snake, she licked her wound up to her ear and back.

"So be it," she said with a distinct voice—somehow both masculine and feminine—that somehow came from every direction.

Her image withdrew from the realm of the mirrors and materialized before my eyes in flesh and bone. I didn't understand how it was possible—Sidney was still alive. She tramped down the throne toward me. I stepped back, looking around for an escape route, but wherever I looked, she was in front of me, walking, getting closer with each step, staring at me with her piercing eyes.

Her image superimposed over the surrounding crowd, and I realized she had inhabited the reflection of my eyes, just like she'd done with Empress. I closed my eyes, but in the blackness, she continued to approach me.

She passed her deformed hand in front of me and held my face. I wanted to yell, but she shushed me. I wished to gouge my eyes out to stop her. It petrified me.

She was fear embodied. She was absolute terror.

"Maia!" Her image transfigured into Jase's.

It was him, staring at me with the luminous eyes that adorned his fine-featured face. It was him wearing his football jacket.

"Don't you love me?" He ran his thumb over my lips.

I lost my breath.

"Don't you want to be with me?" Jase squeezed me against his chest in a cocoon of safety and confidence. "Maia, I love you." Those were the words I had always wished to hear. "Please don't go. Stay with me and I'll love you forever."

But those were not Jase's words. It was a deceit. A deceit perpetrated by my own mind.

No.

This was the demon I'd created, feeding it with my fears.

"No! I was wrong. Jase doesn't love me, and neither does Sidney, and—*it's okay*. All that matters for me is that I loved fiercely, even if it was brief. Now get out of my head!" I shoved him away. "I have a promise to keep. I have an appointment with Death!"

"You coward," Jase said as his twisted voice receded.

"I'm not running. I'm not ashamed of it anymore. All of this has showed me what really is important: the people that I love. And I'll sacrifice myself for them."

Jase's image melted grotesquely, and I opened my eyes back to reality.

"Grab her!" my mother ordered, and a masked man held me from behind.

"Let me go!" I struggled until I elbowed his jaw, partially breaking his mask. Beneath the facade, his lidless eyes looked at me with fury, and his lipless mouth revealed sharp teeth. He growled and dumped me on the floor. The mask fell entirely, revealing his true nature—he was a Sheireil. I shivered, realizing that all this time I'd been surrounded by a thousand Sheireils. I'd even danced with them.

The beast raised his heavy hands, but I rolled aside in time to elude his fists as they shattered the tiles. The Sheireil yowled, covering his eyes in suffering.

The reflection! He saw his reflection on the marble floor! I remembered Sidney's words back in the mirror's labyrinth: *"Sheireils can't bear to contemplate their reflection."* That was the reason why they had to wear the masks.

Even though the entire floor was an immense mirror, it was impossible for me to expose the ghastly faces of every single one.

They came after me, growling, jerking. I crawled backward in an attempt to escape, but I knew my effort was futile. I would reach the stairs of the throne soon, where a greater evil waited for me, laughing, delighted with the macabre entertainment.

But then a hand caught my wrist.

It was Alek's bony hand, reaching out of the projection. A Sheireil charged after me, but Alek dragged me into the reflection just in time to dodge the attack of the monster.

I spaghettified inside a kaleidoscopic tunnel that twisted in on itself. Something trapped my leg during my passage—it was *her* following me. Her sword severed my leg, which had been stretched paper thin. After a second that felt like an eternity, I crossed to the other side, coming out of the water's reflection into the fireflies' forest, where Alek, riding Empress at full speed, propelled me up over the saddle.

"Are you okay?" he asked me, helping me sit behind him.

I was about to answer, but the pain from my leg overcame me. My white bloomers were cut from my knee down to my calf and stained with my blood.

"Now you understand there is no such thing as escape, my dear. We are bonded together—*forever*," she said, floating alongside Empress. Alek shot his revolver, but she disappeared before the bullet hit the water.

I caught my breath. "I'll be fine," I said, wishing it were true. "Are you ok?"

He jolted his shackle. The gilded chain was broken, but there was no sign of his Dragunov.

I fastened my arms around the hollow raincoat. "I'm sorry," I whispered.

"Suffering is nothing to be ashamed of."

"I wish I were like you."

"You are like me," he said, peeking over his shoulder. "A survivor."

"No. I'm a fool. I believed in her and messed everything up. She killed Frank and captured Sidney…" I fought my tears. "Now I have to save him and my grandmother too. And I don't know where to start."

"You have to get to Touriel."

"But what about Sidney—"

"Trust me for once in your life, kid."

He was right. All this time I had distrusted him. But among the crazy people in this mad world, he seemed to be the sanest of all.

"Hold on, *ditya*." Alek hauled the reins. "We need to get out of this place before her next attack."

Empress sped up, but the bright forest appeared endless. I searched for the reflective surfaces I had on me—the remaining pins on my hair, a pearled bracelet—and dumped everything. But my efforts would be meaningless until we were able to escape this waterlogged forest.

Alek halted Empress suddenly.

"Why are you stopping?" I asked, but he hushed me.

Everything was dead quiet. Nobody was in sight. No trace of her. But that was not comforting. She could be anywhere and everywhere at the same time. The water level increased a few inches with a tide that carried a thick mist. The fireflies composing the foliage started fluttering, and suddenly everything went dark.

"Alek, what happened?" I could see nothing, not even Alek sitting ahead of me.

"Shhhhhhhhhhh, silence."

I heard a faint rattle, as if somebody was winding up a crank. I glanced up, hoping to see at least the faint light of the starts percolating through the foliage, but there were none. Not even the slightest shade of gray.

Then the tune of a music box started to play, but I could not identify the direction from where it was coming.

The melody was soft and sad. It made me remember a music box my gran owned when I was a child. It was a wooden box with a lid at the top that hid a mirrored surface where a small ballerina made of resin danced around to the tune of the music. It was so hypnotic and magical for me at that short age that I even thought the doll was alive, until the day it fell from my hands and broke, revealing the magnet inside.

"For the living, Death is an enigma." Her disembodied voice echoed as if we were inside a cavern. "It's uncertain what is expecting you at the other side. But one thing is for sure. You'll have to confront the faces of all those you murdered."

"Hold tight to me," Alek instructed.

A blinding light shone ahead of us as if it were the exit of the cave, casting the bar-shaped shadows of the birches.

"Maia, has Alek told you about his little secrets?"

As my eyes adapted to the light, I realized with terror that we were not alone in the forest anymore. We were surrounded by people hanging from the trees, arms extended as if they were crucified, heads hanging over their chests, but instead of nails, silky thread held them from branches as if they were puppets. Their lower halves were wrapped in a cocoon, as if they were larvae in a pupal state.

The man in the cocoon closest to us raised his head. His face was bluish, as if he were frozen. He opened his eyes and mouth, which were sewn with silky threads like old cloth that had been mended. The man stared at Alek, and his mouth erupted with words without moving his lips or tongue, as if the voice were coming from his entrails.

"*Dzhumla*," he said with a throaty voice. "*Dzhang Atshawúnkey*."

"What?" I said, unable to understand a word.

"It's *Pashto*," Alek said nonchalantly. He elaborated when he noticed my confusion, "It's a language spoken in Afghanistan."

"What did he say?" I asked, but Alek was lost in his thoughts. "Alek!" I shook him. "What did he say? Did you kill him? Did you kill all these people?" I said, horrified, looking at the tens of cocoons hanging as far as the darkness surrounding us allowed me to see.

"*Sentence, Warmonger*, were his words," Alek said.

Sentence? And I remembered *Sentenza*, Alek's nickname during his years in the army.

Alek pulled Empress's reins, and she started cantering in the direction of the light. As we progressed, the people trapped in the cocoons woke up and started shouting at us. From all the gibberish I could not understand, I recognized only a few in English.

"You monster," screamed a man. "Murder," said another. "Please, don't kill me!" begged a frightened man. It was like a parade, but Alek didn't seem bothered. He had visited Hell, after all.

Empress advanced, but the light appeared to be always at the same distance.

"Have you forgotten them?" my mother asked. "Don't you recognize their faces?"

"I've told you. I recognize only one," Alek said solemnly. "Every time I pulled the trigger, I saw only one."

Her maniacal laugh echoed as if we were in a tunnel.

"Aleksandr," a male voice said behind us, and Alek halted Empress. He was a middle-aged man, but his gray hair made him seem older. He was trapped in a cocoon like the others, but his eyes and mouth were not sewn with silk threads. "Aleksandr, my son!" he said, speaking with joy.

"Is he your father?" I remembered the heartbreaking story he'd shared with Sidney.

Alek looked at me askance and dismounted.

"Alek, wait!"

Alek raised his hand, signaling for me to stop, but I was worried about what could happen. I feared the worst.

"Aleksandr, son, have you come to rescue me?" Alek's father said with relief, but Alek stared at him, unmoved. "This is so painful. I can't hold on any longer. I'm so tired. I just want to rest, but I can't fall asleep… or *they* will come for me… They are ruthless," he said with wide, unblinking eyes, as if creatures were waiting for his eyes to close. "Please take me away."

"There is no *they*. It's only you." Alek finally broke his silence. "And that was the problem. There was always only you. Neither my mother nor sister nor my brothers. You cared only for yourself." Alek chuckled. "But do you have the slightest idea of how hard it was for me? I not only lost my father but also my mother, because I killed the man she stupidly loved," Alek shouted. "Even when I did what was right."

"Oh, Aleksandr, my son, I didn't know—"

Alek's hand clutched his father's throat. "Do you think it was easy for me to explain to Kiska what you did to her? And not having something to say when she asked *why*?" Alek squeezed, strangling his father, who looked at him with bulging eyes.

I didn't know what to do. If I should intervene.

Finally, Alek's trembling hand released his father's throat, and he turned away.

"No! Please, release me from this suffering!" Alek's father babbled, trying to catch his breath. "They are coming, I can hear them."

And he was right. Something was coming. I could hear the splashes of horses' hooves galloping in the distance. *Could it be the centaurs?* My hand reached for the bump on my neck, but there was no tingling. They were not Sheireils. "Alek, we need to go!"

But instead of listening to me, Alek confronted his father. "Did you release my sister when I begged?"

All the cocoons hanging around us wriggled, squeezing the

hosts inside. Their heads shook violently, and blood started dripping from the tails. The dripping quickly escalated to a continuous stream that dyed the shallow pool crimson.

"Alek, we need to go now!"

But it was too late. I heard a swoosh, and a spear flew at us at high speed and landed in Alek's chest, piercing through his rib cage and protruding from his back.

"Alek!" I screamed in panic, and Empress neighed and reared, almost dropping me.

Alek fell backward, and the spear anchored in the mud, leaving him impaled, arched halfway to the ground. Alek tried to reach his revolver, but an arrow hit his hand, and it fell from his grasp.

A chariot rolled in, pulled by two white horses, driven by a man in copper armor who carefully aimed at Alek with bow and arrow.

"You don't mind having a rematch against Achilles, right, Alek?" my mother's voice said enthusiastically. "The mob still clamors your name at the arena."

Arena? So the story told by Alek was true: he'd competed against Achilles and his immortal horses, Balius and Xanthus, and he'd won.

"They still clamor my name because they still fear me, and you should too," Alek said, and with a swift movement of his hand, he reached for his knife and threw it at Achilles, who tilted his head to evade it. Achilles's face, framed by the T-shaped visor of his helmet, turned enraged, and he shot an arrow at Alek's head, but Alek blocked it using his arm. The sharp tip of the arrow stopped an inch before Alek's eye, trapped between his forearm's bones.

Achilles pulled the reins of the chariot, heading toward Alek, driving it to pass by his side so that the spinning blade attached to the wheels would cut him through. Alek propelled himself using his feet and pivoted, using the anchored spear to avoid the blade. Alek used his hands to flip and fell to his knees on the ground. With mobility restricted by the spear shaft still lodged in his chest, Alek crawled on all fours to grab his revolver as Achilles turned around his chariot with difficulty, maneuvering through the birches and cocoons.

Alek ran toward me, removing the spear from his chest. "Maia, ride!" He whistled, and Empress ran off at a speed to allow him to catch us.

I held on to the saddle's pommel and turned back. "Alek, he is coming!" Achilles loaded his bow with three arrows at the same time and shot, hitting Alek's back, thigh, and calf.

Alek kept moving, shooting his revolver. The bullet tracked its target and perforated Achilles's chest, erupting at his back, leaving a hole from side to side. Achilles clutched the reins to prevent himself from falling back. He looked at his wound, which closed as his skin regenerated. Then he smirked at me.

"Move forward!" Alek instructed me to make room for him as he ran parallel to Empress. But when Alek prepared to jump, Achilles grabbed a spear from the arsenal in his chariot.

"Wait—" I was unable to finish as the spear burst through his coat. Alek lost his footing and grabbed my wounded foot to keep his balance. I was able to fasten myself to the saddle to hold Alek's weight as he was being dragged by Empress.

A discharge of pain advanced through my spine and to my head. Balius and Xanthus were matching Empress, and the chariot's wheel blade was getting dangerously close to Alek's feet.

"Alek, aim at his heel!" I babbled amid my pain, remembering Achilles's weak spot.

Alek extended his arm, aiming at the carriage, and pressed the trigger. The bullet passed effortlessly through the wooden carriage and blew off Achilles's leg, which spun in the air.

"It's not real!" I said, startled, realizing it was a copper-made prosthetic leg.

"Did you think that Achilles would fall so easily by the same trick twice?" My mother laughed out loud. "He sawed off his foot himself!"

We were *doomed.*

Achilles prepared to impale Alek with his spear, but Alek anticipated the movement with a shot of his revolver. This time the bullet zigzagged above us, cutting the silk threads of cocoons hanging from the branches. The cocoons fell, knocking Achilles off his chariot, which flipped over, pulling Balius and Xanthus down.

Just when I thought we had escaped, I turned ahead and collided against a cocoon. Everything rotated 360 degrees, until my head hit the waterlogged ground.

Moments later, I barely opened my eyes through the bloodied water and saw the limping silhouette of Achilles heading toward Alek, and I drifted unconscious.

CHAPTER 21

I AWOKE SOAKED IN A DARK RED PUDDLE. Alek was still standing, but he was pinned with spears and arrows from side to side of his ribs like a voodoo doll. Exhausted, he caught his breath and started extracting them one by one.

"Alek!" I tried to stand, but my wounded leg failed.

"Don't move," he gasped, picking up his damp hat from a pool and hobbling to me, still carrying weapons nailed in his chest. "I'm sorry."

"I'm fine, it doesn't hurt anymore," I said.

"That doesn't mean you're not hurt. You are losing your sense of touch." I had forgotten about my degradative condition. More than three days had passed since I'd crossed abroad. "You have less than two days before everything goes dark."

That meant I had just one more day to finish my mission, otherwise my sacrifice would be lost, and my gran would die.

"I can't make it ten steps ahead like this." I could hardly limp.

"You'll have to." Alek cut a strip from my bloomers and tied it tight around my thigh to stop the bleeding.

"Alek, what happened? Where is Achilles? Is he dead?"

"Not quite." Alek glanced to where Achilles was hanging from a tree with a noose of silk thread around his neck. Choking, but not dying. "He can't die, but neither can he cut the line. The only option to free himself is chopping off his own head."

Empress neighed, heading toward us.

"She's back!" I said, glad to see her safe.

"A loyal steed will gallop through the valley of death, race against the devil, and descend into the ardent depths of Hell for its master," Alek said, caressing her head. "Now, up." He helped me to climb up the saddle, but I could not sit properly. "Can you ride?" I shook my head. I could not straighten my back, but I could not tell if a bone was broken.

"But I can hold on to you—I don't bite, I promise." I painfully laughed at my misfortune.

Alek looked away, and I understood that he wasn't planning on coming with me.

"I don't even know how to ride," I protested while he collected two spears.

"She will take you to the gates of Touriel. If they are closed, follow the road by the cliff; there is an entrance on the seaside." He tied a spear on each side of the saddle.

"No—no," I said with watery eyes. "I won't leave without you."

"Battle is not over yet, girl."

From one pool, a feminine figure emerged, born out of the blood.

"We have to run."

"No, you have to run," he said, binding me to the spears so I would not fall. "My trail ends here."

"But you can't stay, she'll kill you."

Alek smiled.

"You still have to avenge your son," I said, trying to appeal to his fatherhood.

Alek untightened his fist, showing the creased photo he had held during the entire fight. "I'm counting on you for that."

"What? I don't know him!"

"But you will," he said with bright hope in his eyes.

"What are you talking about?"

"I'm sorry, Maia, for keeping the truth from you all this time." Alek delved into the saddlebags and took out the small radio he'd used in the cabin. "It was the only way."

"Wha—" I recalled his words back at the bonfire: *So you have to put up a scarecrow. The crows cannot gouge his eyes out, cut his tongue, or feed from his entrails. A man that patiently waits below sun and rain, restless from dawn to dusk. What crows fear the most is a man without a soul.*

"Lovelock, do you hear me? Over," he messaged, but there was no answer. "I'm sending Maia over. So, I ask you—I beg you," he corrected, "protect her."

I sobbed, hearing his words.

"I'm counting on you, Lovelock. Next time, I promise we will toast on bourbon—*tovarishch*." Then he dropped the radio, and it sank in the reddish mud.

"Heartbreaking." The blood-born woman opened her eyes—it was her. "I'm sorry to interrupt such a tender moment, but the hunt is over."

"Leave now, girl!"

"I will not abandon you!"

"Don't worry, my dear," she said. "I'll find you." She winked at me.

Alek drew his revolver. "There is still one bullet left."

"One bullet?" she mocked with her dual voice.

"It's all I need to make you pay for what you did to her." Alek squinted.

"Who do you think you are to threaten *me*?"

"I'm the one who frightens the night!"

"And I'm the light that gives birth to the darkness. I'm the shadow of the sun. I'm who whispers in the silence. I'm knowledge. I'm everything you will ever feel and desire. No man can frighten me, because I'm terror. You dared to betray me and missed pitifully," she said, licking the wound on her cheek.

"I didn't miss, because I wasn't aiming at you. I aimed at your pride." Alek tipped the brim of his hat.

"You missed against Vandella. You failed to deliver as stipulated in the contract. But you are a chained dog, and your chain still hangs from my hand. I can pull it to claim your soul once more."

Bloody chains and shackles emerged from the puddle, trapping Alek's extremities.

"I didn't miss. My bullet didn't kill him tonight, it's true, but it will—*eventually*. After traveling the cosmos, at the end of the times, one night it will return and pierce his heart. One day. But not today. He is still needed. All nights are the same for a timeless, remember? I fulfilled my contract with you," he declared, and the chains melted, setting him free.

She observed him, exasperated.

"My soul doesn't belong to me anymore, but it doesn't belong to you either. There is a pledge to be claimed by the new owners, and I'm only one bullet away. So come here!" Alek goaded. "I will leave this existence with an ear-to-ear grin, knowing that legends will be told for the centuries to come about the man who cheated the hidden one, the one who walks among snakes, *Sathariel,* the Seventeenth Watcher."

Was she a Watcher? A Fallen?

Sathariel smiled viciously. "Maia, dear, why do you look so surprised?"

I remembered what Sidney had said back in Betheli's square. *"You can't trust appearances here."*

"Why do you use the likeness of my mother?" I demanded. "Where is she?"

"Because this is what you desire the most, don't you? To be reunited with your mother, to be loved by her. And I'm here to fulfill your desires, because above all, I'm love."

"You are not love, you are hate incarnate!"

"I'm solely what the *Will* wanted me to be." Sathariel extended her hands, and wings grew from her back, not made of blood—it was feathered angel wings. "After the most beautiful among the creations had been completed, the *Will* whispered, 'Love,' but not even the *Will* could avoid craving me, the most perfect being. Fearful, the *Will* also whispered, 'Hate,' in an attempt to rectify the mistake, believing that feeling aversion for me would counteract the effect.

"It was me who taught my fellow angels the meaning of love, and they ended up falling for the mortals, because that was the purpose entrusted to me by the *Will,* right?" Sathariel's face turned serious. "But the *Will,* enraged with me, stopped whispering to me and finally banished me." The blood forming her body started boiling as her hatred increased. "The *Will* punished me with this hollow existence, believing I would remain unseen beneath the reality. But little the *Will* knew, mortals would follow the steps of Narcissus and would look at their reflection over the pond and ask *why.*" Sathariel morphed her face into a younger version of me, bald from the chemotherapy, as I saw myself in the hospital mirror years ago. "And I'll always be there to answer the questions the *Will* would never return."

"Stop!!" I yelled, my mind flooded with all the unpleasant memories.

"Now you finally understand, Maia, why we'll always be together? Every time your heart rushes with craving or aversion, I'll be there with you." Sathariel smiled. "So you'd better choose well: Love me, and I'll love you in return. Hate me… and—"

"Let her alone," Alek said, pointing at her. "It's me who you are fighting." He pulled back the hammer of his revolver. "Now crawl here like the snake you are."

Sathariel morphed her face into that of Alek's father. "How considerate, little son of a bitch," Sathariel said with a Machiavellian smile.

Alek shot his revolver, but Sathariel's chest opened, creating a passage from side to side, allowing the bullet to pass through without causing harm.

"Predictable, as always," Sathariel said. "Now, come back under my dominion!" Sathariel's angel wings extended, plucking themselves, revealing a frame comprising long spider legs. The spider legs clasped around Alek, the tips burying in Alek's bones.

"Alek!" I screamed, terrified, but instead of suffering, Alek smiled, as if he were enjoying it.

"I told you, there is a pledge to be claimed. Did you forget?"

The loud sound of a gong resounded.

"The last bullet has been shot," the voice of the Third Mother echoed through the forest. "It's time for the harvest."

"It's time for you, stranger, to fulfill the pact and pay the price," the voice of the First Mother informed, and the bones of Alek's rib cage started to pulverize and floated away, carried by an unseen wind. Alek was paying the price for exchanging his soul to have the right to kill Sidney, but he was also being freed from Sathariel's dominion.

"Noooooooooooooooooooooooo!" Sathariel shrieked.

"I would love to stay to chat, but I'm needed elsewhere." Alek tipped the brim of his hat. "Maybe next time, *Suka*." He winked at Sathariel.

"I'll find you and drag you back to your prison of woe where you belong."

Before fading away, Alek turned to me. "Go save your grandmother, *ditya*." He whistled, and Empress took me away.

"Alek!" I gazed behind with effort, and the last thing I saw was

Alek's empty clothes falling on the puddle.
The bells tolled, and the light at the end of the tunnel vanished.

CHAPTER 22

MY TIREDNESS OVERCAME ME, forcing me into a cyclic slumber. It was the same dream over and over. My golden velvet *nightmare*.

I unjammed the door and escaped from the ballroom to the terrace, where Sidney strolled gallantly at the world's end. I hurried, calling after him, my voice drowning in tears. With each step, the floor tiles detached and floated, blown around by the hungry maelstrom.

After an agonized wait, my fingers finally reached his hand, and Sidney turned around, welcoming me in his cozy arms.

"I'm sorry," I said, losing my breath.

"Cry no more." His fingers collected the tears from my cheeks. "There is nothing to forgive." He wrapped his left arm around my waist and his right arm around my neck and held my face from behind, lifting my chin so our lips could meet.

We kissed, revolving like dancers, carried by a twister of debris.

Sidney floated away from my arms, pulled toward the sky upside down. Our lips were the last to be detached, but our eyes never left each other as he ascended through the whirlwind. My hands stretched, trying to reach him. Sidney parted, carrying with him the pearls of my tears.

It was powerful gravity that separated us. The force carrying the volition of the *Will*. The edict banning our union, proclaiming that a timeless and a mortal woman shall never be together.

Sidney's green, starry eyes vanished inside the blackness.

The maelstrom forgave me this time, leaving me standing on a fragment of land, dejected, wearing the mark of his lips and with my heart pounding his absence.

My tears were wiped by a thin, forked tongue coming over my left shoulder.

I revolved around and saw Sathariel smiling wickedly. I wanted to holler, but she shushed me, and before my eyes, a collection of images passed in a frenzy. It projected my past, the season of weakness I endured with cancer, comforted only by the caring hand of my granny. Then it showed my present, composed of my odyssey to the hereafter. Each memory from my past and present represented a page of an ancient leather hardcover book engraved with the word *Resilience* formed by multiple strokes of a knife. I held the book, with my index finger following the embossed title, feeling the grief and despair that emanated from it.

My eyes opened briefly as I drifted in and out of consciousness. The landscape traveling by Empress changed, as if all seasons were contained in a day, from the icy winter to the warm summer, as the sun rose to the zenith and was eclipsed by the moon.

My left arm floated, carried by the wind, but I felt nothing—my sense of touch had totally abandoned me, freeing me of the pain of my wounds. My hearing was also coming and going intermittently. I assumed it would be just hours away before I started losing my sight as well.

My blurred eyes focused, and I realized my hand was not being carried by the wind but pulled by the bone-white claw of a winged Sheireil flying alongside me. Startled, I jerked back, and my hearing returned with the strident howl of the flock that flew over me.

Empress sped up, trying to outrun them, but the creature was fiercely clenched to my wrist. I pulled with all my strength, but I could not break free.

"Together again, my dear." I heard Sathariel's voice coming from over my left shoulder and saw her reflection in the pupils of the demon.

The creature bit at my head, and I barely dodged, my mobility restrained by the straps that anchored me to the saddle. The demon prepared its next assault, when its chest burst, surprisingly. A sparkling dot emerged from the explosion in pursuit of the remaining Sheireils that, one by one, nosedived to the ground, turning into ashes before landing.

"Alek!"

I supposed I had to be glad, freed from the menace of the Sheireils, but instead I was on the brink of tears.

The silver dot waving through the sky must have been Alek's final bullet, which had elevated toward the sky like a falling star finding its way back home. Alek had foreseen I would need his help. He had used a bullet to save me instead of trying to save himself.

I gathered my remaining strength, and I broke away from my binding.

"Thank you," I said, embracing Empress's crest. "I'll never forget it."

Up ahead, my destination appeared—*Touriel.* The imposing volcano emitted an immense cloud, like the mushroom of a nuclear explosion. As scared as I was, I rejoiced at the thought of finally putting an end to this.

Scared birds flew away from treetops, and the drums rattled, portending the arrival of the Sheireils riding centaurs, ravenous and ruthless, that came out after me from the woods surrounding the road, as if they were expecting my arrival.

I secured the bridle and hauled it. "C'mon, Empress, please race for me like you did for Alek."

The road opened onto a vast plain ending in a cliff at the seaside.

I observed with dread how the centaurs of the wild hunt shadowed us. The entire night of riding had left Empress exhausted, unable to outrun them this time. So I armed myself with one of the spears attached to the saddle and prepared for the confrontation.

A burst of bullets riddled the first line of my pursuers, and three military jeeps flanked us.

Lovelock's company!

The infantry opened fire on the stampede, which counterattacked with arrows and spears.

"Maia!" Bill drove parallel to me. "Follow us! We have a plan."

I was elated to see them again.

Two arrows thrust into Duncan's chest, and he fell from the turret of Lovelock's jeep.

"Duncan!" Lovelock retaliated, enraged, discharging his machine gun aimlessly. "Damn you, bastards. Bill, now—send the signal to Germanicus!"

Bill shot a flare gun into the air.

A battle horn blew, and an army of men descended the slope, commanded by a warrior in golden armor and red cape riding a white horse that carried a golden eagle as a banner, just as described by Mr. Mankell in his history lectures.

"*Ad victoriam!*" yelled the Roman general Germanicus, signaling ahead with his *gladio*, leading his eclectic army of timeless warriors as he once had in life with his Roman legion against the barbarian tribes.

Germanicus's offensive bravely clashed against the centaurs. But in spite of their courage, the scale quickly tipped in favor of the Sheireils, who were superior both in number and in skill.

"There is no escape, my dear," I heard Sathariel's distinct dual voice and saw her faint reflection moving across the military-green body of the jeep driven by Lind.

"Lind, look out!" I flung the spear, but she reached the engine's vents before I could hit her. I heard a bell tolling, and the jeep blew into the air, covered in flames, amid her guffaws.

"Maia, jump!" Bill beckoned, but I shook my head.

Sathariel wanted me and would not stop until she achieved it. She would joyfully kill every single one of them to make me suffer.

"Go away! Leave me! You have to escape, please!" I ordered.

"We will not abandon you."

"You have to." It was my fight—my war. "I'm sorry, girl, but I need you one more time." I clenched Empress with my heels and veered onto the cliff. As I hoped, the beasts followed me, disengaging from the fight with Germanicus's army. I followed the narrow road mentioned by Alek at the fireflies' forest, forcing the Sheireils to jostle as they funneled in behind me. The centaurs at the edge slipped over the precipice, falling hundreds of yards before smashing against the rocks in the sea. Germanicus seized the opportunity, ordering the battalion to charge and shove them over.

A jeep ramped onto the road, ramming the centaurs, pushing them onto the precipice.

"Maia!"

"Bill, what are you doing?"

"I have an idea." He unveiled the rear of his jeep, which was full of explosives. "I'm gonna blow up the road. Follow me."

Bill jammed the gas pedal with a stick against the seat and trapped the wheel with another. He jumped to the back and removed the lids of the wooden boxes packed with explosives.

"Ready!" he said, picking up a fragmentation grenade. "Make room for me."

I aligned Empress with the side of the jeep, and Bill was preparing to jump when a winged Sheireil hit his back. He fell prone on the seats, tossing the grenade onto the Jeep's hood.

"Bill!"

The beast landed on the windshield with threatening claws and went after Bill, dripping cords of saliva. I extended my hand to grab the angle of the windshield to jump in to help Bill, when I saw Sathariel's reflection slashing the stick that was anchoring the wheel, driving the jeep out of control.

Empress had to slow down to avoid being crushed against the rock wall that the jeep scraped. Bill reached for his rifle just in time to push it against the muzzle of the beast over him. The jeep zigzagged, threatening to drift off the road at any second.

I unfastened the remaining lance from the saddle and wielded it with my left hand. I was too weak to battle the creature, so I propped it against my stomach and tangled the bridle in my right hand. I observed the jeep reeling and waited for the precise moment… then I pulled the bridle. Empress galloped parallel to the car, and I charged the Sheireil like a medieval knight in a jousting tournament, thrusting the spike into its neck. The force of the blow pushed me back until the stick broke.

The Sheireil retracted in agony, trying to remove the pike, but Bill shot it and it fell to the road.

Bill stabilized the car, and I aligned Empress with the jeep's hood. Leaning over, I stretched to pick up the grenade. My fingers secured the grenade before Sathariel's reflection appeared. Her sword bulged through the metal hood, piercing its way out.

"Maia, look out!"

I maneuvered away, evading the blow.

"Maia! Throw me the grenade," Bill said, dodging her attacks, which chopped the windshield like paper.

Even without knowing his plan, I knew it wasn't a good idea, but the clock was ticking. I tossed the grenade on the seat.

"Now get out of here!" Bill grabbed the grenade, but escape

was futile. Sathariel was present in the reflection of each piece of the shattered glass lying on the Jeep seats. It was impossible to predict where the next lunge would come from.

"Bill!"

He picked up a backpack and pulled the pin off the grenade. "Come on! Come after me!" Bill challenged an enemy he could not overcome. Actually, no one could. Then I finally understood his plan was to blow himself up too.

"Bill, don't do it," I begged.

"You coward, you would never have the guts," Sathariel said.

"Bill, don't listen to her!"

"I'm no coward." Bill smiled as a farewell.

Despite my wishes, Empress raced.

"Turn around! Empress, please!" I tugged the reins, but she disregarded my commands.

I could only glance behind.

The sword emerged from the reflection, but before it could hit him, Bill jumped off the cliff. He spun back in midair and dumped the active grenade over the explosives, and the jeep disappeared, consumed by a huge fireball. The invisible wall of the shock wave shook us, and the deafening noise left my ears hissing. The explosion collapsed the road, dragging the voracious stampede over the precipice and blocking the rest of the Sheireils.

Amid the destruction, Bill hung from his parachute, floating smoothly like a seagull as he glided safely into the ocean. My heart rejoiced, seeing him out of danger.

The ground shuddered, and the sky rumbled with such intensity that it brought my eardrums back online. A burst inside the crater of the peak exhaled an endless torrent of ash. The detonation of the explosives must have triggered something. A shower of meteorites landed, breaking off chunks of stones that collapsed down the slope.

"Come on, girl!" I petted Empress's crest, guiding her toward the entrance of the tunnel up the road. "We are almost there." I drove Empress amid the rain of debris.

A piece of the hillside exploded, coughing magmatic rocks that rolled down, threatening to collapse on the road, blocking our way to reach the cave that led to the interior of Touriel. Empress slowed down with a loud neigh followed by a squeal, frightened by the flaming stones.

"No, no, no! We cannot go back now. I know you can do it, girl. It was you who crossed the valley of death. It was you who beat Achilles's immortal horses. C'mon, girl, you are the only one who can do this. Please trust me, Empress!"

Empress swung her pointy ears up, as she always did when she heard Alek's whistle.

"Alek?" I looked around. *Could it be that he was calling for Empress?*

Empress raced like a Ferrari, eluding the stones that collapsed on the road. She jumped powerfully from slab to slab, floating so gracefully in the air that I could swear she had wings.

A curtain of dust and fiery rocks rained down on us, but Empress reached the cave entrance before we were buried alive.

Shaken and relieved, we continued through the dim tunnel, which was scarcely lighted by torches embedded in the walls, until we arrived at the junction with the main tunnel. Empress reared up, avoiding ramming into the scared people carrying their oil lanterns. The pilgrims were everywhere. It was a gallery ornamented in the fashion of a Greek mausoleum, with marble statues and reliefs of human figures fighting angels—all beheaded.

"Calm down. We're ok!" I reassured Empress.

The tunnel followed by the pilgrims continued down a crowded stair; it was too steep to make my way on Empress. I would have to go the rest of the way on foot. But my capacity to walk was uncertain, since I could not feel my body. My leg was not well, and my wound had soaked my clothes in blood. All I had was my determination. I dismounted and slid down Empress's side, but my hurt leg was incapable of keeping me up, so I hit the floor.

A group of pilgrims surrounded me, trying to help.

"Stand back! Don't..." I said, discouraging them. My past as a cancer patient trying to prove my ability to take care of myself came flooding back. "I can do it on my own." I leaned against the wall and tried to control my body. With tremendous effort, I finally was able to stand up. But on the first step, I collapsed again.

"Maia!" An old woman fought her way through the crowd. It was kind Mrs. Thompson. "Oh, my goodness!" The cigarette fell from her mouth.

"Mrs. Thompson, how's vacation?" I winced, trying to look as normal as possible.

"Maia, what happened?" Mrs. Thompson helped me up.

"I-I fell from the horse."

"But Maia, you hate horses."

Empress squealed.

"Well, not anymore. Not after everything I've been through. Empress just saved what I have left of life." I petted her forehead. "I need the rest to save my grandmother."

"Emma? What's wrong? She was perfect last time I saw her, healthy as a teenager, even made me jealous."

I could not avoid laughing. "She is as enthusiastic as a teenager, that's for sure—and stubborn as well." My spirits faded. "But the truth is, her life is in danger… and I'm the only person who can save her."

She stroked my cheek. "If only your mother and Emma could hear you speak like this, Maia, they would be so proud. They love you so much."

"That's why I need to finish the pilgrimage." I tried to walk but had to lean on the wall.

"Come, hold on to me. Unless you feel uncomfortable, being held up by an old lady."

"I'd be delighted. You have helped me walk before."

I remembered watching the video of my first steps. It was shot in the backyard, surrounded by the great oaks. Mrs. Thompson walked behind me, holding my hands, while I tottered, trying to coordinate my feet. After my initial clumsy steps, I straightened, and she released me. I waddled into the arms of my grandmother, where she welcomed me with a warm embrace.

"Let's go, Maia."

"Wait, wait." I turned back to Empress and petted her forehead. "No words are enough to thank you for what you did for me. You are the most incredible horse I have ever known—no, you are the most amazing, loyal, and kind lady I have ever met."

Empress nickered and rubbed her head against mine.

"Now, I have one last mission for you. I want you to ride after him, do you hear me? You saved Alek once, and I know you can do it again. No place is too far, and no task is impossible with a spirit like yours. Find him. And tell him thank you."

Empress blew and pricked her ears. She reared up and galloped down the path, followed by the pilgrims. People stepped aside, as- tonished and admiring. She disappeared among the throng, carry- ing with her a piece of my heart.

"I also have someone to find and an impossible mission to fulfill," I said, beholding the stairs following the endless tunnel.

Mrs. Thompson held my arm, supporting me like she did when I was a baby, and we started our ordeal, descending one step at a time. Hundreds of people, elders, men, women, and children, surpassed us, all eager to arrive at our ultimate destination.

CHAPTER 23

AFTER HOURS OF EFFORT, we made it to the end of the stairs, where the tunnel opened to a massive cavern. It was so big that the light of the pilgrims' lanterns faded in all directions of the nebulous entrails of Touriel. There was a thick, ashen fog that not even the eternal fire of the lanterns could break through. Quickly, we got lost in the abysmal quiet of the haze.

"Don't worry, Maia. Keep close to me. The road will find us," Mrs. Thompson assured me.

It was difficult to believe. Everywhere I looked, a monotonous gray wall surrounded us. The ground was our sole reference, but I discovered that the lantern light rays refracted, projecting waved patterns at our feet, as if we were standing on the seabed, with the sunlight passing through the waves. I picked up a fistful of dirt.

"It's sand—like from the beach," I concluded after a close examination.

"Maia, Maia." I heard an elusive voice whispering my name but could see no one.

"Is he calling you?"

"Who?"

"Your boyfriend, the boy you introduced me to at the square," Mrs. Thompson said.

I stared at her, bemused, but I could not hold her gaze, and I looked away.

"Don't worry, honey. You don't have to tell me."

"No, it's okay, but he is not my boyfriend."

"But do you love him? I saw the way you looked at him."

I went mute, feeling stupid.

"Then there is nothing to be ashamed of," she said, interpreting my silence.

"It's not that simple—"

"Have you told him?"

I shook my head. "It was not the right moment. Circumstances, you know. Maybe—"

"Maia, you can't hold yourself back from living life because of circumstances. You cannot deprive yourself of the good moments, waiting for the bad moments to disappear. All we have in this life is the capacity of living those moments, good or bad, and if you don't squeeze life out of each moment, you might let the happiest times pass."

She pulled out a pack of cigarettes, putting one in her mouth. "Maia, you asked me how my vacation is going." She opened the lid of the lantern and lit up the cigarette with the eternal fire. "Well, I laughed out loud at the jokes of your grandmother, I loved my Edward passionately, I mourned his departure, I suffered cancer. And I watched you suffer from cancer, too, which was what hurt most—but at the end, it was you who taught me to overcome my disease."

"Me?" I asked, bewildered, unable to imagine myself as the role model for anybody.

"Yes, it was looking at you, so young and fighting so fiercely for your life, that gave me the strength to endure. You were my rock in my moments of frailty."

My sight blurred. I ran my fingers over my eyes and found my tears running, even though I had lost the ability to feel them.

"My vacation has come to an end, Maia, and I look behind and realize I have enjoyed the trip—I have enjoyed my life. I embraced the good and the bad. 'Life is a privilege you don't claim until it is taken away from you,' my Ed said."

Mrs. Thompson hugged me. "Don't wait until the end of the book to start enjoying your story, because you don't know which will be the last page."

"Thank you…"

"You should go after him," she said, handing me the lantern. "You found him once. I know you can do it again. No place is too far, and no task is impossible, with a spirit like yours. Find him. And tell him what you feel."

Mrs. Thompson walked away.

"Wait, where are you going?"

"The wait is finally over," Mrs. Thompson said, smiling.

The silhouette of a man materialized behind her—it was Mr. Thompson. They contemplated each other with the enthusiasm of teenage lovers.

"Why did you take so long, my love?" she asked in tears.

"I was never really gone." Mr. Thompson hugged her. "I walked ahead of you, but our hands never separated, and I never removed my eyes from you." He kissed her forehead.

Mrs. Thompson smiled at me. "Don't think, girl, just go."

I nodded.

They walked away holding hands until they vanished in the fog, leaving behind the memories of a passionate life in the form of two trails of footprints on the sand, overlapping one behind the other during hardship, but never split.

I resumed my plodding walk, this time convinced that I would arrive at my destiny. The voices calling my name got louder, but there was no sign of my destination. I stopped, frustrated, thinking that the voices were only in my imagination. I smacked my ears and realized my hearing was coming and going. I could not see the sky nor feel the tiredness of my body, but I knew night had passed, and I was on the verge of complete hearing loss. I had to hurry; my eyesight would be next. I would be trapped here, disconnected from the outside world. Until the end.

In my fatalistic despair, I looked behind and found a staircase of stone leading upward. But it was different from the one that had brought us here—narrower, just wide enough for a person to walk through. "The road will find us," I said, remembering Mrs. Thompson's words, so I decided to follow it.

Eventually I made my way out of the hazy cloud. Once above the surface, I realized the mist was like an ocean, which explained the sand at the bottom. The vast ocean was contained inside the boundless cavern—and it was alive. Human faces formed and dissolved on the agitated surface of the watery mist, some happy, others sad, a few peaceful, but most in pain. Hand-shaped waves smashed against an old wooden quay attached to the stair, lit with lanterns at every post. In the distance, a broken barge sailed across the nebulous sea, manned by a figure covered with raven feathers that spread white powder across the water.

I continued my ascent. The staircase led me to the ceiling of the cavern through a rock tunnel lit at the end. As I crossed the threshold, I realized the gilt light beams were a product of the lava. I was on top of the magma chamber of Touriel. The steps ended on an agora surrounded by destroyed pillars that rested on a rocky boulder atop the molten rock. Beyond the plaza, the staircase continued a stretch, leading to the magmatic precipice.

On the last step, a floating hooded cloak—Samael—admired the giant sculpture of a crucified man carved into the volcano's inner wall, just like the sculptures in the valley of the Watchers. The giant was eyeless, and from his mouth emerged a glowing stream of lava.

Samael's darkness looked at me. "Hast thou found thy way back, Little One?"

"I'm here to reclaim what belongs to me," I said, pointing to the gold medallion that dangled over his chest.

"Maia Foster, daughter of Dario and Luvena, I welcome thee!" the angel of death said, extending his ever-changing arms.

CHAPTER 24

"WELCOME BACK TO THE FLOCK," Samael said with a sepulchral voice.

"Give the medallion to me."

"Thou art confused." He descended from the broken stair.

"I'm here to save my grandmother, and you will not stop me."

"Even if I give it to thee"—his chameleonic hand stroked the medallion—"wouldst thou dare to throw thyself into the burning pit?" A geyser of lava sprouted violently through the gorge of the volcano.

Three out of five colored orbs in the medallion had turned opaque gray, and the fourth was dimming, announcing the impending total loss of my sense of hearing. My clock was ticking before my eyes, but finally my goal was in reach. I could throw myself into the raging inferno, so Gran's life could be forgiven.

Even though I was scared, I realized my misfortune had become my ally. Since I had lost my sense of touch, being scorched to death would not be painful. I just had to close my eyes until everything went dark. But first, I had to recover the medallion. I was in no condition to fight, so my only chance was to persuade him to willingly give it to me.

"I'll sacrifice myself for her gladly," I answered with determination, dropping the lantern on the floor.

"Poor creature, I'm afraid thy grandmother needs no salvation."

"What do you know about salvation, when you have tortured your own son?"

"Torture? That is what death is for thee? A torture?"

"I saw him suffer."

"He begged for death." Samael floated to me. "Just as thou didst."

"You are lying," I said, diverting my eyes to avoid seeming too obvious about my interest in the medallion.

"How is it that thou hast forgotten how thou wrecked the car, hoping to kill thyself?" I flinched. "Art thou here to consummate thy suicide?"

"I-I—" *Damn,* he knew too much, but I also knew how to play smarty-pants.

"Why art thou so anxious to terminate the unique real possession thou hast?"

"You know why I wanted to kill myself," I said, furious. "Because of the curse you cast on me."

Samael ran his reshaping hand over me, and the lymph nodes in my neck and my belly bulged, magnetized by him. "The seeds of life can rot the apple by doing nothing more than giving life. Canst thou blame life for giving life?"

"Cancer is not life—it's misery. And you are responsible. Death is your creation, and in cancer, you've made your masterpiece. Bravo!" I clapped sarcastically. "Why did you create something so vile and miserable?" I extended my hand, stepping closer to the medallion. "No, no, no, wait, don't tell me. I already know. It's because you find amusement in inflicting suffering. You really enjoyed torturing me and the entire cancer ward. You were enraptured with each excruciating dose of chemo, with each killing ray aimed at our bodies, with every procedure. Why should I be surprised, when you are capable of tormenting your own son?!"

Samael was silent. Not even his breathing was audible.

"You are just a compassionless, sadistic pig," I added, trying to regain my breath.

I had let go of all the words locked in my heart for years. For one moment I felt feathery—freed.

Samael's arm roulette halted on the hands of a young male. His right fist uncurled, revealing a razor blade held in his fingertips. I backed up. He sliced his left wrist and repeated the procedure on the other arm. He dropped the razor, which sank in a blood pool formed on the floor. Even though I couldn't feel them, my hands were quivering.

"I know how death feels. Every time somebody dies, I die myself. With infinite mercy, the *Will* punished my sin as a Fallen, making me embody both the murdered and the murderer, and by doing so, the *Will* showed me that an artist cannot capture on a canvas the feelings which he doesn't know. The artist must feel them through him at each stroke—transformed by them. It doesn't matter how painful they can be, the artist will fall in love, not with the pain, but with the miracle of feeling—the miracle of life."

The languid arms paled as he contemplated the bloodstained hands, until they completely bled out and dangled, motionless.

"Life is preceded by the miracle of death. There couldn't be life if there were no death. There was darkness before light. Unbalance before balance. Purpose before will."

"You are sick. Death is no miracle. Where is the miracle in snatching away the mother of a newborn? Where?" I grabbed the cloak and shook it. "Where? Where?" I repeated endlessly, with my eyes flooded. "Where is…"

"In sacrifice," Samael finally replied. "Thou, as a stillborn, should know that better than anyone," he said, referring to the fact that I was born with the umbilical cord wrapped around my neck. Asphyxiated.

I shook my head in denial. "No. No. I lived!"

"Maia, thy questions deny the fact that Death is the sole answer to all of them."

"You monster! Murderer!"

"I just carry the *Will*." Samael came close to me, his breath blowing my hair. "I'm just a puppet that performs in the third act. A hollow doll. My lines are given to me. All names that have been and those that shall be. All who have been called back."

I took advantage of his distraction to snatch the medallion from his chest with my left hand. A stream of sensations flooded my whole being through my arm as I regained my lost senses and, with them, the terrible ache of my wounds. But it was too soon to celebrate. Samael's hand trapped my wrist before I could snatch it away. I pulled, using the weight of my body, but I could not free myself—it was pointless.

"Maia," he said, coming closer, as if he were planning to devour me. "Thy name has been whispered to me."

I heard a creak—the bone in my wrist—and cried, feeling pain once again. My fingers twisted, releasing the medallion into Samael's hand. Losing it numbed my senses again, but not my despair. *Everything is lost now,* I said, blaming myself for ruining my only chance. I closed my eyes, expecting the worst.

"Let her go!" a voice ordered.

It was Sidney, climbing the stairs, dressed in an off-white jacket and jeans.

It took me a couple of seconds to convince myself I was not hallucinating.

"You are alive," I mumbled, blissful that he had survived Sathariel. I could not feel my heart, but I was sure it was racing for him.

Samael released my hand, and I fell into the arms of Sidney.

"Are you all right, Maia?" Sidney stared at me with his mesmerizing olive-green eyes.

"Now I am." I smiled.

"Thou walkest before me as a mere mortal." Samael floated away from us, enraged. "Haughty. Naive. Ungrateful. Commanding thy father against the *Will*."

"How are you so sure that this is not what the *Will* wants?" Sidney inquired.

"Her name has been pronounced."

"So was mine. I was found guilty of my crimes. Sentenced to death."

"Yet thou art here, miraculously saved by the deceit of a wayward that dared to defy the high ones," Samael said, referring to Alek's defiance in postponing Sidney's execution.

Sidney stood. "So do I. I defy them! I question the high ones!" he yelled furiously.

"Inquiry is a human virus, a disease that leads to anxiety and remorse."

"Then I'm infected."

"No, the purpose after thou wast named is not this. You are confused, my son. It's the mask that thou holdest to, this name that thou flauntest, which cloudeth thy judgment. But it is just one from the thousand thou hast."

"A thousand masks can't hide the true nature that dwells in my heart—a human nature."

"What is it that she hast done to thee?" Samael asked, enraged.

Sidney looked down at me, lying on the floor.

"Is it her beauty? Her body? Her passion? What hast thou seen in the mortal girl, to sacrifice eternity?"

After a long silence staring at me, Sidney answered, "What did you see in my mother?"

Death didn't reply.

"What did you see in a mortal girl, Father? Her beauty? Her body? Her passion? Or it was her naivete and sparkling curiosity for the question *why* that tempted you against the commandments of the *Will?*" Sidney walked to his father. "Maybe it was because you had asked yourself the same before. *Why? Why not?* And you dared to do it, even knowing the consequences. The punishment to the *Grigori*. The damnation of your offspring." Sidney turned to me. "Everything just for a feeling."

I could not really grasp the situation that Sidney had lived his entire existence with the strict borderlines that prevented him from experiencing something that was so normal for us, like harboring a feeling. But I also had been a victim of denial myself. I was denied having a family, to be healthy, to be loved. So I could understand Sidney's pain and eagerness for the experience of love.

"Father, you made me what I am—the half-human harbinger of Death. You made me your shadow, your instrument. But you committed a grave mistake. You never rid me of my human heart," Sidney said, with tears running down his left cheek. "I can feel." He wiped his tears and presented them to his father. "I have felt the joy, the pain, the love, the suffering of each soul that I have brought aboard. And now you are expecting me to forget it? To repress it?"

"I know how thou dost feel, my son." Samael's hand reached Sidney's cheek. "I deviated from the path, fell prey to seduction. I experienced firsthand how persuasive Sathariel can be. But after the sweetened seduction, it will accuse thee and judge thee with equal dedication. This is the reason I—as thy father—know what is best for thee, and I will not allow thee to commit the same mistake I did. Even if I have to force thee to abide."

Sidney averted his face away from the caressing hand of his father.

"She has to go now. Step aside, Son."

"I will not."

The vacant blackness inside Samael's hood stared at Sidney.

"So be it. Thy murderer awaits," Samael whispered with a sepulchral tone. "Ravisseur!" he called.

From the gloom of Samael's sleeve, an animated tattoo of a striped snake with fiery coal eyes and threatening fangs crawling up his forearm toward the back of his hand appeared. The hand clutched, and a bright sword materialized. It had a gold-engraved handgrip and a crystal blade that fragmented light in the entire spectrum of a rainbow as he waved it, like a prism.

"Ravisseur..." Sidney's eyes filled with fear.

Samael had embodied Ravisseur? He was Sidney's murderer?

A mouthful of magma was violently expelled by the stone giant, signaling a new eruption of the volcano.

"Sidney, look out!" I warned as Samael slashed Sidney's shirt and jacket when he tried to escape the blow. "Please stop, you are going to hurt him," I begged, but Samael continued his assault on Sidney, who evaded the blows, sidestepping and rolling away the best he could.

"Life is unfair," a voice came out from under Samael's hood, but it was not his elder voice, it was a younger one—Ravisseur's. "If you want to survive, you ought to force your way through, thrusting steel and toasting with the blood of your victims."

Sidney grabbed a standing torch and fought back, swinging the wrought-iron rod in all directions, but Samael circumvented the assault, twisting and reshaping as easily as a piece of fabric.

Samael counterattacked with a powerful thrust, but Sidney trapped the blade between the iron bars at the tip of the torch. Sidney twisted it, disarming him. The sword was launched into the air, falling just yards away from me.

I limped after it, but the sword had become invisible. I knelt and fumbled for it, hoping to get lucky and brush against it.

I heard a scream—it was Ravisseur. Sidney had burned the hand holding the medallion. The gold piece fell, bouncing on the cobblestones. Sidney went after it, but before he could reach it, Samael stopped him, stabbing him with a long dagger that appeared suddenly in his hand, plunging it between his chest and shoulder.

"Nooooooooo!" I screamed.

"Now you know how pain tastes. You are the lucky one," Samael said with Ravisseur's voice. "Now you know how it feels to be alive. To be human."

Sidney stared at Samael's hood, as if he could see Ravisseur's eyes within the murkiness.

I could not watch him suffering without doing anything. I hammered the harsh stone blocks around me with my right hand, trying to find the blade, watching how my fist got sticky with threads of blood.

"That's what you wanted, right?" Ravisseur demanded.

"No. You are wrong. I didn't want to be a human—I am human," Sidney clarified, trapping the blade with his bare hand. "And if you want to kill a human, you should aim for his heart." Sidney dragged the dagger down to the center of his chest. "But you should be aware that as long there are heartbeats, a human will fight for what he loves"—dark scales grew out of the wound, trapping the blade—"until his final breath."

Ravisseur released the handgrip, surprised.

Sidney removed the dagger and tossed it away. He snatched the medallion and ran up the stairs.

What?

I lost my breath, realizing what he was planning. He was going to sacrifice himself to take my place.

"Sidney, no! Don't do it! It's my sacrifice to make," I implored, but he did not listen to my words and continued up the stairs.

"Touriel, Mountain of God, Eighteenth Fallen!" Samael called with his guttural voice, "Listen to thy brother. Wake up from thy entrapment and quench thy thirst for freedom."

The whole volcano trembled, fissuring the walls. Flames ignited in the eye sockets of the stone giant, and with a deafening bawl, the titan came back to life. Touriel was one of the Watchers, punished, chained to fulfill a penance that would only end along with Sidney's existence, since he was the last of his species—the damned offspring, the sole remnant of the original sin. Sidney's life kept all the Fallen bound to their miserable existence, even his own father.

With colossal strength, Touriel broke the chains that had kept him trapped and fell waist-deep into the molten lake, causing waves that splashed against the agora where we were standing. His fiery eyes searched for Sidney and howled with threads of lava. The awakening of the colossus didn't stop Sidney, who continued his ascension on the stair until he was deflected by Touriel's powerful backhand blow—as if he had smashed a troublesome insect—tossing him against the stone floor.

Touriel's humongous right fist hammered to crush him, but Sidney rolled away barely in time to escape, only to meet Touriel's left hand, which trapped him.

"C'mon, c'mon, c'mon!" I hurried myself, grabbling for the sword, until finally the blobs of my blood revealed its location. I clutched the hilt, and the blade materialized.

"I will not allow you to kill him!" I charged against the Watcher and stabbed the back of his hand. Molten lava splashed out of the wound, and I had to step aside to avoid being burned by the torrent. Touriel squealed, releasing Sidney, and then slapped me off. I flew into the air and landed fifty feet away.

Dazed, I shook my head and saw a big shadow descending on me—Touriel's palm coming to crush me. I held up the still-smoky sword and closed my eyes, expecting the worst.

A thunderous crunch enlivened my ears. I opened my eyes slowly, still fearful that the sound had been produced by the cracking of my bones, but peered up to see Sidney standing by my side with his arms up, containing the pressure of Touriel's hand.

"Sidney!" I yelled, aiming the sword at the huge hand he was straining to keep from crushing us.

"No! Don't do it, or you will be burned by his blood," he said with a labored voice.

He was right, but I didn't care. The only agony I felt was Sidney's suffering. The unbearable pressure brought Sidney to his knees.

"You have to go! I will not be able to hold this much longer!"

"Why? Why are you willing to sacrifice yourself for me?"

"Because..." His arms succumbed, and the overwhelming hand rested on his shoulders, burying his knee in the stone. "Be-be-cause—I promised I would," he finally said.

"No! I'm not abandoning you."

"Don't be stubborn! Take the medallion."

The medallion dangled from his hand, within my reach. All I had to do was take it and run into the pit...

But I could not take the medallion.

"I'll not accept your sacrifice." *Forgive me, Gran.* "If you die, I'll die by your side."

"Why can't you just follow orders?"

"Because I'm a spoiled brat, remember? A spoiled brat who is not willing to live without you."

Despite the humongous pressure resting over his shoulders, Sidney showed me his smile one last time. I embraced him, resting my head against his chest. His heartbeats were faint. My hand covered the wound on his chest to prevent him from bleeding out. But I was fooling myself. It was just a matter of time. A minute more. Seconds, perhaps. I was totally convinced that I would give up everything to share his remaining moments beside him. I would change the eternal by the ephemeral. I would choose him. A thousand times I would choose him. No matter the price.

"Stop your crying, Maia," he said as I wept, incapable of sensing my tears. "Princesses don't cry. Princesses endure, not because they are fearless but because they are brave," Sidney repeated the words he'd said to me back at the fair when I was a toddler.

"I'm not a princess. Princesses live happily ever after."

"I'm sorry to meddle in your fate, but I have a promise to keep." Sidney's muscles bulked, tearing his shirt and jacket, and his veins popped as he pushed himself up and stood with difficulty. His skin became covered with dark scales, and two dragon wings emerged from his back and surrounded me.

"Why are you doing this?" I pleaded.

Sidney's mesmerizing olive eyes rested on me, making me feel the same spark as when we first met at the hospital. Even though I couldn't hear him, I read his lips when he said, "Because I love you."

It wasn't just his words; everything had silenced—*I finally lost my hearing!* I covered my ears and squeezed them, hoping to find a switch to turn them on. But it was futile. Once more, destiny mocked me. Of all the sounds I could have missed during a lifetime, I'd missed the words I desired to hear the most—*I love you, I love you, I love you,* I repeated to myself.

Somehow, amid my deafness, the sound of Sidney's heart had lingered in my ear. I could hear it, still throbbing with hope.

His scaled hand formed a sharp claw that he used to thrust into Touriel's mammoth hand. His wings shielded me in a cocoon from the splatter of the magma. Sidney endured the scalding blood until Touriel retracted his hand, then vanished from my side and took to the air, waving his scorched wings. He landed on Touriel's forearm and ran up the arm, cutting it with his claw, dodging the attacks of the Watcher. With each step, his heartbeats grew feeble and sluggish, until it was almost imperceptible. At the end, Sidney landed a jaw-twisting hit on the titan, before the sound of his heartbeats extinguished.

There was only silence.

The dragon scales of Sidney's mighty armor transfigured into soft black feathers, and he nosedived like a shot bird.

"Sidney! Sidney!" I cried, unable to hear myself.

Touriel caught Sidney with his thumping hand before he crashed in the magmatic lake. The titan looked at the tiny man resting on his palm—the one responsible for his misfortune. The flames in his hollow eyes invigorated as he clenched his fist, squeezing Sidney with raging strength that ceded by degrees as his thirst for vengeance was satiated. Relieved, the giant tossed Sidney's lifeless body onto the platform.

My quivering hand reached my mouth. I refused to accept what was going on. I could not feel my heart, but I knew it was crumbling.

Touriel howled thunderously, reviving my ears—apparently, I was not totally deaf yet. The fiery eyes of the Watcher extinguished, and the giant was paralyzed again, reverting to the lava-spitting sculpture.

Samael, who watched the assassination, floated to the body of his son.

Rabid, I propped myself up on the sword. "You bastard. You killed him! You killed your own son."

"Thou ought to be exultant," Samael drawled. "He finally fulfilled his desire."

My abhorrence for him invigorated my exhausted body. I limped and thrust the sword into Samael, right in the obscure vacuity of his hood. It was difficult to tell, but it didn't feel like I hit anything.

My sight blurred, and I realized Ravisseur's tattooed hand had stabbed my belly first with his dagger.

I dropped the sword, which disappeared before hitting the ground.

"He was your son, he was your son!" I jolted the floating cloak, still trapped by the dagger, but there was no reply from Samael's nor Ravisseur's voice. Then I dared to do the unimaginable. I pulled Samael's hood back to find who was hidden in the insoluble darkness of Death and unveil the mystery of Ravisseur.

"It's impossible." I shook my head, stepping away, openmouthed, unhooking the blade from my flesh.

Ravisseur was truly him, as Frank had said.

It was the man with whom the only thing I had in common was

my surname.
It was *Dario*.
It was my father.

CHAPTER 25

"WHY?" I FELL TO MY KNEES. "Why?" I asked repeatedly, with the burden of a life of resentment aged by his abandonment, disinterest, and detestation upon my shoulders.

My father looked down on me, haughty and unmoved.

"Why not?" he said harshly, as his countenance got lost in the murkiness draped by the hood.

Then the roulette started again. Samael's hands revolved in the infinity of possibilities as he floated away.

It's my fortune, then, to die at the hands of my father? I finally understood the enigma of Death, the job he had been enslaved to as a punishment for giving birth to Sidney with the First Mother. Condemned to embody all murdered and murderers. Destined to feel the sorrow and the guilt from Abel and Cain until the last corpse—including his own son.

"But it was your duty," I said, and Samael halted. "A father should always protect his son."

The white marble cloak morphed into soft fabric, and Samael's true hands stretched out and his bare feet landed on the cobblestones. His translucent skin showed the veins and muscles inside his extremities. He removed his hood, revealing his hairless head. The pumping arteries branched like scars across his face. It was like seeing the fetus of an old man. He observed me with dilated pupils through his closed, lashless eyelids.

"Shall a father and a mother rejoice of giving life to a baby as a product of love, or feel sad, because by bestowing life they are condemning the newborn to a certain finale?" he asked.

"Your son was eternal."

"So are the rocks and mountains." He waved his hand, pointing at Touriel. "Mountains have to witness the day and night passing by through inert, hollow eyes. Observing the rise and downfall of men, wondering how people often feel enslaved to an existence they didn't ask for. Mountains didn't ask to be mountains, just like men didn't ask to be men. Yet a mountain would exchange an inert eternity for wearing a man's skin for a day. Just out of curiosity. For what is mortal? Having a limit is what gives meaning to the limitless."

Samael glanced at Sidney's body. "My son questioned the same. He was rebellious and harbored doubts. A thousand infinities were not enough to satiate his curiosity. He had to taste mortality." He stared at me. "He had to taste *thee*."

"No."

"He had to taste the mortality of an ungrateful and rebellious girl that even sown on a field of love refuses it, disowning thy own existence."

"No!"

"It was thee." His pupils constricted, staring at me. "He is dead because of thee."

"No, all this was *your* doing. Sathariel's doing. I-I tried to save him—" I stuttered, trying to deny it, but internally I punished myself, remembering it was me who chained and betrayed him. It was my hurt pride fueling my revulsion.

It was me.

"Maturity is assuming thou art solely responsible for what happens, by act or omission. Something that thou should have learned during your life, but it's too late now. Thou hast been called. Thy name has been whispered to me."

Samael extended his arms, and his tunic opened and expanded, creating a portal to the dark and hypnotic maelstrom that devoured my dreams.

"Now, Little One, come into me," he said with a charming voice. "Close thine eyes and come to me. Release thyself from the good and the bad, the felicity and the suffering, your desires and afflictions. Preoccupations will bother thy soul no more. Become one with the end. Embrace the miracle of death."

Samael was right.

I was tired.

I was tired of pretending, of trying to show myself strong, of fighting to be better in order to be liked. I was jaded from inhabiting my prison of solitude, of my addiction to nostalgia.

Maybe it was time to let go.

I beheld Sidney's body one more time and shut my eyes.

It was time to return to nothing.

I opened my arms to receive sweet and heartwarming death.

"No end is worthy of your sacrifice, my dear," I heard Sathariel's seductive voice over my left shoulder. "I can save you, and you will live in me—*forever*. All you have to do is call my name."

"Sidney," I whispered unconsciously.

"I can give him to you," she answered with a silken voice.

A voice broke my trance. "Don't listen to it, Maia!"

I opened my eyes and saw Samael's chameleonic hand about to touch me.

A hooded figure ascended through the stairs to the agora.

"Peach—" I whispered.

"Don't you dare touch her," she ordered, and the floating marbled cloak retreated.

Peach walked over and knelt before Sidney. Her fingers tenderly stroked his lifeless body. "Thank you," she sighed and collected the medallion from his hand.

"A substitution is about to take place!" Peach stood and declared.

"Wh-what are you doing?" I asked, disconcerted. "The medallion is not yours!"

Peach's steely blue eyes fixed on me. She leaned down and cupped my face in her hands.

"Hush, hush, my ruddy bear. Everything will be fine now," she said, pushing up the corners of my mouth with her thumbs to draw a smile, and kissed my forehead.

"Wha—"

Peach walked away with difficulty.

"I'm here to take the place of my granddaughter," she said, wearing the medallion. "I'll be her substitute in death."

My mind could not conceive what my ears were hearing.

"Emma Niemeyer, daughter of Hans and Frieda, I welcome thee."

She removed the hood, and her cherubic face turned into the creased and withered face of my grandmother. Her once crinkly golden hair became white, as if decades had elapsed in a second. But her eyes were the same, radiant and profound. And she comforted me with the same gentle smile.

"Wainwright. It's Emma Wainwright now, after my late husband."

My mind flooded with questions.

I remembered Peach slapping me for my disobedience at the graveyard and her concern that I continue the pilgrimage—*she even left flowers at my tomb!* I remembered her hugging me in tears at the campfire and whispering, "Don't worry, my dear, this will end soon." She'd scolded me for putting too much salt on my food the same way she had when I was a kid. I remembered Sidney's uneasy attitude when he was with me in her presence—*he was kissing her granddaughter at the river!*

Then, the memories of her conversation with Sidney at the cabin replayed in my head. "But what if she refuses at the end? And tries to stop us? You promised me," she said, and Sidney candidly replied, "I'll fulfill my promise." The very same promise she'd begged behind the hospital curtains the night before Sidney met me.

I recalled Peach testifying before the Four Mothers, where she admitted how she'd deceived me with the intention of trading her life for mine, and how she'd persuaded Sidney to do it. "I'm the culprit! Punish me!" She'd admitted her guilt to the deaf ears of the audience, especially mine.

Her sole crime, *Love*. Unconditional love for her granddaughter.

"There is nothing to forgive about love," were Sidney's words when I was blinded by my prejudice.

"You did all of this only to save me?" I demanded.

"I'm sorry it had to be this way, Maia," my gran said with a breaking voice. "Sidney never betrayed you."

I glanced over to the man who'd endured perjury, judgment, and punishment, giving up not only his eternity, but his mortal life, in order to save me.

Now he lay motionless at my feet, lifeless.

I was a fool.

Not a fool. I was the stupidest person who had ever walked the earth.

I'd had him and lost him.

"It was me, Ruddy Bear, everything was me. I'm sorry for misleading you, my dear, but it was the only way you would accept."

"B-but, why?"

She gasped. "Because I could not sit there and watch you die."

"I wish you'd let me die!" I caressed Sidney's hand. "At least he would be alive. You made him promise that he would do everything to save me, and now he is dead."

"No," my grandmother corrected me with tears in her eyes. "I made him promise that he would restore the smile that the cancer robbed from you and that he would do everything to preserve it after I had gone."

"What?"

"Yes, my dear, you have to live. You still have much to laugh about." She smiled tenderly before marching, with the weight of a lifetime upon her shoulders, to cast herself into the flames.

"No! Please! Don't do it!" I forced my way up, but I fell prone to the ground. My legs resisted giving a single step more.

"Halt!" Samael stepped in her way. "Thy name has not been called, Emma. It's not thy time yet."

From Death's hood, darkness escaped like stripes of black cloth that wrapped our reality like a cobweb. The cobblestones covered with snow and the glowing magmatic cavern transformed into a dense, starless night. Two arms emerged from Samael's cloak holding a machine gun, and a group of ghostly Nazi soldiers appeared on both sides of him, pointing their weapons at my grandmother. "Step aside, girl," one said with a young voice and a bold German accent.

"No, I will not," my granny said firmly, standing in front of me. "You have punished me enough, making me outlive all the people I have loved. You stole from me my daughter Luvena, my husband, Ghislain, my family. And you robbed me of my children, who were innocent. No. I will not falter." She opened her arms. "So you'd better aim well at my heart, because you will have to tear it apart before I will step aside," she said, walking to the firing squad led by Samael.

"Step aside, girl!" he said, aiming at her with shaky, hesitant hands. "I'll not repeat myself."

"Shoot!" my granny incited. "Put an end to what you started."

"No!" I yelled.

They pressed their triggers, releasing a burst of bullets that crossed my grandmother, tearing holes in her cloak and dress as the spent shells clacked on the floor.

The firing ceased, leaving smoky barrels.

"Gran!" I cried, terrified.

My grandmother stood on her feet, not moving an inch, with a wide smile across her face, as if each wound were something to be proud of.

"Impossible!" Samael's trembling hands reloaded the magazine, appalled to witness such a miracle. The troops flinched in disbelief.

The silence was broken by the harmonious laughing of children.

"She's here!" the voices announced spiritedly.

Samael's hands dropped the machine gun and convulsed. The soldiers vanished, and Samael drowned in a shrill shriek of anguish. Seven light figures emerged from his hood, one by one, vanquishing the insoluble darkness of the spell of night that had possessed Touriel. The once ominous marbled cloak fell to the cobblestones like an old rag. Empty. Defeated.

The figures were seven children, all younger than ten, six boys and a girl, who ran into my grandmother's arms.

"*Pfirsich! Pfirsich!*" all yelled, surrounding her.

"*Meine kinder,*" my granny cried, squeezing the heads of the little ones against her chest. "*Danke! Danke!*" she repeated endlessly, with her eyes covered in tears.

The children had numbers tattooed on the backs of their hands. *13, 27, 44, 49, 66, 68, 88.* I remembered the story shared by Lovelock at the bonfire back in Pahana Forest.

"One day, we found a girl in the forest covered in blood. She was a *kraut* pursued by her own kind. She had escaped from a concentration camp, where she had discovered the horrors that hid behind the steel doors. Children with their skin pale as chalk, with numbers tattooed on the backs of their hands, subjected to experiments and the cruelest tortures. In her bravery, she devised a plan to liberate the children, but her plot was exposed. She was able to escape with seven children. Six lucky little boys and a girl, for whom a young girl, just like you, stood before a Nazi death squad with open hands, offering her life to protect them as if they were her own."

I'd shared my entire life with my grandmother, and I barely knew her. At that moment, I finally understood who she really was. She had been a warrior her entire life. And I knew she had sacrificed for those children as she did for me. There was no room for doubt. There was nothing but love and devotion in my gran's heart. And witnessing the love the children had for her, they became my family.

"Will you be with us forever?" asked the smallest.

"Yes," my granny answered. "Now we will be together, forever."

"*Kommen! Kommen!*" the kids pulled her arms, as if they were conducting her to a playground.

"I need to go," my granny said to me.

Her image turned blurry in my eyes, saturated with tears. I did not want her to go. I loved her; I loved her so much.

"Who is going to tend your flowers?" I said, still rejecting her sacrifice.

"I raised them strong; no more care is needed," she said, squeezing the medallion. "The only thing left is to have a happy life and have offspring that you will look after with the same love as I did."

I had to let her go.

I closed my eyes, squeezing out my tears, and nodded. "Thank you."

"Please don't cry, Ruddy Bear. One person shedding tears in the room is enough," she said with tears running down her cheeks.

She nodded and walked away amid my choking sobs, holding the hands of the singing children, climbing the stairs until the last step.

Then, finally, I saw through her eyes how she had felt all this time, looking at me during my disease—climbing and descending the steps of the broken stair that was my life.

I held Sidney's icy hand against my chest as I said goodbye to the other half of my heart.

My grandmother looked at me from the top. Smiling. Radiant. Content. Fulfilled. As I had never seen her before.

"Responsibility is about fulfilling promises," I said, smiling.

She had done it again.

Even in such a dreadful situation, she'd managed to draw a smile out of me. But no surprise—after all, she was my superheroine, and making me smile was her superpower.

My granny leaned forward, and her figure disappeared.

I closed my eyes.

CHAPTER 26

I OPENED MY EYES to the 100%-polyester-germproof-light-blue curtains. I was in my hospital bed, entangled in tubes and cables.

Am I alive? I asked myself, reluctant to believe what had happened. *It was all a dream?*

"Gran?" I babbled through the tubes.

The curtain was drawn, blocking my view of the armchair.

No answer.

"Gran!" I said louder, but nobody replied from the other side.

I pulled away the cords imprisoning me amid a cacophony of beeps. I tried to sit, but an acute pain in my bandaged leg impeded me.

My leg, I said to myself, remembering how I'd gotten injured escaping from Sathariel.

It was real! I thought, convincing myself of my sanity. *But that means… Shit.*

"Gran!" I scrambled out of the sheets and rotated on the bed with great effort, until finally I reached the curtain and drew it open.

The armchair was empty, neat and not recently used.

My chest tightened.

Darrell appeared beside my bed, wearing Mr. Farrell's Yankees hat with *that* look.

No words were needed.

She was gone forever.

I wailed, while he and Gary tried to comfort me.

The nurses came into the room and forced sedatives on me as I kicked and cried and babbled until darkness fell.

Two days later, I was discharged from the hospital on crutches.

Dr. Wolk took me to drink a hot strawberry tea and later pushed my wheelchair through the park as he recounted the events of the past days while I was on the brink of dying.

He told me the story as it was recorded by the surveillance cameras of the hospital, describing how that fateful night I'd abandoned my bed, pushing my IV pole, and strolled down the hallway, oddly without being noticed by the nurses at the station or anybody else in the hospital. "Like you were a ghost," Dr. Wolk said. Then I descended the stairs a couple of stories before losing consciousness and rolling down the stairwell, hitting the bottom—hence the wound on my leg.

According to the nurse who discovered me, I was in shock, and by the time I reached my bed again, I was in a coma. They plugged me back into the tubes, hoping for the best, because there was nothing left to do for me in my condition—besides pray.

Three whole days passed by with no sign of improvement. "Your grandmother wouldn't abandon your side for a second, watching after you day and night," Dr. Wolk said.

And it was during the third night when my granny passed away—her heart stopped. The nurses found her by my side, in a dead slumber after countless tiring nights of vigil. She went into an eternal sleep with her fingers intertwined with mine.

Over the next few days, the swollen lymph nodes in my body had reverted back to normal sizes. Dr. Wolk said it was "inexplicable." After more than a decade of struggle, the cells in my body that were killing me somehow had decided to make peace.

"It was a miracle." Dr. Wolk went short of words, trying to explain what had happened.

Suddenly, I, who didn't believe in miracles, found myself living one.

But I knew it was no miracle.

It was *sacrifice.*

It was the sacrifice of my beloved grandmother; of my love, Sidney; of my dutiful Frank; and of Alek. All of them had died for me. And they were all gone.

"You are free now… truly free," Dr. Wolk said. "I know it's not easy to say it, but I have crossed the same path. Forget of all this, Maia. Turn the page and start anew and enjoy your life."

It was my desire fulfilled. The opportunity to start with a clean slate, to finally be normal.

But looking behind at the road I had traveled, at all the sacrifices, it was unfair to forget.

"No, Dr. Wolk, I'm a survivor. I'll never hide, and I'll never forget. I will enjoy my life carrying my scars. I owe it to her." My eyes turned watery, but I didn't feel ashamed this time.

"I know how much you miss her. Treasure the good moments you had with her."

I shook my head. "I'm treasuring the bad." Dr. Wolk's expression puzzled. "It was during my weakness and hardship that she was closest to me."

A nostalgic grin appeared on his face, as if my words made him rewind into the past. Dr. Wolk had pursued medical studies for the sake of saving his mother, but I believed the very same moments of hardship he'd endured beside her had made him devote himself to being a doctor.

"Sorry, I forgot to give you this," Dr. Wolk said, rummaging in the pocket of his jacket, and handed me a creased photograph.

It was the photo of me in Sidney's arms at the amusement park.

"How did you get this?" I asked.

"The night that the nurse found you in the stairwell, you had it with you, pressing it against your chest."

How did I get it? Perhaps Gran had it? But I had never seen this picture before. Could she have hidden it from me?

The past and motivations of my grandmother were still an enigma. But even with its intriguing origin, that photo was a ray of light that illuminated my clouded heart.

"And you were carrying this too," Dr. Wolk said, handing it to me.

I extended my hand to receive it, but when I noticed a gilded bell dangling from his fingers—the exact same bell used by Sathariel—I drew my arm back. The bell fell down, bouncing and jangling, rolling slowly until finally stopping on the ground.

My heart throbbed at the pace of the rattling drums.

"Is everything ok?" Dr. Wolk asked, picking up the bell.

"Yes," I said, pushing down all the awful memories of Sathariel. Because even if *she* existed, that meant Sidney wasn't a product of my imagination.

And I knew, somehow, somewhere, he was alive.

I felt it in my heart.

And I was certain that one day he would return, and the two of us would ship off into an endless journey to where the stars collide with the sea.

CHAPTER 27

SHELLY PARKED HER BRAND-NEW HONDA CIVIC.

"Are you sure you will be ok all by yourself?" she asked. "It's a ways away... and on those crutches."

"I'll be fine," I said, squeezing her hand. "Thank you. Thank you for everything." I hugged her like the sister I never had, with my heart full of gratitude for taking care of the last wish of my grandmother while I was still in a coma at the hospital.

Shelly helped me out of the car, handing me the crutches and the backpack containing a small shovel and the *Masdevallia coccinea*—my gran's mountain orchid. She leaned on the car and watched my slow and shaky walk to the entrance of the cemetery.

The clouds parted, and I was able to glimpse the setting sun, tinting in blush the pale headstones. I hobbled through the cemetery with effort, wishing to never reach my destination—or even better, wishing to find her grave empty. That everything had been a terrible misunderstanding and my gran was waiting for me at home, cooking dinner.

But she was there.

I put my crutches aside and fell on my good knee, and my hands squeezed the still-loose dirt. Her headstone read: *Taken too soon, loved for an eternity.*

The very same epitaph I had read on my grave in the here-after.

"Gran… why did you have to go?" It was all I could articulate before breaking into tears.

I cried and cried, shedding countless tears, until my eyes had dehydrated.

I wanted to take the shovel and dig her out of the ground, but I just dug a small hole, enough to plant the orchid that miraculously had survived the frost, as she'd anticipated. The only flower beautiful enough and with the fortitude to match my grandmother.

The purple-flowered orchid rose over the barren soil as a scream of hope amid the uncertainty of dying. As a ray of light growing from where her heart should be.

I stood on my crutches and gave a last glimpse to her final resting place.

"Most people carry their secrets to the grave, but there are others, like you, whose secrets lead you to the grave," I said to her. "Thank you."

"Maia?" someone asked behind me.

"Yes?" I turned with difficulty.

"I'm sorry," said an old man with a mournful voice, probably my gran's age, pushing a walker. "Your friend told me I could find you here." I didn't know who he was, but from the way he looked at me and at her gravestone, I knew he must have cared about my gran.

"Did you know her?"

"Sorry. William Hurlbart," he said, extending his gentle, wrinkled hand.

William Hurlbart? His name resonated in my head. *William… Bill… Bill Hurlbart.*

"Bill?" I answered, disconcerted, looking at the same eyes of the soldier boy I had met in Lovelock's company. "Bill, is that you?"

"Yes, people call me Bill," he answered, fascinated.

"Don't you remember me? It's me, Maia."

"The last time I saw you, more than ten years ago, you were a little girl."

"No, no, no. You were hanging from a tree in the forest after you jumped from a plane, remember?"

"That's how I met your grandmother seventy years ago," he said, looking at the grave that displayed her birthdate. "In an unforgettable war, in an unforgettable place. I was in the 508th Infantry Regiment—"

"The 82nd Airborne Division," I interrupted.

"I'm flattered, knowing your grandmother told my story."

"Yes. No. Well…" I halted. "I don't know how to explain it. But when I was dying, and I saw my grandmother at my age, I saw you, and Lovelock, Duncan, and Lind…" Bill looked awed. "You don't believe me, do you?"

Bill remained silent.

"Do you think I'm crazy?"

"I was there," he finally said. "Netherlands, 1944."

"You think I'm crazy." I sighed, disappointed.

"No. I don't think so." Bill gently smiled. "I have also been *there*. In the whispering forest. Pursued by the nightmarish beasts. Last time was six months ago—third cardiac attack." He caressed his chest. "But same as you did, I came back here, for some reason—I want to believe. I feel sorry that you had to relive such memories of your grandmother. But as dark as it might have seemed, there was always a silver lining. And for me, like for many people struggling in such times of uncertainty, that ray of light was your grandmother."

"How? What did she do? Please tell me!" I implored.

"I know how you feel, Maia, overwhelmed by questions about your grandmother. I felt the same way when she disappeared after the war, vanished without a trace. She changed her surname. She moved to America. She tried to forget her past…" Bill's eyes glanced at my gran's grave with nostalgia. "I searched for her for more than fifty years, all in vain. My tired heart finally gave up hope of finding her alive, but then one day, as a conspiracy of destiny, I found her in the most unthinkable of places."

I saw in his eyes how his mind transported him to that moment when he found my grandmother.

"I should have cherished her, but I blamed her. I hated her for abandoning me," he said with red-rimmed eyes. "But your grandmother listened attentively to my words without defending herself. When I was done, she said, 'I never wanted to cause you this suffering, not to you, not to anyone, yet this was the burden I had to endure. I'm not asking you for forgiveness, nor understanding, but respect. Maybe it was not the wisest decision, but it was my decision in the end.' And she was right."

Bill's trembling hands reached for a package inside his bag, hanging from his walker.

"She gave me this," he said, handing me the stained manila envelope. "She told me that the answers to all my questions were written there."

I unraveled the cord and extracted a bunch of documents in German, and finally a book. An ancient leather hardcover book engraved with the word *Resilience* with the stroke of a knife. It was the book I had seen in my dream before my arrival at Touriel.

"When I finished reading it, I tried to return it, but your grandmother refused. She asked me to deliver it to you. That was more than ten years ago, and now I'm fulfilling my promise… after her passing."

I squeezed the book against my chest, admiring the orchid on her grave.

Bill's hand rested on my shoulder.

"Thank you, Bill. Thank you for saving me."

And he smiled tenderly.

I said goodbye to him, not knowing if we truly had met in the past or if we would meet in the future in that distant, timeless place.

DESPITE HAVING ONLY BEEN GONE for a few days, I was a stranger in my own house. Without Gran, it felt huge, cold, and lifeless.

"Maia, are you sure about this?" Shelly stood at the doorjamb. "You can stay at my house until you feel better… We can have girls' night every day!"

I smiled briefly, remembering all the silly things we'd done wearing pajamas. "Thanks, Shelly, but… I want— I need to be here." My heart sank at the sight of the vacant chair where my gran used to sit every morning to drink her coffee.

"I know." Shelly squeezed my shoulder. "I'll leave this in your room." She lifted the backpack containing my clothes and the manila envelope Bill had given me at the graveyard.

"You can leave them on the table."

"But the stairs—"

"Don't worry, Shelly. I'll manage. Crutches are temporary." I hugged her. "Thank you for everything you've done for me."

"That's what friends are for."

I nodded, and we both grinned.

"Please call me if you need something."

"I will."

Shelly closed the door.

Alone, I sighed, looking around. "What am I supposed to do now?"

I somehow still expected the always-wise response of my gran, but the empty house did not answer.

I grabbed the manila envelope and sat on the armchair. I dumped its contents over the coffee table, including the mysterious ancient, leather hardcover book. I brushed my fingertips around the outline of the word carved into the cover: *Resilience*. The word transmitted the despair of the hand that had engraved it. I browsed through. The first third of the book was missing, the remains of the torn pages still stuck to the binding. The first available page contained a dedication from my gran, so I assumed the discarded pages were unimportant. I read it aloud.

"'My dearest Maia'…" My voice broke at the thought of hearing her voice. "'By the time you read this, you will be clouded with questions, many of which not even I have an answer for. Sorry, I should have told you this before, but I lacked the courage. I kept silent, hoping my past would never haunt you, that you would not inherit my curse. But watching you lying prostrate in the hospital bed, my little Ruddy Bear, is what encouraged me to write this, heartbroken. Because you have the right to know the truth. The secret buried in my chest for so long. Maia, you must know how I met the Harbinger of Death…'"

Continue reading Peach's story in the exciting sequel *Vandella: Resilience.*

For more information about *Vandella: Resilience*, please visit my webpage, **www.mchlanda.com**, and subscribe to my newsletter to be informed about my upcoming novels.

ACKNOWLEDGMENTS

My foremost thanks are for my parents, for believing in me when nobody else did and for always being willing to sacrifice themselves to support me to reach my dreams. Without your love, compassion, discipline, and drive, this book would only be an idea tangled in the cobwebs of my mind.

My dearest appreciation to my brother, my first teacher and role model. Thanks for your constant support through the years, especially for bringing this book to reality. Your annotations and ideas as beta reader helped me to push my creative boundaries.

My heartfelt thanks to my editors, William Boggess and Julie Tibbott, for guide me through the editing journey, always pushing me to tell my story in the best way possible. Your continuous efforts to mentor my writing craft have helped me to become a better writer than what I envisioned when I started writing this book.

Special thanks to Natasa Lekic and Dan Alaxandar, for helping me to connect with the right people to bring this manuscript to fruition.

To my friend Ernesto Barba, for your skillful art to capture my imagination in the oil painting used to create this beautiful book cover.

To Lara Kennedy, for proofread the manuscript with the keenest eye, even to the smallest details.

Thanks to my readers, who have followed my blog posts over the years. Your encouraging words have helped me to overcome the challenges of writing this novel.

Finally, my sincere appreciation to all of you who have influenced me. This book in some degree is a byproduct of my life experiences. So all of you have contributed to create *Vandella*.

ABOUT THE AUTHOR

M. CH. LANDA is a longtime blogger and author of *Vandella* and *Vandella's Chronicles* series. Death and the hereafter play a key role in the legends and traditions within the folklore of Mexico, where he was born. From a young age, he took *fabulism* to heart, endowing his stories with the duality of reality and magic. When he is not writing, you can find him watching a movie (his first passion), working out in the gym, reading a book from his endless list while he tastes a wine, cooking a new recipe, or hanging out with family and friends.

For more information, please visit:
www.mchlanda.com

Or follow him on Social Networks:
Facebook—M. Ch. Landa
Twitter—@MChLanda
Instagram—@m_ch_landa
Goodreads—m_ch_landa
TikTok—@m_ch_landa